A Body in the Borderlands

Helen Cox is a Yorkshire-born novelist and poet. After completing her MA in creative writing at the York St John University, Helen wrote for a range of publications, edited her own independent film magazine and penned three non-fiction books. Helen currently lives by the sea in Sunderland, where she writes poetry, romance novellas, the Kitt Hartley Yorkshire Mystery Series and hosts The Poetrygram podcast.

Helen's *Mastermind* specialism would be *Grease 2* and to this day she adheres to the Pink Lady pledge. More information about Helen can be found on her website: helencoxbooks.com, or on Twitter: @Helenography.

Also by Helen Cox

Murder by the Minster
A Body in the Bookshop
Murder on the Moorland
Death Awaits in Durham
A Witch Hunt in Whitby
A Body by the Lighthouse
Murder in a Mill Town

HELEN COX

A Body in the Borderlands

QUERCUS

First published in Great Britain in 2023
This paperback edition published in 2024 by

QUERCUS

Quercus Editions Ltd
Carmelite House
50 Victoria Embankment
London EC4Y 0DZ

An Hachette UK company

A CIP catalogue record for this book is available
from the British Library

PB ISBN 978 1 52942 154 5
EBOOK ISBN 978 1 52942 153 8

10 9 8 7 6 5 4 3 2 1

Typeset by CC Book Production
Printed and bound in Great Britain by Clays Ltd, Elcograf S.p.A.

Papers used by Quercus are from well-managed forests and other responsible sources.

In memory of Roger Brough,
who had many of his own Solway adventures

CHAPTER ONE

Joe Golding was just starting to wonder if he'd made a terrible mistake in seeking work experience at Hartley and Edwards Investigations when a blonde woman walked through the door of their offices on Walmgate. Something about her, though he couldn't quite say what, made him sit up straighter in his seat. The long, crimson coat she was wearing to ward off the October chill was finely tailored, judging by the lines. But no. That wasn't what had caught his attention. Perhaps it was her walk? The way in which she almost seemed to tiptoe towards his makeshift desk, which stood between those of Kitt Hartley and Grace Edwards. The pair ran their small investigative agency in the historic city of York and the cases they had worked on in the past seemed to have spanned everything from infidelity to serial murder. After Joe had approached Kitt, and she'd learned about the recent difficult turns in his life, she had kindly agreed to let him shadow her and

Grace for a couple of months to see if he had a future in the business.

Although life at the agency was certainly different to the years he'd spent in investment banking in Manchester, he privately admitted it hadn't been quite what he'd imagined. For one thing it wasn't as busy as he'd expected. The enquiries that had come through had all been by phone or email and had seemed quite petty in nature. The boss of a local delicatessen who wanted proof one of his employees was pilfering from the cash register had been the most dramatic situation Joe had dealt with so far.

Why did he have the strange feeling that things were about to change gear?

Perhaps it was because the woman who had just entered the building was the first face-to-face prospective client the company had had in the two weeks Joe had worked with them. The only other visitations had been from Kitt's best friend Evie, Kitt's partner – a local detective inspector by the name of Malcolm Halloran – and an older woman called Ruby Barnett who seemed to think she had psychic powers. From what he could tell, Ruby was a friend to Kitt. Even if she struggled to keep her patience with the rather bizarre prophetic predictions Ruby was prone to making.

On one of her many unannounced calls, Ruby had told Joe that he was about to meet somebody who would bring new excitement into his life. He had tried to pretend that such a prediction was of little to no interest to him. But after everything that had happened over the last year, he knew a consuming distraction was what he needed more than anything. And perhaps the woman who had just walked in, the woman who was so timid she had even yet to say hello, was the spectre Ruby had been referring to.

She wasn't quite a damsel from a Raymond Chandler or Dashiell Hammett novel, which is how Joe had pictured the private investigation game before he had spent the last fortnight processing forms and trawling through credit reports. At least Kitt, who worked as a librarian as well as an investigator, had the decency to commiserate with him over that. She was as big a fan of Chandler and Hammett as Joe was. In fact, there seemed to be almost no book in material existence that Kitt wasn't interested in. The agency walls were lined with books on profiling and forensics and chatting about their mutual love of mystery novels had taken the edge off some pretty dull administrative tasks.

In all of Joe's years working in a grey office behind a beige desk, reading a good mystery had been a way of escaping the spreadsheets and the drudgery of meetings. After reading an article online about the sleuthing success of Hartley and Edwards Investigations, an idea had formed in his mind. He had been made redundant not long after the death of his wife, Sarah. The promise of bringing some of the intrigue and excitement into his life that he had merely read about all these years was a tempting one when he didn't know which way to turn. After his initial anticipation and squaring all the details of his work experience away with Kitt, returning to similar menial office work as before had been something of an anticlimax.

But now, this woman ... she had an expression on her face that at once suggested some drama might be afoot. She may not quite have been Anne Riordan incarnate but she still had the air of a character Raymond Chandler might write about. She was tall, Joe guessed five foot eight easily, and yet she seemed strangely small in stature. Almost as though she was willing the ground to swallow her up and it was, slowly, millimetre by millimetre, granting her wish. Joe also noticed her hand tremble as it clutched at the strap of her black leather handbag. Quickly, he ran his hands through his dark brown hair in a bid to vaguely neaten it up. He was about to open his mouth to greet her, and hopefully set her at ease, but Kitt beat him to it.

'Can I help you?' she said, fixing her frost-blue eyes on the woman. Kitt was much shorter than their walk-in and yet somehow commanded a more formidable presence. Perhaps it was the combination of her fiery red hair and poker-straight posture, but anyone who came into contact with Kitt Hartley knew within the minute that she didn't suffer fools gladly. Likely, this was an incredible asset when dealing with some of the less desirable people she might meet in her line of work.

'Yes ... I ... I would like to speak to Kitt Hartley directly if you don't mind. It's a – a very difficult matter.'

The woman's voice was surprisingly plummy to Joe's ears. She wouldn't have sounded the least bit out of place in a 1940s radio broadcast. She was definitely from somewhere a lot further south than York.

'I *am* Kitt Hartley,' Kitt clarified.

'Oh . . . you're . . .' The woman looked between Kitt and Joe. 'I'm terribly sorry, I don't know why, I thought Kitt was a man. How embarrassing.'

Grace, who revelled in any misfortune at all that might befall Kitt, no matter how minor, started to giggle at the mix-up. Whenever she laughed, her brown curls bounced as though they were somehow in on the joke too. Although of Indian heritage, Grace had lived in Leeds all her life and Joe had found, given that they both came from places a little bit further west, she had a similar sense of humour to him. When it came to Kitt, however, Grace seemed to take her fun to the extreme and Joe had been left at a bit of a loss over how to respond to it. Kitt was a North Yorkshire lass, and they were, in general terms, quite notorious for giving little of themselves away and making jokes so dry they were arid. As such, Joe found it difficult to know whether Kitt found Grace's pranks funny or downright annoying. Important intel when a person was trying to ingratiate themselves with a new boss – even if the arrangement was only temporary.

Kitt shook her head at her assistant. 'Thank you, Grace. No need to be ordering me a fake moustache off Amazon just yet.'

'Would I?' Grace said, barely keeping a straight face as she uttered the words.

Kitt glared for a moment, unwilling to credit Grace's innocent act with a verbal response, and then turned back to the woman who had mistaken her for a man.

Joe braced himself. It had come up, more than once, that during her shifts at the Vale of York University Library Kitt specialized in the Women's Studies area. A thoroughly researched mini-lecture on gender expectations could well have been in the offing but it seemed, on this occasion, Kitt was more interested in what brought the woman to their door. Likely, she too could see just how nervous the woman was.

'No need to worry about it in the least. Quite a common mistake, actually,' Kitt said. 'It is sometimes used to shorten Christopher, as in Marlowe, you know, but in my case it's a childhood nickname, short for Katherine. And you are?'

'Oh.' The woman pushed a hand to her temple and shook her head. 'I *am* sorry, I don't know what I could've been thinking. Walking in and not introducing myself. My name is Caroline. Caroline Lewis, if you need the full details. Which you probably do. I'm sorry to be in such a state. I . . . I can't think straight at the minute. That's what I've come to see you about.'

'Do take a seat, Caroline,' said Kitt, gently. She had taken the same tone when Joe had told her about his wife's death.

There was something warm and golden about the note in her voice. It brimmed with kindness and couldn't fail to set a person at ease. 'These are my associates, Grace Edwards and Johan Golding.'

'But you can call me Joe,' Joe quickly corrected.

Kitt shot him a knowing look but didn't comment on his rather blatant attempt to cosy up to their new prospective client.

'And you can all call me Carly, everyone does,' she said, tucking a strand of her bobbed blonde hair behind her ear as she spoke.

'Well, Carly, whatever you have to say, this all sounds very serious,' said Grace. 'As is tradition under such grave circumstances, I'll put the kettle on.'

'Lady Grey for me, if you're making,' Kitt called after her. In Joe's limited experience, Kitt was never one to miss an opportunity for a cup of tea.

'What else?' Grace called back with a smile.

'And as this tea run is for a client, bring the good biscuits,' Kitt added.

Grace made a little fist punch that she just about managed to conceal from Carly, but not from Joe.

Once the tea had been made and the good biscuits had been handed around, Kitt opened a notebook and offered their visitor a tender smile.

'Thank you for the tea,' Carly said, after a few sips. 'Always calms your nerves.'

'That's why we make a point of never being without it,' Grace said. Her broad West Yorkshire vowels somehow sounded more pronounced when discussing the topic of tea.

'Now that you're a little calmer, do you think you can tell us about why you've come to see us?' said Kitt. 'If it's a difficult subject, just take it one step at a time. There's no rush and best you make it as easy on yourself as possible.'

Carly looked down into her drink and nodded. Her hair fell into her face as she did so, and again she scraped it back behind her ears. 'Yes, of course. You've all been very patient with me. A lot of people would have just demanded I came out with it. But it's quite hard to talk about. It's . . . it's my uncle, you see.' At this point, Carly's voice broke and she seemed close to tears. She apologized and swallowed them back.

'No need for sorrys,' said Kitt. 'Just take your time.'

After a few deep breaths, Carly felt able to continue.

'My uncle, his name is Ralph Holmes. He was away on holiday on the outskirts of Carlisle. Just near the Solway Firth from what he said when I saw him before he left. And, well, he's . . . he's gone missing, I think.'

Kitt gave the smallest of nods and waited a good few moments before speaking, giving Carly time to add anything else she wanted to. When it became clear she was waiting for Kitt to prompt her, only then did she ask her next question. 'I'm so sorry to hear about this. Let's break the information down into small chunks to make it a bit more manageable for you to talk about. Best thing we can start with is building a timeline. When was the last time you had contact with your uncle?'

'Three days ago,' said Carly. 'Well, not exactly contact in the strictest sense of the word. He left a voicemail on my mobile.'

'Do you still have it saved?' said Kitt. Joe could hear the hope in her voice. He was still learning a lot of the trade basics but Kitt had, on one of their many tea breaks, talked to him at length about how useful recordings were – video and audio – to their work.

Without another word, Carly reached into her handbag, pulled out her phone and dialled voicemail. She hit the speakerphone button so that Kitt, Grace and Joe could all hear what was about to come.

'Message received on Friday sixth of October at ten twenty-six p.m.,' said an automated voice. The next voice they heard was that of Holmes. Joe could tell from the deep, almost gravelly nature of it that it definitely belonged to an older man.

'Carly, it's Ralph. I'm sorry not to be able to tell you this in person, that would have been much better. But I've had time to think while I've been out here. The scenery is so . . . well, it's difficult to describe the effect it has on you. It's probably lost on a young person like you but to an oldie like me . . . The way the firth borders the marshland. It almost feels like you're standing at the end of the earth. And it . . .

it gets you thinking. About your life and, well, everything. So, I just wanted to tell you . . . I won't be going back to that old rented dump in Bethnal Green. I know that'll be a bit of a shock to you, but I just can't face it any more. My life, it wasn't supposed to turn out this way. Lonely old man. No wife. No kids. No connections or prospects. In the last few days, I've come to realize what nobody ever wants to realize. I prefer my life when I'm away from it. So, I've decided I'm going to stay away . . . for good. Go somewhere and start afresh. Don't know where yet. I might let you know when I'm settled but if you don't hear from me again, know that the odds are I'm a lot happier in my new life than I was in the old one. I love you very much, and even though I may never see you again, I always will. Take care of yourself.'

A beep sounded out. Joe, Kitt and Grace exchanged a look with each other, but after what they had just heard not one of them knew quite what to say.

CHAPTER TWO

Carly was the first one to break the silence.

'I know what you're all thinking,' she said, looking between Kitt, Joe and Grace in turn. 'You're thinking, what is this mad woman talking about? Her uncle hasn't disappeared. He's gone off somewhere of his own accord. Started a fresh life, just like he said.'

Carly paused then, letting those words settle. Joe had to admit, he didn't quite think Carly was mad but he wondered why, based on a message like that, she'd jumped to the conclusion that her uncle could be classed as a missing person. He tried not to let the confusion show in his face but had no idea if he was succeeding on that score.

'The thing is,' Carly said, when nobody else spoke, 'I know my uncle and he just simply wouldn't do such a thing. What he says in that voicemail, well, it doesn't make any sense. Not one bit.'

'You will know your uncle better than we do. But what

do you mean by that, exactly?' said Kitt. She was doing a good job of keeping her voice level. Not betraying any feeling, one way or another, as to whether she thought Carly's initial claims about her uncle going missing were true or erroneous.

'Well, he doesn't hate the place he has in Bethnal Green for starters. I've never once heard him speak that way about it. He loves it. He said often how he wished he could afford to buy it. He's never been short of money but London house prices, you know what they're like. Even as someone quite prosperous he couldn't afford to buy the place on his own. I've heard about it countless times so him referring to it suddenly as a "dump" is totally out of character. I can't make any sense of it whatsoever.'

'He did say that the scenery up there near the firth had given him a bit of a change of perspective,' said Kitt. 'There's a chance he thought he was living where he wanted to be all that time and has only now had a change of heart . . . but I'm just playing devil's advocate there. What other inconsistencies are there in the message he left?'

Carly paused before continuing, seemingly a little taken aback by Kitt's ability to immediately provide a rational explanation for her uncle's behaviour. 'It doesn't sound like him, is all,' she said. 'He's never been a lonely man. He comes from a good background and had plenty of opportunities to marry, settle down, but he didn't take any of them. He always said he preferred his own company. That married life wasn't for him. So, all this talk about no wife, no prospects, et cetera . . . it doesn't ring true, not to the man I know at least. It's like he's had a personality transplant or something.'

'Without wishing any offence, are you sure that's how he really felt deep down?' Joe said, not sure what kind of reaction he might get for asking such a question. But even he understood enough about private investigation to know it was one that needed to be asked. 'Sometimes people put a brave face on things, perhaps particularly men, because they feel like they can't tell people what's really going on. Maybe he was too afraid to seize the opportunity of marrying someone in case they left him or died . . .'

Joe trailed off then and momentarily met Kitt's eyes. They were full of unmissable sympathy for him. For the fact that even when he was trying to focus on somebody else's problems, he was still somehow drawn back to the death of his beloved Sarah.

Carly shook her head. 'The police said the same thing when I went to them. It was obvious they weren't going to do a thing. That's what made me desperately google *Private Investigation North England*. And then I found you and . . . I had hoped you'd have more of an open mind.'

'I assure you,' Kitt said, 'all minds in this room are open.'

'According to Kitt, my mind, and my mouth, are always a bit too open,' said Grace. A cheeky comment that drew a grudging, momentary smile from Carly.

'But we do need to ask lots of questions at the outset of a case,' said Kitt. 'Even the uncomfortable ones, I'm afraid.'

'And in defence of my open mind, and mouth, to help you as much as we can, we have to be open to all of the possibilities,' said Grace. 'All of them. Including that this situation is what it looks like on the surface. That your uncle really has just decided it's time for a fresh start. We have to be sure when we take on a case that we're not wasting the client's money.'

'I see,' Carly said, raising her eyebrows. She clearly wasn't thrilled that the team hadn't launched into action, but Grace was right. If Carly's uncle had taken off of his own accord, it would be exploitation to charge her, knowing that in all likelihood he was safe and sound. Joe hadn't known Kitt long but a person needn't know her for any time at all to understand she'd have no hand in any kind of exploitative business.

'You must have been very close to your uncle, for him to ring you directly about this,' Kitt said.

'I thought I was.' Carly offered Kitt a half-smile. 'It's just me and him in the family, you see. He is my mother's brother. I don't have any siblings and my parents are already . . . gone. So, there's only us two left really.'

'I'm sorry you've had so much loss in your life,' Kitt said, with a sad shake of her head. 'Given the work I do, I'm no stranger to the fact that there is so much pain and grief in this world.'

'My mum died when I was very small so I've sort of come to terms with that one,' Carly said. 'Though I do sometimes wonder what would have happened if she hadn't been in that traffic accident. My father I only lost a year ago to illness.'

Joe did what he could not to wince at this revelation. The notion of losing a loved one to illness hit a little too close to home just then.

'Me and Ralph had always been on good terms,' Carly continued, 'but after Dad died, that's when we got a lot closer.'

'The prospect of losing your only remaining family member must be difficult beyond words,' Kitt said.

Carly paused, digesting this comment. 'Well, yes, but . . . I mean, that's not . . . that is not why I want to go after him. If I genuinely thought he was going off to some new and wonderful life, I'd let him go. However . . .'

Carly trailed off. Kitt offered her a polite nod but Joe could tell she wasn't that convinced by what she had heard. And in Kitt's defence, she had a voicemail from a man claiming he was going to start a new life. And only the word of Carly that this was out of character. Carly may have another motive for wanting to get in touch with her lost uncle, and it may not be a pleasant one.

Carly sighed and for a moment looked very close to tears. 'Nobody's going to believe me, are they? I'm telling you, my uncle wouldn't leave a message like that. He must have been put up to it.'

'By who?' said Grace.

'I . . . I have no idea,' said Carly. 'I've just got this idea in my head that won't go away. That someone's done something to him. Something bad. Perhaps they – whoever they are – forced him to call me and convince me he was going away. They couldn't have known they'd get my voicemail . . . When I didn't pick up he would have been forced to leave the most convincing message he could.'

There was a pause as everyone in the room digested the story Carly was weaving in her head. She seemed pretty sure of herself but she had no evidence. Joe waited to see what Kitt's next move would be.

'So, if I'm understanding right, you think that someone might have wanted to harm your uncle and you truly think he might have left the message under duress?' said Kitt. 'That perhaps he was somehow coerced into making you believe he was leaving, starting a new life somewhere?'

'That is the only scenario that makes sense to me,' said Carly. 'That someone put him up to this. Or threatened him in some way.'

'But why would someone do that?' Kitt pushed.

'I . . . I don't know,' Carly admitted. Her hands seemed to grip the teacup in her lap that little bit tighter. 'I wish I had something more concrete. Really, it would make this a lot easier if I did. All I can tell you is that something is wrong.'

Kitt let out a long, slow sigh before speaking again. In

the short time Joe had known Kitt she'd only done this on one or two occasions. At first, he'd interpreted it as a sign of exasperation but he now knew it signalled contemplation. She was weighing up Carly's narrative, and by the expression on her face, she was trying to suss out Carly on a personal level to boot.

'Before we go any further, have you tried going to the place where your uncle was staying to see if he's already left for this mystery new life he talks about in the voicemail?' she asked at last.

Carly shook her head. 'I would have done that. That was my first thought. But I didn't know exactly which B&B he was staying in. Just that it was out on the Solway coast somewhere. Near Bowness-on-Solway, I think. But he didn't tell me the name of the boarding house before he left. When I realized I couldn't go after him myself or at least try to catch him before he left, that's when I went to the police. I thought they'd be able to check into it all a lot quicker, you know, get to the bottom of it.'

'But they couldn't help you because of the voicemail,' Joe said. Given that Kitt was dating a police officer and had other friends she'd mentioned on the local force, it seemed prudent to say 'couldn't' but in truth it sounded to Joe like 'wouldn't' would be a better word.

'I suppose it was naive of me really, to expect them to put in police time when there's no real evidence anything had befallen him. I just thought if I went to them and explained this was out of character, they might do something . . . But the officer I talked to said there was nothing they could do if someone took it upon themselves to start a new life somewhere else and wouldn't entertain the idea that he was being coerced in any way. As far as they were concerned, my uncle had given me notice of the fact that he was going away and wouldn't be returning so there was no need to be suspicious.'

'That must have been difficult for you to hear,' said Kitt. 'But if you weren't able to offer them a reason why someone would try to coerce him, then they probably felt they didn't have much to go on.' Again, her tone was gentle. She likely didn't want Carly to think she was dismissing her again.

'I do understand that,' Carly conceded. 'Like anyone else, I've seen enough TV to know the police only have so many resources and that cases like this are extremely far down the pecking order. The last thing I want is to stir up trouble. But the truth is, there are many aspects of my uncle's life I couldn't tell you a thing about and he might have had difficulties I was completely ignorant to. I've never really understood how he earns his money, for example. He's always changed the subject whenever I brought that up. The strangest thing. Most people understand that what you do for a living is a pretty standard topic of conversation. But not him. He'd never be drawn.'

'That is a bit suspicious, like,' said Grace. 'As you say, difficult to get by in a conversation, in this country at least, without people asking how you put bread and butter on the table. And even if they're into something they shouldn't be, most people are savvy enough to either speak in broad terms or make up a believable cover story.'

'I agree it is a bit odd that he wouldn't discuss his work,' said Kitt. 'But it's important not to jump to conclusions in the absence of any factual information. Your uncle could have been hiding something. But he could just as easily have been a private person, particularly if he was of an older generation, and preferred to keep his financial affairs to himself.'

'I suppose that's true,' said Carly, a small sigh escaping her lips as she spoke. 'Quite a lot of people don't like talking about money. It can be a sore subject to those who haven't got much of it. But . . . I'm sorry, I know you're sceptical, and I suppose I can't much blame you for that, but I just can't shake this feeling that he is in some kind of trouble. If he is, I doubt he'd have the heart to tell me or ask for help. He was always protective of me even before we were the only two members of the family left standing.'

'One thing that is a little bit strange is that your uncle seems to think he has to cut off contact with you just to start afresh somewhere new,' said Grace. 'There's actually no reason why he couldn't have started a new life somewhere and still kept up with you.'

'That's true,' said Kitt. 'That's an aspect that doesn't quite add up. It could be that he just felt he had to cut all ties for it to be a truly fresh start but it does seem a tad . . . dramatic.'

'I haven't been able to think straight ever since I got this voicemail,' said Carly. 'But now that you say it that way, well, the whole thing makes even less sense. Of course he could have started a new life somewhere and stayed in touch. He must have done all this for some other reason. Maybe he went along with some strange scheme or was perhaps even murdered for owing the wrong person too much money. Oh, I know it sounds mad. I don't even want to think about that last possibility. Saying it out loud makes me feel sick, but every last scenario has raced through my head since I received his voicemail message. I feel like he's out there somewhere, waiting for me to do something. To be there for him like he was there for me, and I just feel so . . . so . . .'

'Helpless,' Joe finished. He was no stranger to that feeling. Even as he spoke it a series of images flitted through his mind that he did everything to block out. He could recognize another person in the same position easily enough.

Carly nodded. 'Yes, that's just the word. Helpless. Look, I may not know everything about my uncle, but I do know this is not like him. Not like him at all. Something is wrong. Maybe something truly terrible. And whatever it is, I can't uncover it on my own, so what do you say? Please. Will you help me?'

CHAPTER THREE

'You're looking a bit smug about life,' said Evie, just as Joe hit send on an email to Kitt. Evie was Kitt's best friend and had popped by on her way home from work after Kitt had sent her a text saying she couldn't make a drink after all because she was working late.

In Joe's experience, most friends would have accepted this information and gone home or elsewhere to make their own entertainment.

But not Evie.

She was currently perched on the edge of Kitt's desk in a vintage tea dress and cardigan, sipping on a gin and tonic from supplies she'd brought to the office herself. Joe had learned very quickly that Evie was a quirky little soul. She loved anything old-fashioned and often slipped outdated language into casual conversation. Being a tender thirty years old, Joe was sometimes left scratching his head at their meaning, even despite being quite an avid reader.

'Just got the result of the financial background check on the client we had in today,' Joe said, folding his arms behind his head before leaning back in his chair and smiling in Kitt's direction. 'There's nothing untoward in Carly's credit history. Seems she's good at paying her bills. No adverse credit. None of the red flags you were looking for.'

Joe's spirits lifted as he verbally confirmed what he had suspected would be the case all evening. Given how slow life at the agency had been over the past couple of weeks, he had hoped that he, Kitt and Grace would make plans to leave for Carlisle the moment Carly had left the office.

But no such luck.

If anything, Kitt and Grace had very much played down the prospect of Carly's plea leading to a case of any kind. They seemed convinced that they'd discover something concerning in Carly's background checks. Sure, her story was a little bit strange, even Joe had to admit that. A beloved uncle takes it upon himself to disappear and cut off all contact for no discernible reason while holidaying near the Scottish border. With such a bizarre starting point and nothing much to go on, they had no real idea what they could be getting into if they did launch an investigation. But there had been a look in Carly's eyes Joe recognized from the numerous occasions he had looked in the mirror after Sarah's death. In his own deep brown eyes, and in Carly's green eyes, he'd seen a mixture of confusion and desolation. Almost as if the eyes themselves were asking: how on earth did this happen and what the hell do I do now?

Nobody had been around to help Joe answer those questions for himself. Despite all the well-meaning text messages from people who called themselves his friends with stock phrases like *here if you need anything*. On the few occasions he had tried to reach out, the same people had found themselves too busy to take his calls. Too busy with their own partners and kids to meet up for a pint or give him a hand in sending Sarah's countless books about baking to the charity shop. Too busy to sit and help him make sense of the grief he never thought he'd be dealing with a mere three decades into his life. Sixty, maybe. Or seventy-five. Or maybe deep down he always thought he'd be the one to go first. Even six months later he was no closer to knowing what to think about the whole thing. But he wasn't going to sit by and let someone else go through the same kind of pain unaided.

Granted, despite Carly's concerns for her uncle's health, there was no concrete evidence that anything sinister had befallen Ralph Holmes. But Carly was convinced something was wrong and it seemed to Joe that the least they could do was settle the matter for her, one way or the other, so that she could find some closure.

'So that's no strikes for Carly and none for Ralph Holmes either,' said Grace.

'Sounds like another case is afoot, comrades. Tally-ho!' Evie said, before taking another sip of gin.

'Hold your horses,' said Kitt. 'Especially given you've had more than three sniffs of gin and aren't going to be working this case. I'm still not quite sure about this.'

'Far be it from me to agree with you about anything, not much fun in that, but I know what you mean,' said Grace. 'On the surface at least, we've no reason to disbelieve what Carly is saying but I have to say, the whole thing does have a distinct stink of fishiness about it. I just can't tell whether the smell is coming from Carly or her uncle's supposed disappearance. Maybe he'll be like that guy who faked his death and tried to canoe to Panama.'

'That was for insurance money,' said Kitt. 'And Ralph Holmes's finances seem in good order. There's no obvious reason why Holmes would need the money.'

'Mmm. Maybe the smell is coming from Carly's story then,' said Grace.

'Well, after all the cases you've worked, if you've got your reservations, maybe it's best to follow them,' said Evie. 'Never can be too careful about who you trust.'

As she said this, Evie instinctively rearranged her blonde hair around her face. She had some facial scars around her temples and it seemed to Joe that whenever she played with her hair it was in an effort to try and conceal them. It would have been beyond rude to ask what had caused them. She worked in the beauty industry so it could have been anything from a botched Botox procedure to an abusive ex-partner, and many possibilities in between. It was, frankly, none of Joe's business how the scars had come to be there but the way in which she spoke about being careful about who you trust made him wonder if she had, at some point, trusted the wrong person.

'To be honest, I'm still hazy on why you think someone would make a story up like the one Carly told us,' Joe said, reverting his attention back to Kitt.

Kitt smiled a funny little smirk. 'Let's just say in the time I've been investigating it's proven prudent to know who you're dealing with at all stages of the case. On paper Carly seems above board but there are some things official records can't tell you.'

'Like what?' Joe asked.

'Like whether Carly's the kind of person who gets her kicks by messing people around,' said Grace.

'Or is prone to exaggeration,' said Kitt. 'And without medical records we can't confirm that she's not suffering from some condition that might make her believe the extraordinary, induce paranoia, if you get my meaning.'

'She didn't seem to me like she was paranoid per se,' Joe said. 'Like you said, more worried about her uncle. But you're right, it's not something we can confirm either way. We can't know for sure if these people who might be intimidating or otherwise harming her uncle exist at all. She said herself, she just had a feeling something was wrong.'

'The whole thing sounds a bit rum if you ask me,' said Evie.

'Although nobody did ask you, I share your sentiments,' Kitt said, flashing a wry smile at her friend. 'Bearing such caveats in mind is always a good working principle. Especially when the client is in possession of a voicemail from her uncle telling her that he's perfectly fine. If there's no case to investigate, then it would be wrong for us to take the money off Carly at any rate. If she is suffering from some kind of paranoia, the last thing she needs is some charlatan investigator rinsing her for every penny she's got.'

'Have you ever had a case like this, where somebody has seemingly disappeared of their own accord but it actually turns out it was against their will?' Joe asked. He couldn't get his head around the idea that such an occurrence was in any way common.

'There was the job we worked in Durham,' said Grace. 'Me and Kitt worked it a few years back now. The police had been unable to solve a missing person's case. It had gone cold, you see, and one of the theories they worked to was that the girl in question had actually disappeared of her own free will.'

'But she hadn't?'

At this question, a grave expression passed over both Kitt, Grace and Evie's faces. It told Joe everything he needed to know about the ultimate fate of that particular young woman.

'The big thing I don't understand about Carly's story,' said Grace, 'is the motive bit. Carly seems to think that someone made her uncle leave that voicemail and then either kidnapped him or worse. If you are going to do someone harm or even go so far as to make them disappear somehow, why would you take the time to get the victim to make a voicemail? And more to the point, how do you even get them to agree to that?'

'In instances where a hostage complies with the kidnapper's instructions, it's usually because the kidnapper promises they'll let them go free if they do what they say. Of course, this is almost always a lie,' Kitt explained.

'Sadly, I know from personal experience how true that is,' said Evie. 'If he has been kidnapped, he probably will do anything his captors tell him to. In my case, I was forced to write a letter confessing to several murders. I don't see how that is much different to being forced to leave a voicemail like the one you're all describing.'

Kitt reached across and squeezed her arm while Joe bit his tongue. It was wrong to ask who kidnapped Evie and why when it was clearly a sensitive subject. But had this happened because she was involved with one of Kitt's previous cases? Just how much hot water could he be getting himself into here?

'I hear what you're saying, Evie. Obviously you'll know from what you've been through what it's like,' said Grace. 'I do think this particular instruction – to leave a voicemail at that specific point in the timeline – is a bit weird, though. Most people who make other people disappear just hope nobody will notice. But leaving that voicemail immediately drew Carly's attention to the fact that her uncle wouldn't be around any more. I know she didn't know where Holmes wore staying but the kidnappers – if they even exist – aren't forced to know that. What if she had driven straight up to his boarding house to try and stop him and found some piece of evidence or other that she was able to pass on to the police? It's a terrible risk immediately alerting people to the fact that you're going to make somebody disappear.'

'I agree it is quite strange behaviour,' said Kitt. 'But if Ralph did make that voicemail under duress, for whatever reason, whoever made him do it possibly thought Carly was naive enough to just take the voicemail at face value. Hoping that she would let the matter go and wouldn't bother looking for him. Certainly, that's the only thing that springs to mind. Otherwise, as you say, it would be a bit silly.'

'Carly said that she's the only family member Ralph had left,' Joe said, musing. 'So, if something strange or illegal was going on with him, then she was the only loose end. The only person who would notice Ralph was missing.'

'Until his rent was due at the end of the month,' said Kitt. 'His landlord or landlady would almost certainly notice his absence. And even though he lived alone, he must have had friends who would notice if he was missing.'

Joe sighed and considered how to phrase his next words without giving away the fact that they were deeply per-sonal. Maybe some people were lucky enough to have friends checking up on them all the time but since Sarah had died, Joe had learned what living alone could really mean for some people. 'He might have had his rent set up as a regular payment. I know I do. And yes, he might have had friends but they might not be the kind who text updates all the time. Or wouldn't think anything of the radio silence because Holmes was slow to reply to messages. If either of these things was the case, perhaps it's not so strange to hedge your bets and try to head off any suspicion about Ralph's whereabouts before you make him disappear. Carly said it herself, if such people exist, they couldn't have known he'd get her voicemail service. They were probably hoping she'd pick up and that they'd have a real-time conversation in which Ralph reassured her. But they had to settle for a voicemail when she didn't answer.'

'A plausible scenario,' said Kitt. 'But this is all complete speculation until we find out more about Ralph's movements in the Carlisle area. He told her he was on holiday there.'

'But if any of Carly's fears are true, then that must have been a lie,' said Grace. 'We need to consider the possibility that he didn't tell her the truth about his trip to the borderlands.'

'I agree,' said Kitt. 'We also need to ascertain what he actually was doing there. Whether he was off for a stroll along the Hadrian's Wall Path or if that was a cover for more shady business. And if there's a reason why her uncle might find himself mixed up with the wrong people, I want to know what that reason is. Carly may not have felt comfortable asking him about that but we have our methods of finding out exactly how he made his money.'

'So many questions,' said Joe. Inside, however, the excitement about the possibility of the case actually happening returned. Kitt was starting to talk as though they were already working it.

'Indeed,' said Kitt. 'We'll have to manage which answers we pass on to Carly and when carefully, however. Given our reservations about her. People don't always reveal the true reason why they're looking for a person upfront. Sometimes they feed you a sob story but are really trying to recover money from the person you're tracking down, or find a lover who has left them, or, in the worst-case scenarios, they actually intend to inflict harm on the individual they send you out to find.'

'This has all happened to you in the time you've been running the agency?' Joe said, trying not to let his surprise show too much in case Kitt decided he was far too green to be going on a real-life case with them anyway. It hadn't really entered his head that someone would go to such lengths to find a person but now that Kitt mentioned all this, he realized the naive assumptions he'd been working under.

'No, not all of them,' Kitt said. 'Some of these cautionary tales come from the PI training I did before we started the agency. Others come from fellow PIs who work across the country with different specialisms. We all try and share information as much as possible, at least with the other businesses we deem reputable. Such cooperation can sometimes save lives.'

'And you think one or more of these motives might apply to Carly? That she really wants to find her uncle to inflict harm on him, for example?' Joe said.

Kitt took a deep breath before responding. 'According to birth and census records, she is who she says she is. She's given us adequate identification of name and address and there are no legal or financial red flags that might suggest she's in some other kind of trouble. Of course, we can't access her medical records but based on my own assessment of her I'd say she seemed sound of mind – if a little bit rattled, and understandably so, after the disappearance of her uncle. So, in short, at the very least, I suppose I believe she believes she's telling us the truth.'

'So, we are headed to Carlisle, then?' Joe barely dared to get his hopes up even as he asked the question.

Evie nearly spat out her drink at this comment. 'I didn't realize the case was in Carlisle. There are some absolutely spiffing vintage shops there. Oh, go on, Kitt, please take the case!'

'Evie, it makes no odds, does it? You're not working this one with us. You have your own job to go to,' said Kitt.

'Yeah, but I've got Wednesday off. I could come across on the train, do some shopping and meet you.'

'You could do that any time,' said Kitt. 'I don't need to be working a case in Carlisle for you to hop on a train there.'

'I know that, but this gives me a valid excuse to have coincidentally walked past a vintage shop when I take all my purchases home and my wife sees them,' said Evie.

Joe had never met Evie's wife, but from what he understood she was married to Halloran's work colleague, DS Charlotte Banks.

'Charley giving you a hard time about the amount of shopping you do again?' Kitt said with a smirk.

'I'm the mistress of my own fate,' Evie said ruefully. 'I've married the only woman on the planet who has the shopping habits of a monk.'

'Yes, well, for the record, Evie, this decision has nothing to do with your desire to go shopping, but first thing in the morning we will head to Carlisle,' said Kitt. 'After all this admin I definitely need a good night's sleep before I can think clearly again. But my library shifts aren't until the weekend so we can at the very least make a good start on the case before then. And I'll have to let Halloran know that he's looking after Iago for the next few days.'

'Ha,' Grace said. 'You're going to be popular.'

Evie giggled at the idea of Halloran and Iago battling it out for dominance of the cottage in Kitt's absence.

From what Joe had gleaned, Iago was a black cat Kitt had nurtured since he was a kitten. All the stories he'd heard about the feline since working at the agency confirmed one thing: Iago and Halloran were mortal enemies.

'Don't I know it,' Kitt replied.

'So, I should start booking our holiday on the west coast, then?' said Grace.

'Holiday?' said Kitt. 'Exactly how relaxing have you found the other investigations we've conducted where travel has been involved?'

'Not very,' Grace admitted, her whole expression dropping as she remembered.

'Thought so,' said Kitt. 'But in terms of getting the bookings sorted, there's no time like the present. Yes, we're reserving judgement until we know more but if Carly's uncle really has disappeared under dubious circumstances, then there's not a minute to waste. Every hour that passes on a case like this means the trail gets colder. People will start forgetting that they've seen him, misremembering conversations they might have had with him. And if something terrible really has befallen Carly's uncle, we'll never forgive ourselves for hesitating.'

CHAPTER FOUR

Ralph Holmes had been right about the landscapes that bordered the Solway Firth. Scotland was clearly visible beyond the silver water which marbled what greenery was still left on that crisp October day. But even with another settlement in plain view, the meandering nature of the coastline did make this stretch feel like the end of the earth. Scotland, another universe.

Granted, Joe had had to keep his eyes on the winding country roads for the most part. When he, Kitt and Grace had looked closer at the transport links in the Carlisle area the night before, it was clear they were going to need a car to get around the coast on a schedule that suited them. Consequently, Joe agreed to drive them in his blue Nissan. To his surprise, however, he found himself having to concentrate harder than he could ever remember in the whole time he had been driving while navigating the unfamiliar road through the Pennines. Sheep on the road. Sharp bends.

Unexpected bouts of thick fog. The hazards had been plentiful and even now as they neared their destination, the lack of road signs by which to navigate along this stretch wasn't helping matters.

The council had taken pains to post regular signage about the dangers of the tidal firth. The fact that it flooded the road. That taking a leisurely swim in the waters was highly likely to end in a drowning. That quicksand lay in wait across the marshland, poised to swallow you up. Signage designed to actually point you towards wherever you may be headed, however, was in short supply.

Even from the glimpses he'd caught, though, Joe had already decided that this part of the world was a lonely place. Perhaps it didn't help that autumn was beginning to cast its spell on the shrubbery. Hawthorn berries and rosehips were already reddening the hedgerows. Joe did what he could to push the thought out of his head that those little dots of red resembled blood spatter. But Carly's desperation the previous day had really hit him, deep down. She'd imagined coercion, kidnapping, murder. And now he was too.

As if this wasn't enough to put Joe on edge, they hadn't seen anyone since passing through the small village of Burgh by Sands some miles back now. They had passed several houses, a couple of farms, but no people. No other cars. Nothing to distract you from your own thoughts. A fitting backdrop for a person to ponder their life and the way they've been living it. Just as Holmes claimed he had in the voicemail he left.

'Managed to pull anything up about crime in the area yet, Grace?' Kitt said, who, after losing a game of rock paper scissors with Grace, had been relegated to the back seat of the car. In Kitt's defence, she'd taken the defeat admirably and had taken the opportunity to stretch out and read a well-thumbed copy of *The Thirty-Nine Steps* by John Buchan. A title Joe had read so long ago he could barely remember the resolution now.

'It's been tricky,' said Grace, from her prime position in the passenger seat. 'Signal has been patchy most of the time and, well, then there's the queasiness factor.'

Joe shot Kitt a quick quizzical look in the rear-view mirror.

'Grace doesn't travel well,' Kitt clarified.

'I'm sorry, you should have said. I'd have . . . well, I don't know what I'd have done because there isn't really a way around the Pennines but maybe if I'd known, I could have . . . driven easier . . . or something.'

'Thanks, but it really wouldn't have made any difference,' Grace assured him. 'I don't even bother mentioning it in advance of a journey any more. It comes and goes, so it's not all bad. At any rate, even despite those obstacles, I have pulled up a couple of things that might be of use or interest while we're here.'

'Good going when you're not one hundred per cent,' said Kitt. 'What have you got for us, if you're up to relaying it, that is?'

'Yeah, I'll manage. For one thing, at first glance, there seems to be an unusual number of shootings in the area,' said Grace.

'Shootings?' Joe heard himself parroting the word. Somehow that was almost the last thing he was expecting to come out of Grace's mouth. Guns were rarities in the UK. Had he unwittingly wound up working a case in the gun capital of England? He thought himself pretty clued up. He read the news on a regular basis and did what he could to keep up with current affairs but he'd always assumed rural areas didn't have issues with weapons like guns and knives.

'Mmm,' said Grace, who seemed completely unperturbed by the discovery she'd made. 'Sometimes people have shot themselves, sometimes other people. But then, on reading more about the issue, it seems that the weapons used were all shotguns legally owned by farmers. And the shootings were nearly always by accident.'

'*Nearly* always?' Kitt said, her nose crinkling.

'So far I've only found one case where there was a deliberate shooting. A farmer shot the man his wife was having an affair with. But this seems to be an isolated incident,' said Grace. 'Not sure I'd dare get into bed with someone if I knew their spouse was armed, like.'

'People do a lot of questionable things for love or passion,' said Kitt. 'Still, I'm glad you've sussed that out. It's worth knowing that there are a number of deadly weapons in the area. We've passed several farms and I imagine most if not all have at least one firearm for controlling livestock, or threats to their livestock.'

'Guns,' Joe said again, shaking his head, this time voicing his concerns aloud. 'Not something I was expecting to encounter on a trip to such a quiet idyll.'

'There's no rule to say we will encounter any,' Kitt said. 'But forewarned that they are within reach of some residents here is forearmed . . . No pun intended.'

'There's something else too,' said Grace. 'In my rigorous searching, I stumbled across a serious drug case a couple of decades back now. Some of the locals managed to arrange for drugs to be dropped from a plane near Anthorn airfield.'

'I didn't know there was an airfield near here,' Kitt said. 'The area doesn't exactly seem like an international hub for transport.'

'It's not used for commercial flights or anything. From what I can tell, it's been turned into a transmitting site to communicate with submarines now, for the navy, I think,' Grace said. Joe glanced over, just for a second, to see her reading off her phone. 'I'm not even sure if the runway is still functional and, if they've uncovered things like that before, odds are they've tightened security to make sure the same kind of racket can't happen twice.'

'I would think so,' said Kitt. 'If it's a navy-owned facility, someone getting something like that past them wouldn't look good.'

'You're not wrong,' said Grace. 'Anyway, the details about

this drug case are scarce because the news story is from so long ago. I don't know how they arranged the drop or anything. But if there were drug rings here back then, there could still be now.'

Kitt nodded. 'Once a drug ring is established in an area, the leader and the exact smuggling MO may change but the general make-up of the group tends to stay the same.'

'How do you know so much about drug rings?' Joe asked, wary of what the answer might be.

'*Drug Rings for Dummies*, haven't you read it?' Kitt said.

'You're joking,' Joe replied. He was unable to look at Kitt directly because a cow up ahead couldn't decide which side of the tarmac it wanted to be on. Consequently, he had to keep his eyes on the road.

'Yes, of course I'm joking,' Kitt said. 'It's just something I've gleaned from Mal over the years. Not that York is exactly a hotbed for drugs. But there are people, and cases, like there are anywhere, of course.'

Joe nodded. Living with a detective inspector must be incredibly useful for a PI. Although on this particular trip, DI Halloran had had no choice but to stay in Kitt's cottage and look after Iago as requested because he was currently working a big fraud case back in York.

'Drugs and guns it is then,' Kitt said, before pursing her lips. 'As yet, there's no reason to suspect Ralph Holmes was involved with anything like that, of course. But given how cagey he was about how he made his money, we have to at least consider the idea that there was another reason for his visit here than leisure if we're thinking there's a chance that he fell victim to foul play.'

'What if we don't find anything?' Joe asked. 'I mean, what if we ask around but nobody offers information? Or there just isn't any evidence that Ralph was doing anything other than having a nice holiday in a scenic part of the world?'

Kitt shrugged just as the car rumbled over a cattle grid. 'We'll make sure we dig as deep as we can before we give up. But if it's a dead end, it's a dead end and we'll have to tell Carly as much. No matter how hard you try, sometimes there's just nothing to go on and there's no honour in stringing a client along under those circumstances.'

Although Joe nodded his agreement, he didn't relish the idea of going back to Carly empty-handed. She had seemed so desperate, and Joe was no stranger to desperation. When Sarah was dying of complications related to her diagnosis of lymphoma, he'd have given anything for someone to come along with a wonder cure and save the day. But nobody had any answers. And that was one of the most unthinkable things about the whole experience. That nobody on the planet could help. Joe was determined to find something. Even if it was evidence that Ralph Holmes was perfectly safe and sound, living his dream life in a new location. News that would surely bring Carly peace of mind, even if she would miss her uncle.

'Oh, excellent,' Kitt said all of a sudden, 'the pub is open.'

During Joe's musings, the car had passed the welcome sign for Port Carlisle. Carly had said her uncle was staying near Bowness-on-Solway, or so she thought, and this was the nearest village to that one. Last night when the trio had been making plans about where to start, this place had seemed the best candidate. Their plan was to begin with the closest settlements to Bowness-on-Solway and work their way further out if no information immediately presented itself.

'Well, now you know, Joe, what a terrible drunk Kitt is.' Grace teamed this comment with her trademark infectious giggle, which had not once failed to bring a smile to Joe's face in the time he'd been working at the agency. 'Yes, it's such a tale of woe really,' she continued. 'I've done my best to hide it from you as long as possible but she just can't help herself when it comes to the sauce. The cat is out of the bag. We've tried every last kind of intervention. Alas, nothing has worked.'

The ludicrous nature of Grace's insinuation about Kitt had Joe chuckling. But, as usual when it came to winding up Kitt, her joke made little sense. 'Grace, Kitt made it very clear last night that we were going to start at The Solway Inn in Port Carlisle to see if anyone had seen Ralph Holmes . . .'

'If you are trying to use logic against Grace, Joe, let me tell you right now it's pointless. She doesn't care that she sat through that briefing nodding away, she just wanted to make a ridiculous joke about me. For Grace, that is always the top priority.'

'You say that like it's a bad thing,' said Grace, turning slightly to flash Kitt a cheeky little smirk. 'Anyroad, I'm not really convinced there's going to be anyone in this pub. I'm reserving my excitement for a lead that might actually pan out. Haven't seen a soul for miles.'

'Maybe that's because they're all having a lunchtime drink in their local watering hole,' said Kitt, though Joe noticed her tone sounded unusually wavering. There was something about this place that had you quickly believing you were the last surviving souls on earth. Even when faced with the welcoming lights of a roadside pub.

'Only one way to find out for sure, I suppose,' Joe said, pulling up near the pub and switching off the engine.

'When we go inside, follow my lead,' said Kitt, putting on the trilby she always wore when she was headed outdoors. 'We need to be careful about what we do and say in public from here forward. Word soon circulates in small places and who knows what kind of situation we're getting involved with here.'

On that less than cheery note, they exited the car and made their way up the gravel path to a beautiful old tavern built of sandstone. The pub's name hung in large gold lettering over the entrance and the door was constructed of heavy dark wood. Joe watched as Kitt gave the handle a sharp tug. The door shuddered open and Kitt and Grace stepped inside. Joe was about to follow them but paused and looked back across the water to take in his first proper view of the firth, undistracted by unexpected sharp turns or pheasants with a death wish.

Water and sky dominated this space. The very smell of water hung in the air – a dampness that invaded the lungs the second you dared draw breath. Human beings had barely made a mark on the landscape, save for the odd fence built in a vain attempt to keep cattle off the road. Such a desolate place was surely a good environment to conduct shady business, should you have any. There was very little chance of anyone noticing or witnessing whatever it was you were up to. And if things should go awry, if the ruthless characters involved turned on each other, there would be no one to hear the cries for help. Let alone a nearby ambulance or police car to offer assistance. Out here, if something terrible befell you at the wrong time of night, you really would be on your own.

Joe closed his eyes and shook his head. He tried to tell himself he'd just read too many detective novels. But looking out over the liquid horizon, another rationale for the voicemail Carly had received surfaced in his mind. Perhaps Holmes wasn't going to start a new life. Perhaps he didn't make the voicemail under duress either. Perhaps he had merely got himself into deep water and the message was a coded plea for help.

CHAPTER FIVE

After the sting of the October chill outside, Joe welcomed the warmth of an open fire burning in the hearth of the small pub. Fuelled by several large logs, it was roaring away and he had an immediate urge to walk over and hover his hands over it. This small comfort would be particularly welcome given the freeze that seemed to fall upon the room as Kitt, Grace and Joe entered. The pub was relatively modest in size, probably no bigger than twenty-five feet in each direction, Joe would guess. Every visible wall was adorned in yellow fleur-de-lis wallpaper and the entire place smelled vaguely of cigarette ash even though nobody could have legally lit up in the place for almost twenty years.

A small collection of people Joe presumed to be locals sat around the bar, which was panelled with dark wood. Only one or two of the customers chose to sit on outlying tables made of the same brown mahogany. Yet regardless of whether they perched at the bar or lolled at a table every face in the building seemed to turn towards them as they walked through the door and there was not a smile to be found among them.

Joe felt something in his chest tighten at this reaction. Wasn't this stretch of the coast a regular walking route? Part of the Hadrian's Wall Path? That's what Kitt had told him at least and she was not known for dishing out false information. If tourists were such a common sight in these parts, wouldn't the local people be used to strangers popping their heads round the door for a drink to keep them going on their hike?

Joe searched his mind for an explanation for the somewhat inhospitable behaviour on show. The main walking holiday season would have ended early September. Perhaps things slowed down here in the winter and unfamiliar faces were of more interest. Or perhaps those who lived locally preferred to enjoy their peace and quiet during the autumn months, without the intrusion of tourists. Joe tried to make one of these two rationales stick. Above all else he tried not to link the way in which these people were looking at them with the thoughts he had had upon entering the pub. If Ralph Holmes had visited this specific venue, had he endured the same response when he'd wandered in for a quiet pint? Had it somehow led to trouble?

Despite the undeniably frosty greeting, Kitt spoke as though nothing was amiss. Joe had no idea how she was managing it when the sour looks they were getting were so off-putting. 'Hello, folks, sorry to disturb you but we're parched.'

'You don't have to be sorry for bringing business through my door,' said a woman slouching behind the bar. She was an older lady with white hair piled up in curls on top of her head. Her outfit was a mish-mash of leopard print and neon pink fabric but what most caught Joe's attention was how many bangles the woman wore on her wrists. She had very thin arms and the row of bangles on each arm reached almost to her elbows. Joe was amazed she could even lift her arm to pull a pint with that much bling weighing her down. 'You'll have to forgive the gawping codfish,' the woman continued in a weary voice. 'They don't see much excitement, you know.'

'Watch yerself, Donna,' said a broad man with a shaven head sitting at the bar. He was wearing a grey tracksuit and Joe could tell from the way the fabric strained around his biceps that he kept himself in shape. 'I don't have to spend my money here, you know.' Though the man's tone was one of only faint agitation, Joe couldn't help but notice how angry he looked. His complexion had reddened and his thick eyebrows caved heavily into a frown.

'Oh, I know,' Donna replied, seemingly unaffected by the man's irritation. 'But I also know you're too bleeding lazy to walk on to Bowness for a pint so you'll just have to take what's dished out. Now, let me get on and serve these people, will yer? Or do you fancy being barred?'

Unwilling to push his luck with the landlady any further, the man in question turned back to his friends and began a quiet conversation. Donna's face transformed in an instant from one of quiet warning to a generous smile as she beckoned Joe, Kitt and Grace to the bar. 'Now, sorry about that. What can I get for you, pets?'

'I'm on the lemonade because I'm driving,' Joe said. 'But I am gasping so a pint if you don't mind.'

'After that journey I could do with a G&T. How about you, Grace?' said Kitt.

'Count me in,' said Grace, before slyly whispering to Joe, 'See, I told you she can't keep off the sauce.'

Kitt heard Grace's whisper but seemingly didn't glean the actual words as she merely flashed her assistant a look designed to remind her that they were here on business and trying to gather some important information.

'Coming right up,' Donna said. 'Are you here on a little holiday? Not the best time of year weather-wise but the views are still quite something even in the rain, no denying that.'

Kitt's smile faded at this. 'Oh, I wish we were here to admire your marvellous scenery. You're probably used to it but I . . . I've never been anywhere quite like it.'

Donna grinned as she poured the tonic into the gin glasses, revealing a set of uneven, yellowed teeth. 'Just about everyone says that, and I know what they mean. I used to think the same, a long time ago when my parents first came to live here. I take it you're here on business by the sound of things, then?'

'Quite serious business,' said Kitt. 'We're rather concerned about a man who was staying here recently. He's not been contactable for some days, which is very out of character. A family member hired us to try and locate him.'

Joe wasn't sure if he was imagining it but the room again seemed to fall eerily silent as Kitt said this.

The man who had given Donna some grief just a few moments ago cast his thick-eyebrowed stare back in their direction.

'We do hear some sad stories around here,' Donna said. 'I've been in charge of this pub nearly forty years, and I've seen some terrible things in that time. The firth's dangerous, you know. People come here on holiday because it looks so beautiful and I keep telling them, beautiful things can be dangerous.'

'I'll drink to that!' said a lone man sitting at one of the outlying tables. He threw his balding head back and his few remaining straggles of brown hair were swept this way and that as he cackled, raised a glass of whisky and took a gulp. 'Gotta watch who you trust in this world,' he added.

'Yes, Bernie, thank you for the life lesson,' Donna said, rolling her eyes at the man before returning her attention to Kitt. 'Ex-navy, that one. Full of conspiracies about the world. I should know better than to say things like that around him. Mind you, I'm amazed he even heard me say that, he's a deaf old bugger.'

'Oh dear,' Kitt said with a little chuckle at the way Donna had spoken about the man. 'I'm sure that's a bit of a challenge when you're taking his drinks order.'

'Oh, he has the same thing every time he comes in, they all bloody do. And as for the hearing, I'm starting to go the same way so I probably shouldn't take the piss out of him for it. Anyway, back to your missing man ... I'm sorry to tell you that nine times out of ten, if someone goes missing round here, it's got something to do with the water. I've had some near misses with it myself when the tide has come in unexpectedly fast. And I'm very cautious. To be honest, though, I'm a bit surprised the police aren't already searching the marshes if there's somebody missing.'

Kitt paused at this comment but, despite the opening for an interjection, Joe and Grace remained quiet, remembering Kitt's instruction to let her lead. Was Donna digging for more dirt on their missing person just so she'd have a tale to tell to the customers who came in later? Or did she have some other motive for casually pressing for the fuller picture?

'It's a bit of a complicated situation, unfortunately,' said Kitt. 'The police seem to think the man in question might have disappeared of his own accord.'

'But ... you're still looking for him?' said Donna. Her smile had faded now and she was giving Kitt a sidelong look.

Again, Kitt paused. That was the second time Donna had angled for more information. It could just be nosiness, of course. But the way in which she asked, almost as if she hoped Kitt wouldn't notice she was probing, made the hairs on Joe's arms stand to attention.

'His relative isn't convinced he would just up and leave,' Kitt said, slowly, carefully. 'So they've sent us here to try and ascertain what happened to him.'

'Is there a name?' said Donna. 'I do get a lot of folk in and out of here but some of them do tell you their whole life story within about a minute of settling themselves down on a bar stool. Maybe I know the person you're looking for.'

'His name was Ralph,' said Kitt. 'Ralph Holmes.'

'And here's a photo of him,' Grace said, turning her phone towards Donna. One of the things Kitt had asked Carly to provide them with, alongside her number and the details of the best time to contact her, was a photograph of her uncle. She'd sent one over straight away on WhatsApp and Holmes looked quite different to how Joe had imagined him, based on the sound of his voice. For some reason, the deep, gravely tenor had left him envisioning someone rather portly but Holmes was broad and toned. By the number of wrinkles around the jaw, Joe would have put him in his fifties but he was in very good shape and his tanned skin suggested he holidayed in hot climates quite regularly.

'Do you remember seeing him at all?' Kitt asked Donna. 'Take your time, take a good look at the photo.'

'Oh, I don't need to. I recognize him right off the bat,' Donna said. 'It was a week or so ago I saw him in here.'

'That's wonderful luck for us, that you've seen the person we're looking for,' said Kitt. 'Can you remember if it was exactly a week ago or a little less?'

'Let's see . . .' Donna narrowed her eyes, thinking. She cast a glance at the man with whom she'd had a confrontation earlier, who was still very obviously eavesdropping. 'No, it was definitely a week ago today. On Tuesdays I only work the day shift, you see. My son works the evening and I remember the day I saw him, I was looking forward to my night off.'

Joe tried to determine how far what Donna was telling them aligned with what Carly had told them. Holmes had definitely been up here, seemingly on holiday. He'd been alive and perfectly well on the Tuesday. On the Friday, however, he would leave Carly a voicemail that was so out of character she would start to imagine the worst. What had happened on the Wednesday and Thursday in between?

'Did he talk much?' asked Kitt, and there was no missing the hopeful note in her voice.

Donna pursed her lips, then shook her head. 'I'm afraid not. He kept himself to himself.'

'Oh,' Kitt said with a sharp nod. 'What about his composure or behaviour? Did you notice anything unusual about him?'

'I'm putting up with this motley crew every day, and

you're asking me if I notice unusual behaviour,' Donna said with a sneer.

'Yes, I know where you're coming from there,' Kitt said, shooting Grace a pointed look.

'I wish I had something to offer you on that score but I'm afraid there was nothing obvious,' said Donna. 'Though, of course, I don't know how he normally behaves so I can't tell you if there was anything out of character. All I can say is, he just sat with his dog and had a quiet drink in the corner.'

'Oh, he had a dog with him?' Kitt said. By her tone, Joe was pretty sure he knew what she was thinking. Carly hadn't mentioned a dog, and why was that? She must have known her uncle had a dog. And that he was likely to take it on a walking holiday with him given how rural an area it was. Of course, not everyone has the deepest concern for an animal's life, especially when a human life might be in jeopardy, but wouldn't she have been a little bit concerned about what became of her uncle's pet?

Joe tried his hardest not to get distracted by this new development. It threw up quite a few questions about Carly and what she had told them but he had to concentrate on the information that was being dispensed in the here and now if he was to keep up.

'Oh, aye, it was a big Alsatian. Looked like a police dog, you know. Friendly thing it was. He didn't stop patting and stroking the dog the whole time they were here. But he didn't really speak.'

'Don't suppose you know where he was staying, then?' Kitt said.

'Ah, now. I noticed he was holding a door key with a navy blue keyring on it. I recognized it as one given out by one of the local B&Bs,' Donna said with a nod. 'But I only remember because I couldn't believe someone as well-dressed as him had booked into a place like that.'

'A place like what?' Grace said, a nervous edge to her voice. It had come up, more than once, in the time Joe had been working at the agency that Grace was quite the fan of horror films. Given how many she'd watched she was probably imagining all kinds of things about Holmes's hotel.

'There's a B&B at the other end of the village called The Lowland View. Not where I'd choose to stay.'

'From what you've said, I'm assuming it's not a very comfortable place to rest your head for the night?' said Joe. Given that he was on work experience, he was mostly supposed to be observing, and he had done so far. But he couldn't help but notice Donna's comment about the B&B and wanted to probe that just a little more.

Donna shook her head. 'Hasn't had a thing done to it in years. The carpets are probably from the 1900s and Julius who runs the place is hardly a welcoming soul.'

'We'll have a word with him,' said Kitt. 'See when Holmes checked out and if he mentioned where he was going. I appreciate you giving us the lead. We weren't really sure where to start and the family are obviously extremely worried.'

'Well, I hope you find him – alive and well, that is,' said Donna, before lowering her voice almost to a whisper. 'But if your next stop is The Lowland View, just watch what you say to Julius, won't you? He's not someone I'd want to get on the wrong side of.'

Joe resisted the urge to look at Kitt just then. Resisted the urge to give away any of the thoughts that were running through his mind. If Ralph was on holiday and as far as Carly was concerned wasn't short of a bob or two, then why was he staying in the village dump? Was it possible that he had really come to this part of the world to conduct some shady business, and thus had chosen to stay at an establishment that might look the other way?

And what about this dog? As far as Joe knew, dogs were big deterrents for criminals. If something terrible had befallen Ralph and the dog was present, wouldn't its barking have raised the alarm? Or had Holmes's plan to choose indifferent hospitality backfired on him? Had the owner, Julius, turned a blind eye to whatever was going on in his establishment at just the wrong time?

CHAPTER SIX

'This is the place all right,' said Kitt as she looked at a small information plaque pinned to a board outside of The Lowland View bed and breakfast. 'Julius Yeats is the name listed as the owner here.'

Kitt took a step back from the property to fully size the building up. Joe and Grace did the same.

'I see what Donna meant about the cut of the place,' said Grace. 'Not exactly The Ritz, is it? At any rate, it wouldn't be my first choice if I was coming here for a holiday, I can tell you. I did a quick Google search between here and the pub. There are lots of quaint little places to stay along this stretch of the coast between here and Anthorn. Some of them quite makeshift, designed for walkers conquering the Hadrian's Wall Path, but from the pictures I've seen there are much more welcoming places than this.'

Examining the three-storey structure of weathered red brick as best he could in the rising gale, Joe had to agree with Grace's comments. The building barely looked stable. Would it even hold up in the gathering winds which whipped around its corners? Quite a few of the bricks were crumbling to dust. The hand-painted sign bearing the name The Lowland View was barely readable and Joe wasn't sure if it was his imagination but the angles of the walls were somehow off – they all seemed to lean slightly to the left.

'Indeed. Not exactly a dream holiday hotel,' said Kitt. 'If Holmes did come up here for a break away, he didn't have very good taste in accommodation.'

'I suppose there is a chance that it looked better in the pictures online,' said Grace with a rueful shake of the head. 'I've been duped like that a few times myself. Some people selling accommodation through websites think they can pass off a cupboard with an electric fire stuck in it as a sauna.'

'That doesn't sound very health and safety friendly,' said Kitt.

'Funnily enough, I didn't use that particular facility so I can't rightly comment on that,' said Grace.

'You think Holmes might not have been on holiday here, given the quality of the abode?' said Joe.

'I suppose I can't leap to any conclusions,' said Kitt. 'I suppose this could just have been the closest B&B to the places he wanted to visit. But Grace's search for accommodation in the area suggests he had quite the list of options. I don't know. Something doesn't add up. And if Carly's story is to be believed, something must have happened between the Tuesday when Donna saw him in the pub and the Friday when he left that voicemail.'

'You think we can trust what Donna had to say?' said Joe. 'I'm just living by your principle of not trusting anyone on a case like this, but she did seem to be angling for more information from you.'

'I noticed,' Kitt said. 'But I gave her the same information I'd dish out to anyone else, the basics. There's a man missing and his family are looking for him.'

'It was the man at the bar who put me on edge,' said Grace. 'He was obviously listening very closely to what we were saying.'

Kitt shrugged. 'Donna said they were quite stuck for entertainment and distraction. It could be just general nosiness. If any of them played a part in Holmes's disappearance, or know someone who did, the odds are we'll know soon enough.'

'Because they'll come after us?' said Joe, unable to hide the nervousness in his voice.

'Possibly,' said Kitt. 'But I wouldn't think it will be in a very aggressive manner. There were lots of witnesses in that pub to us asking about Ralph Holmes. Harming us in any obvious way would likely be too big a risk for any criminal with half a brain.'

Joe nodded but somehow Kitt's rationale didn't soothe his concerns.

'Anyroad, considering Carly never mentioned her uncle's dog, we don't even know if we can believe her story,' said Grace.

'That was a strange thing to come out of that conversation,' said Kitt. 'There may be a rational explanation for her not knowing about the dog, however, so again we need to reserve judgement for now. We'll ask Carly about the dog when we next speak with her. But, though I regret to say it, we're not going to get to the bottom of anything standing out here.'

'So . . . I suppose we'd better go in then,' said Grace. 'Even though there could be skeletons of guests who never made it out of there alive under the floorboards. Or mirrors that show you your own death. Or a cannibal's workshop in the cellar. Or ghosts that lived in the property before it became a B&B.'

'Grace, for heaven's sake, will you give over,' said Kitt. 'I really think you need to lay off those horror films if you're going to come out on jobs like this. Although if either of you do hear a sudden crack or thud, I'd run straight for the door. No doubt it'll be the roof coming down on us.'

Sensing that familiar tightening in his chest once again, Joe followed Kitt and Grace into the ramshackle old establishment and prayed today wasn't going to be the day that the supporting beams gave up the strain.

A bell rang as they opened the door, and a few moments later a thin man with long straggly hair came through a door behind a small reception desk. There were food stains all the way down the front of his T-shirt, which was emblazoned with a drawing of Foghorn Leghorn. Joe guessed from this that the T-shirt was likely decades old. He couldn't imagine there were many places selling Foghorn Leghorn T-shirts these days. And by the looks of things, this man hadn't washed the T-shirt since he purchased it. Surely this wasn't the owner, Julius Yeats? Surely this was some person he'd had to give a job to because nobody else would work in a building with such concerning health and safety issues?

Whereas one might have expected a hospitality employee working in a difficult financial market to force a welcoming smile, this man took no such pains. At the sight of the three of them, who as far as he knew were prospective customers, his expression came closer to a grimace than anything else. Between this and the frosty reception at the pub, Joe was getting the distinct impression they weren't wanted around here. Was this how it was on every case Kitt worked? If so, Joe wasn't sure if he fancied private investigation as a long-term career after all.

'Good afternoon,' Kitt said, while Joe tried to figure out what he could smell. Rotting meat? He tried to forget what Grace had just said about a cannibal's workshop. Whatever the smell was, it wasn't pleasant.

'Afternoon,' the man replied, his voice utterly flat.

'We're looking for the owner, Julius Yeats. Is that you?' Kitt said. Joe was momentarily surprised by her directness but then he looked at the mould growing in a corner of the ceiling and tried yet again to work out what the terrible smell was and ultimately came to the conclusion that Kitt wanted to be out of this place as swiftly as possible. For his part, he was very much in agreement.

The man's eyes immediately narrowed. 'Are you the police?'

'No,' Kitt said, after a slight pause. No doubt she also thought it was interesting that that was the first assumption the man had jumped to. Was he used to visits from plain-clothed police officers?

'What do you want with him, then?' the man pushed.

'We're looking into the disappearance of this man,' Kitt said, turning her phone to display the photograph Carly had provided them with. 'We believe he was staying here before he disappeared.'

'Oh,' the man said. But offered nothing more.

'So . . . can we please speak to the owner?' Kitt repeated. A slight edge to her voice betrayed her distaste for the way this conversation was going. She had just relayed that a man was missing and the person in front of her had seemingly no interest or sympathy to offer.

'I'm the owner,' the man said at last, much to Joe's surprise and slight disgust. 'But I don't know what it's got to do with me if the fella's gone and got himself lost. I just rent the rooms. I'm not here to babysit tourists.'

'We certainly don't think the disappearance has

anything to do with you,' Kitt almost purred. 'Or your fine establishment.'

Disconcerting a presence as Yeats was, Joe had to work hard at suppressing a smirk at this. He could almost hear how hard it was for Kitt to get the word 'fine' past her teeth. And who could blame her? The walls were the colour of sludge. Joe had the vague sense that they might have been painted beige a very long time ago and over the years they had become so grubby the original hue was no longer distinguishable.

'We are here on behalf of a family member,' Grace said, seemingly sensing Kitt's mild irritation. 'He was travelling with his dog.'

'Oh yes,' Yeats said. 'He was here.'

'I'm glad you recognize him,' said Grace. 'The family haven't been able to get in touch with him and want us to follow up and see if anyone remembered seeing him before he disappeared. In case anyone knew which direction he'd gone in, when he checked out, you know.'

'Can't help you there,' said Yeats. 'He never checked out.'

'You mean, he's still here?' said Joe. He knew it was wrong for his heart to sink at this comment. If Holmes was here, alive and well, he should be glad. But this was his first real case with Hartley and Edwards Investigations. He had hoped there'd be a little more to it than this.

'Nah, I mean, he went out one night and never came back.'

Kitt, Joe and Grace exchanged a look and at once the guilt of wishing for a juicier case hit Joe in the gut. Never came back? That didn't sound good. Not at all.

'Which night was that?' said Kitt.

'I dunno,' said Yeats.

'Think,' Kitt said. The pleasant ring in her voice had evaporated now and Joe was certain she was going to completely lose her temper if Yeats didn't cooperate this time.

Yeats must also have sensed Kitt's blood was about to boil over as he did pause at this and then opened a notebook on the desk. He flicked back a few pages after studying the scribblings inside. 'Wednesday.'

'So, the last time you saw him was on Wednesday evening?' Kitt said.

'Yep. Didn't come back to his room Wednesday night and then we didn't see him again. He was booked in for three more nights. Good job I take payment in advance.'

'Yes, I suppose it is,' Kitt said with a slight raise of her eyebrows. Joe was equally unimpressed that profit and loss were all Yeats could think about when a man staying at his hotel left without a trace and had now been reported as missing.

'Did he leave anything behind in the room?' Kitt said. 'I mean, did it look like he'd taken all of his belongings with him?'

Yeats paused but did eventually answer. 'Don't remember anything being left behind. Why, was there something in particular you were looking for?'

'Anything that might have given us a clue as to why he disappeared ... And none of this seemed strange to you?' Kitt said after a moment. 'That a customer who'd paid up for three more nights just disappeared.' The edge to her voice had returned and there was no missing it. Joe made a mental note never to get on Kitt's bad side if he could help it.

'Strange?' A creepy little smirk slithered over Yeats's lips. 'Work in a B&B for thirty years and you'll see strange. You've no idea the things I've seen. The stuff people get up to. The way people talk when they think nobody's listening. But someone just up and leaving, that's not strange. Happens more often than you'd think.'

Joe glanced around the foyer again and decided that if the rooms were anything like this, he'd understand why quite a few people stayed one night and then didn't come back. Joe wasn't even sure he'd make it inside the building if he turned up here for a holiday and was confronted with an exterior like that. Sleeping in his car would be preferable.

'Often,' Yeats said, 'the people who do it are people who'd prefer you not to report it to the authorities. And so long as they're not doing whatever they're doing on my property, it's none of my business.'

Kitt opened her mouth to say something but clearly thought better of it. She closed her mouth and seemed to be thinking something through.

'Of course, I suppose I could have missed something in the room. If you wanted to take a look for yourselves.'

'We've travelled some distance to look into this matter so it probably is best we see the room,' said Kitt. 'But has anyone new checked into his room yet?'

Yeats shook his head. 'Not many people checking in around here at this time of year. Gets quiet once the season ends, you know. Too cold and bleak for most folk.'

'Has the room been cleaned or otherwise disturbed?' Kitt asked. Joe could hear the hope in her voice again. Yeats hadn't sucked all optimism out of her just yet, although if anyone could do that, he could.

'No point cleaning a room until you've got a booking to warrant it,' Yeats said, almost incredulous at Kitt's suggestion that he may have prematurely had a room cleaned.

Joe wondered how this policy fared when people turned up on spec for a room when they needed one unexpectedly but decided that the less he knew about Julius Yeats's sanitation contingencies in such situations, the better.

'Well then, I think it would be best that we take a look,' said Kitt. 'We'll be no more than ten minutes in there.'

The same creepy smile as before returned to Yeats's face. He didn't say anything aloud. He merely pointed to a sign sitting on the desk, written in thick black marker pen. ROOMS £50 PER NIGHT, it read.

'Oh, we don't want to spend the night,' Kitt said, a note of alarm in her voice as if Yeats somehow might be able to compel them to do so. Joe was with her on avoiding that at all costs. One night in this place would likely give him nightmares for life. 'We just want to take a look for a few minutes. We . . .'

But Kitt trailed off as Yeats pointed to the sign a second time with one long, bony finger.

Julius Yeats might yet be some help to them but it seemed that help was going to come at a price.

CHAPTER SEVEN

Joe couldn't decide if he should feel relieved to step inside the last known residence of a seemingly vanished man, he only knew he was glad to be out of the stairwell.

On the presentation of fifty pounds in cash, Yeats had handed Kitt the key to room six and grunted something about the stairs. Less than a minute in the hallway would convince anyone that the B&B had been designed by someone of dubious taste and disposition. There were paintings in the stairwell, but they were all of people with expressions of misery writ all over their faces. In one or two places, Joe thought he was going to put his foot through the stairs, the boards were so weak, and the lighting . . . Joe wasn't quite sure what was going on with that but the bulbs in the stairway seemed to emit a sickly green glow. Perhaps that was just the kind of light emitted when the fittings hadn't been cleaned in the last century. All of it added to the general picture of eeriness that was forming.

Joe found himself hoping, more than ever, that Holmes really had just run off to a better life and that nothing terrible had befallen him. Enduring some traumatic incident in a place like this would surely leave you in therapy for the rest of your life, assuming you survived it.

Mercifully, the rooms, by comparison, seemed a little less like they belonged in a haunted mansion. More like an orphanage in a nineteenth-century novel. Which wasn't much of an upgrade but at that point Joe would take any ounce of relief he was offered. To say that the room was sparse would have been putting it kindly. There was a bed and a chair. But no wardrobe, no chest of drawers, no place to rest one's things. Bare floorboards and no lampshades. No lamps, in fact, just a single bulb hanging from the ceiling.

'I wouldn't like to see the reviews for this on Tripadvisor,' said Grace. 'I'm guessing it's not possible to award minus stars but I'm sure if you could, some people would've done if they turned up to the borders and were presented with digs like these. How's he even getting away with running a place like this? Aren't there regulations to follow? I feel like you might have got away with offering people rooms like this thirty years ago, but not now.'

'Might not be officially registered as a B&B. It wouldn't surprise me after that performance downstairs,' Kitt said, and then casually added, 'Even if it is, it might just be a front for something else.'

'Like what?' Joe said, his heart beating a little faster at the thought.

'Not sure we should discuss that here. I've probably said too much already. Walls have ears, you know,' she said, squeezing Joe's arm. She could likely tell he was a bit jittery after their ascent up the staircase that had been ripped straight from a Hammer Horror movie. It wouldn't have taken a seasoned profiler to notice. His palms were sweaty for one thing and he was sure his expression would give him away if nothing else did. But it was just a building at the end of the day, if a badly kept one. Why did he feel so on edge in this place?

'OK,' Kitt said, opening her satchel and handing Joe and Grace a pair of plastic gloves apiece. 'We're paid up for the rest of the night so we can do a very leisurely sweep. Go gentle when you're moving furniture around and try to touch things as little as possible. I would sweep for a few fingerprints but, let's be honest, there's no guarantees Mr Yeats cleans the rooms properly even when he has got a con-firmed advance booking so I can only imagine the number of prints I'd find.'

'So that means we're just looking for things that have been left behind?' said Grace.

Kitt nodded. 'And any unusual substances.'

'Like what?' Joe asked.

'Drugs, gunpowder residue, blood spatter.'

Kitt reeled off this in a matter-of-fact manner but Joe caught himself flinch at the mention of blood spatter. Did

Kitt think that Ralph Holmes had been assaulted, tortured or worse in this very room? Yes, of course, he'd contemplated the fact that something bad had happened here, but his mind had only approached that idea in abstract, broad terms. The words blood spatter made it all very specific. And what if they did find something like that when they searched? What would it mean? And how would they break it to Carly? Goosebumps ran up Joe's arms at that thought but he did all he could to refocus. Carly was counting on them, on him. He had to keep his mind on the job, no matter how unsettling it might become.

The trio set to work then, examining the small room and the poky shower and toilet. With so little furniture to move around there wasn't really enough work for three people but Joe did his part. He pushed aside the orange, threadbare curtains to discover three dead bluebottles and a spent match.

'Leave the bluebottles, but bag the match,' Kitt said. 'Anything that might have human DNA on it will have to come with us.'

Joe bagged up the match and then shone the torch on his phone down the back of the lone radiator. The only thing he could see was a lost sock stuck down the back. The sock was covered with so much dust he'd be surprised if it had anything to do with Holmes but, remembering Kitt's prior instructions, he reached down to fish it out and put it in a plastic bag.

'We'd best check the bed itself,' said Kitt. 'It's still unmade, looks like it's been slept in. I suppose it must have been like that since Wednesday if Yeats has got his facts straight. Give me a hand, Joe.'

Following Kitt's example, Joe gently started untucking the sheet from the bed. Between them, they lifted the bedding onto the floor.

'Ugh, that mattress is . . . is . . .' Grace began.

'Putrid,' Joe finished for her. The whole thing was stained brown with what Joe could only imagine was more than twenty years of accumulated sweat.

Somehow managing to ignore the state of the mattress, Kitt gathered up the sheet and shook it out. Nothing came of that so she approached the pillows. Again, Joe followed her cue and, very much against his wishes, he pulled off the pillowcase and turned it inside out to check nothing important was inside.

'The sight of those pillows is making me want to vom,' said Grace. 'What are those yellow stains?'

'Do you really want the answer?' Kitt said.

'No,' Grace admitted in a small voice.

Without wasting even a moment, Kitt began to prod the mattress with her gloved hand and lifted it up at her side to check underneath it.

'Ugh, Kitt,' Joe said. 'I'd keep any physical contact with that mattress sparing if I were you.'

'You always have to check these things. People hide stuff

in and under mattresses all the time,' Kitt said, glancing underneath. 'Just not under this one, apparently.'

The only place that hadn't been checked by that point was the space under the bed. Joe did not relish the idea of blindly putting his hand under there but Kitt had taken the big bullet by examining the mattress, so he really felt it was his turn. He knelt on the floor, again using his phone as a torch to survey the space.

Aside from piles of crumbs, likely swept under there by whatever 'cleaner' Yeats had hired, and a used serviette there was nothing to report. Considering what kind of establishment this seemed to be, Joe felt he'd got off pretty lightly. He wouldn't have been surprised if he'd found a severed hand or a horse's head under the bed in a place like this. Especially after the list of grotesque possibilities Grace had reeled off before they'd entered the building.

'We'll keep the serviette,' Kitt said, holding a clear plastic bag open for Joe to drop it into. Cringing a bit at having to pick up such an object, even while wearing gloves, he dropped it into the bag.

'It's been there a lot longer than a week by the look of it,' he said as he did so.

Kitt shrugged. 'You never know with things like this. The odds are against it amounting to anything but you can't take the chance. There might be a DNA sample on here that proves pivotal later. For now, all we can do is collect what's here and wait for further direction in the case to unfold.'

'Have you found anything, Grace?' Kitt asked.

'Not unless you count a spider as big as your fist.'

'I don't, no,' Kitt said.

'Then it doesn't really look like there's anything here,' said Grace, deliberately keeping her voice low. 'When Holmes cleared out without a word, assuming Yeats was telling the truth about that, it looks like he took everything with him. So where does that leave us? Our big lead was finding where he was staying. Hoping that the person who runs the place could tell us something. But Yeats doesn't know anything useful.'

'I'm not sure that's entirely true,' said Kitt. 'If Yeats's account of what happened to Holmes is to be believed, it patches another hole in the timeline. Donna last saw him on the Tuesday.'

'And Yeats saw him on the Wednesday evening,' said Joe. 'Which closes the gap between sightings of him in public and the voicemail Carly received.'

'Exactly,' said Kitt. 'If Carly's suspicions about her uncle's disappearance are true, we are slowly but surely narrowing down the window where something might have happened to him. It's not massive progress, I grant you. But it does help us focus our questioning a bit better with anyone else we might speak to.'

'Who else might we speak to, though?' said Grace. 'That's my point really. We don't know what he was doing up here, who he came into contact with. Holmes didn't use any social media so I can't employ my usual cyber-stalking skills.'

'Well, for one thing, somewhere out there is a missing dog,' said Kitt. 'We could try asking about that in the main villages in the area: Port Carlisle, Bowness-on-Solway and Anthorn. It's a little less serious to most people than a missing person, so they might open up a bit more about what they've seen or heard.'

'Good idea,' said Grace. 'It's a next step at least, and that's something.'

'Before we do that, though, I think we still have a little unfinished business downstairs,' said Kitt.

'With Yeats?' Joe said. He didn't relish the prospect of another conversation with that ferret of a man.

'I'm not sure we can assume Yeats is telling the truth,' Kitt said, also keeping her voice low. 'He's not exactly the kind of person who invites trust. Grace mentioned that Holmes was travelling with a dog but he didn't say anything about the dog when he talked about Holmes leaving on Wednesday. The first thing we need to ascertain is whether the dog went with him.'

'Well, it's not here, so I'm assuming the dog went with Holmes,' said Grace. 'But yes, best to get visual confirmation on that.'

Kitt nodded. 'Once we know the dog was definitely with Holmes we can start asking around. But I admit, right now, this is pretty much our main hope of finding out what happened to Holmes. Unless someone in the village can give us some sense about where he might have gone next, this is going to be a very short investigation indeed.'

CHAPTER EIGHT

'Oh, there you are,' Yeats said as Kitt, Joe and Grace re-entered the reception area. His voice was unusually chirpy, in sharp contrast to the tone he'd used with them before. Kitt's eyes immediately narrowed and Joe agreed with her apparent sentiment that there was something suspicious about the change in temperament.

'I'm glad I caught you before you went,' said Yeats.

'You are?' Kitt said, her note more one of reserve than surprise.

'Of course,' said Yeats. 'Find anything of interest in the room? Something that might help find your missing man?'

'It's not clear that we have, no,' said Kitt. Again, she seemed to be speaking each sentence carefully, as if sensing some kind of trap. Joe examined Yeats's face more closely. Strands of his hair were stuck to his forehead with sweat at the brow. He could just be someone who sweated a lot, of course, or he could be anxious about something they had yet to learn about him, this establishment or his part in Holmes's disappearance.

'I'm sorry to hear it,' Yeats said but something about his grin told Joe he wasn't sorry at all. 'This might cheer you up though. The moment you went upstairs I just remembered that there was a briefcase left in room six.'

Joe glanced at Kitt to see her slowly fold her arms over her chest. If there was one thing Joe had gleaned about Kitt, it was that she did not suffer being messed around by anyone. No matter who they were.

'How convenient that you only remembered this fact after we'd paid to search the room,' she said, her tone quiet and decidedly icy. She was, in general, so kind and generous a person Joe could hardly believe how quickly she could turn if she thought someone was wasting her time.

Yeats blinked in quiet surprise at the tone but then offered a dopey chuckle that was obviously put on. 'I'm no spring chicken, you know, can't remember everything.' With that, he put the briefcase on the counter. It was quite an old-fashioned item of baggage and tan brown in colour. It had a lock on the top of it situated between two metal clasps.

'I'd lose my head if it wasn't screwed on,' Yeats said, again trying to dissipate some of the coolness coming from Kitt's direction.

Joe decided there and then that Yeats was on his suspect list when it came to the disappearance of Ralph Holmes. Before this he'd just assumed Yeats was a bitter man charging towards his fifties without any prospect of making anything of himself. But now he'd openly deceived them about how much he knew, and what evidence he had on the premises. He also had in his possession an item belonging to Holmes. At least, Joe assumed it belonged to Holmes. Would Yeats dare to present them with a suitcase that had been left behind by some previous, random visitor to room six? He supposed he couldn't rule that out from what he knew of the man. But taking the briefcase at face value, even that raised questions. Holmes could have left it behind as Yeats said. Or, he could have taken it when he had a hand in making Holmes vanish.

The same question they had grappled over yesterday afternoon was still as poignant now, however. Why? Why would Yeats, or anyone, want to make Ralph Holmes disappear? Until they knew that, they would be working on blind speculation.

'Can we look inside the briefcase?' Kitt said.

'Of course you can,' Yeats said, his manufactured smile still lingering, 'for fifty quid.'

'You've already had fifty quid,' said Kitt, placing a hand on her hip.

'That was for the room,' Yeats said. 'This is for the case.'

'This is extortion,' Kitt said through a sigh.

Yeats held up his hands as though he wasn't the one making the rules. 'Says in the terms and conditions of the stay that left belongings will not be returned and become the property of the management. It's my property. I can sell it for what I want.'

Perhaps realizing that it was worth fifty pounds to no longer have to look at Julius Yeats's gap-toothed grin, Kitt opened her satchel and paid him another fifty pounds.

'Pleasure doing business with you,' Yeats said, stuffing the notes into the back pocket of his jeans, which looked just as unwashed as his T-shirt.

At that comment, Kitt paused and stared hard at Yeats. 'You know, you probably think you're really clever. Taking a group of visitors for a hundred quid when they're not even staying with you. But a man is missing and you are profiteering from his family's grief.'

Yeats didn't respond but his grin began to fade as Kitt continued.

'People like you only win out for so long. You may not get your comeuppance today or tomorrow. But one day it will catch up with you. And when it does, I want you to remember my words. Remember you were warned. That people out only for themselves never end up on top.'

With that, Kitt pressed the two silver clasps on the brief-case towards each other. Nothing happened.

She tried again but the case remained closed.

Slowly she looked up to Yeats. 'It. Won't. Open.'

Yeats somehow found the courage to grin even in spite of the way Kitt was looking at him. 'You were saying? Folk like me don't end up on top? Maybe you should listen more carefully to what people say. I said I had a briefcase left in room six. I never said I had the key for it.'

Shaking her head at the man, Kitt grabbed the suitcase and began to storm towards the door. Grace scurried after her and Joe was about to follow when a loud howl sounded out from somewhere behind the door through which Yeats had originally entered. The howl was desperate and lonesome enough to stop all three of them in their tracks.

Joe swallowed, trying to keep his composure, and turned back to Yeats. So, the dog Donna mentioned may not have gone with Holmes when he left on Wednesday night. It could be some other dog, of course. But Joe rather hoped it wasn't. If Holmes's dog was behind that door, walking around the villages with the dog in tow might invite attention from someone who knew what happened to Holmes. Which, though perhaps dangerous for their health, would bring them closer to the truth. At any rate, Joe had to at least check to see what was going on with whatever creature had made that howl. He wouldn't wish an owner and a home like this on any dog. They were far too good-hearted for such a fate.

'Do you have the dog that was staying in room six?' Grace asked before Joe had a chance to.

'Might do, what's it worth to you?' Yeats was obviously having the time of his life. He knew he was in a position of power. That he had things they needed and he was going to exploit that for all it was worth.

Well, Joe had had enough of that for one day.

'The question is, what's it worth to you?' Joe strode up to the counter and looked down at Yeats. Joe wasn't particularly tall but luckily Yeats was quite short, probably no taller than five foot four. Joe had a good five-inch height advantage and thus thought he had half a chance of coming across as a bit intimidating.

Yeats frowned at Joe's previous question. 'How do you mean, like?'

'We told you we're not the police, that's true,' said Joe. 'But we're very good friends with some of them. I wonder if you'd like them to keep a close eye on these premises for you.'

'A – a close eye?' Yeats stammered. By the sour look on his face, Joe guessed such a scenario was not desirable to him.

'Yes, just so you feel safe and secure with running a business where anyone can walk through the door. There are a lot of undesirables these days and I'm sure your friendly, local police force wouldn't want you feeling vulnerable when they could be around more often to help if any trouble brewed.'

Joe stared hard into Yeats's grey eyes in an attempt to let him know he meant business. It was a long time since he'd come this close to a dangerous confrontation but he'd be damned if he was going to watch him take advantage of Kitt and Grace for even a minute longer. The only reason he'd hesitated in confronting Yeats for himself was that really this was Kitt's case and he didn't want to overstep. But enough was enough.

Yeats, having had a moment or two to consider Joe's words, looked over to Kitt.

'He's not lying about our connections with the police,' she said. 'I happen to live with a detective inspector. I'm sure he'd be very interested in making sure you felt the police were giving this place, and you, enough of their time and attention.'

'I've got the dog from room six,' Yeats admitted. 'But if you're looking at him, you're taking him with you. I haven't got the time nor the money for another mouth to feed or for messing around with animals.'

'Fine, we'll take him,' said Joe. 'Just let the poor thing out and we'll be on our way.'

Seemingly keen to see the back of Kitt, Grace and Joe lest they brought friends from the local constabulary with them next time, Yeats opened the door behind the counter and the biggest dog Joe had ever seen came bounding out.

The dog was an Alsatian as Donna had said. He was coloured black and tan, had pointy inquisitive ears and deep brown eyes the colour of rich chocolate. He had that look dogs get when they're trying to get something out of you. Food or petting or a long walk in the woods. He was tilting his head at Joe as if to ascertain whether he was his new owner or not.

Then, however, it seemed the dog decided for himself.

Without any warning at all, the dog leapt onto the desk and launched himself at Joe. The force of the jolt was enough to knock Joe over and in the process of falling backwards onto the dusty, time-worn carpet, he wondered if the dog might be vicious. His fears deepened as a set of powerful jaws and a pair of razor-like teeth leered down at him. If the dog chose to attack Joe, he wouldn't stand a chance.

But then a long, wet tongue proceeded to lick the entirety of Joe's face.

Much as he would have rather avoided a facial cleanse from an unknown canine, Joe didn't immediately bat the poor creature away. He knew it was very likely a show of gratitude for helping the unfortunate mutt escape the clutches of Julius Yeats. The man wasn't exactly kind to humans. Joe didn't want to think what he might do to a dog. There were no obvious signs of abuse on the animal. No scars or wounds. But that didn't mean Yeats had been pleasant to the hound. To dogs that were used to being loved and well-treated even verbal abuse could be traumatizing.

After thirty seconds or so, Joe went to sit up but the dog kept his paws on Joe's shoulders, making it difficult for him to raise himself off the ground.

Beyond the dog's snout, Kitt's face came into view.

'When you're quite finished recreating the beach scene in *From Here to Eternity* with your new significant other, we've got some work to do,' she said.

CHAPTER NINE

'Come on, boy,' Joe said as he tugged at the Alsatian's collar. The dog had blithely followed them out to the car without a lead to restrain him. The second Grace had opened the car door, however, the hound had beaten her to the passenger seat and would not budge.

'Come on, car seats are not for dogs,' Joe said, giving the hound's collar another gentle tug.

At the feeling of his collar being jostled, the dog lowered his ears and growled.

'I don't think he likes that,' said Kitt.

'I don't think it would take a private detective to work that out,' Joe said with a grudging grin. Slowly, he worked his fingers around the collar towards a round, gold medallion that hung from its centre, engraved with the name Rolo. Joe instinctively checked the back of the medallion in case it had any other engravings on it which might help with their case, but it was blank.

'Rolo, come on, be a good dog and get down from the seat,' Joe tried again, hoping that using the dog's name might carry some weight. Unfortunately, Rolo seemingly had no intention of following instructions. Instead of climbing off the seat, he lay down on it.

'Looks like he won't be moved,' Kitt said with a chuckle.

'But he can't sit in the passenger seat,' Joe said. He wasn't particularly precious about his car seats but if they were going to look after the dog, he had to know his place. Otherwise, if the dealings Joe had had with any of his childhood dogs were anything to go by, taking Rolo along for the ride would turn into a chaotic disaster.

'I don't see why Rolo can't sit on the front seat,' Grace said with an impish smirk on her face as she opened the rear door of the car. 'We understand after that intimate scene back in the hotel that you two might want some alone time together.'

'After all, you're still in the honeymoon period. You should make the most of it,' Kitt said, sliding onto the back seat after Grace.

Sighing, Joe closed the front door on the passenger side, walked around to the driver's side and settled in for the ride back to Carlisle. Dusk was closing in now and Kitt wanted to look at the contents of that briefcase without anyone else present. Exactly how she was going to do that without a key, Joe didn't know. But it was time to check in to the hotel and Joe was chauffeur.

As he started the car, Rolo growled at the sudden rev of the engine.

'When we eventually head back home, it's going to be a long journey back to the North East if he growls at the sound of the engine,' Joe said while Kitt and Grace laughed at the dog's antics from the back seat.

'Not like you could very well have left him in that place with Yeats,' said Kitt. 'That place is hardly fit for vermin, let alone anyone else. I'm sure the dog will soon realize which side his bread is buttered. And who knows? If we find Holmes alive, we might be able to return Rolo to him and witness a man-dog reunion worthy of a viral video.'

'Where did you learn about viral videos?' Grace piped up. Joe could see from the rear-view mirror that the mischievous look he'd seen flash across her features earlier still hadn't left her face.

'I'm always confused by these "jokes" of yours, Grace. You're always present at my birthday celebrations. You know I'm only forty-two. Why do you treat me like I'm ninety-two?'

'I don't know,' Grace said, squinting at Kitt and cocking her head to one side. 'You just give off a vibe of somebody who is secretly ninety-two but hides it behind prosthetics and a killer make-over.'

'Oh, thanks a bunch,' Kitt said.

'Sorry to interrupt,' said Joe, though he wasn't in fact sorry at all. Entertaining as Kitt and Grace's schtick was, he had learned that if they were left to continue, the pair entered surreal terrain that could leave Joe wondering what exactly was in the tea at the agency. 'But you said, *if* we find Holmes alive. Does that mean you now believe that he has been made to disappear against his will?'

'I haven't made my mind up about anything yet,' said Kitt. 'It's too soon for that. The contents of this briefcase may or may not be of value, but a dog is always of value to their owner. As is any pet.'

'So what you're saying is, a person might forget a bag, but it's very unlikely they'd just leave behind a pet,' Joe clarified.

'Exactly,' said Kitt. 'Despite some of the terrible headlines you read, most people who own pets do so responsibly. Even those who aren't that responsible would be heartbroken if their pet went missing or was somehow otherwise harmed. It doesn't seem probable to me that Holmes would have willingly left the dog behind.'

'And especially in a place like that,' Grace added. 'Can you imagine? Leaving a creature you loved in that B&B?'

'No,' said Kitt. 'I can't. Which makes it a particularly odd discovery.'

'It seems to me that if you did leave a dog in a hotel room, you'd be expecting to come back,' said Grace.

'But Holmes didn't,' said Kitt. 'Which is why something unexpected likely happened to him on Wednesday night when he left The Lowland View. I watched Yeats look it up in his logbook myself, so the odds are the timeline he's giving us is accurate.'

'I still want to know why Carly never mentioned the dog,' Joe chimed in.

'It's a good question, and one we'll be asking her,' said Kitt. 'But she's not forced to know that he'd taken the dog with him and at any rate, if she believed her uncle was missing, it might have slipped her mind that there was another life in the equation. Especially if she's not a pet owner herself. If you're not used to looking after a pet every day, those things sometimes don't enter your head.'

'I suppose that's true,' said Grace. 'But I'll be interested to know what she's got to say about it anyway.'

'As will I,' said Kitt.

'The reception we've had at Port Carlisle, and the loneliness of the place, is reshaping how I view this whole situation, I must admit,' said Joe. 'Maybe we've just been unlucky, but the people we've crossed paths with have been a little frosty.'

'I know what you mean,' said Kitt. 'But places like this, that are quite lonely and very rural, can play tricks on our minds sometimes. Donna seemed friendly enough at the end of the day and she recognized that the way in which her regulars were gawping at us was off-putting.'

'I suppose,' said Joe. 'I don't know, maybe I'm just still creeped out from Yeats and his version of luxury holiday accommodation.'

'Nobody could blame you for that,' said Grace. 'That place is going to live on in my nightmares for some years to come. Even if we did make it out of there unscathed, I sort of got the feeling that other people might not have done.'

'Yes, well, we need to work on evidence alone, I'm afraid,' said Kitt. 'And although Yeats was acting suspiciously to say the least, I don't yet have any evidence, circumstantial or otherwise, that would suggest he was involved in the disappearance of Ralph Holmes. Yes, he was in possession of his suitcase but there's no reason to suspect him of anything on that basis. He likely did just legitimately find that when he went to check the room had been vacated. Above all, we're lacking a motive for him or anyone else to have harmed Ralph Holmes.'

The car went quiet then as they all considered this problem. If they didn't turn up some obvious motive for someone wanting to make Ralph Holmes disappear soon, Joe had his suspicions that Kitt would call the whole investigation off. She didn't like wasting her time and she wouldn't take Carly's money if she didn't think there was anything in it.

Joe glanced over at Rolo. His chin was resting hard against his paws. No doubt he missed his owner. Wondered why Holmes had left him. A question they were all pondering.

He turned his attentions out towards the mauve clouds as dusk descended on the other side of the water over the low peaks of Scotland. The firth looked almost iridescent in the fading light and Joe couldn't help but marvel at its beauty. But then he recalled Donna's words about beautiful things being dangerous. About how so many people who went missing here were lost to the water. Maybe they were over-complicating this whole situation because Carly had been so sure somebody had a hand in her uncle's disappearance. Could it be as simple as him misjudging the firth on an evening walk one night? If he had drowned, that would certainly prevent him from returning for his dog and briefcase.

But Yeats said Holmes had left the boarding house on the Wednesday evening and Carly received a voicemail from him on the Friday. That left almost forty-eight hours unaccounted for. If Holmes was alive and well on Friday evening, why hadn't he returned to the boarding house to pick up his dog and his suitcase in the interim? No, an accidental drowning didn't add up when you took the timeline they'd built into account.

'I wish I knew where Holmes had been and what he was doing on that Thursday we can't account for,' Kitt said, clearly thinking along similar lines to Joe.

'At least we've managed to narrow down the time we can't account for a bit,' said Grace. 'But yes, I'm with you, the sooner we fill in the rest of the blanks when it comes to his whereabouts, the better. Whatever made him leave that voicemail, whether it was just a choice to start a new life or something more sinister, is likely to have happened on that lost Thursday.'

Joe glanced at the briefcase sitting on Kitt's knee via his mirror.

'Maybe there are some answers in the briefcase. What do you think might be in there?' asked Joe.

'Oh, it could be anything from dirty laundry to wads of cash,' Kitt said.

'Oooh!' said Grace. 'I vote for wads of cash, let it be wads of cash! Then I could get a swimming pool installed on the roof of the agency and get super fit and become a ninja and—'

'Grace, I really don't think that voting on it determines what we'll find in the briefcase, I'm sorry to report,' Kitt said with a gentle smile. 'And frankly, the thought of you acquiring ninja skills is enough to keep anyone up late at night.'

'How are we going to open it without a key?' said Joe, doing what he could to keep his mind on the big questions despite Grace's amusing antics. 'Can it be prised or forced open?'

'I'm not sure about that,' said Kitt. Joe stole a glance in the rear-view mirror to see her hold the briefcase close to her nose.

'What are you sniffing the briefcase for?' The question was out of Joe's mouth before he could stop it, even though deep down something told him he didn't really want the answer.

'Bananas and almonds,' Kitt replied in a matter-of-fact manner. As if this were a perfectly logical response.

'Bananas and almonds?' Joe repeated. Wondering if this was some kind of joke between Kitt and Grace that he wasn't privy to.

'Some explosives have a certain smell to them,' Grace explained, as casually as if she was explaining what time the local bus stopped at the end of her road.

'Explosives!' said Joe.

But he didn't get any further clarification. The next thing he heard was a rattling sound. He again glanced in the mirror to see Kitt shaking the briefcase with an impressive amount of rigour.

'Don't shake it if you think there's a bomb in there!' Joe almost screeched.

'Don't be silly,' said Kitt. 'I'm shaking it because I *don't* think there's a bomb in there. At least . . . the odds are very much against it.'

'Oh well, that's very comforting,' said Joe.

'I still can't get these clasps to budge,' said Kitt, seemingly completely unaware of how perturbed Joe was. 'But luckily, I have read quite a few things about lock-picking in my time.'

'I knew it!' said Grace. 'All this time you've been masquerading as a private investigator searching for the truth when in fact you've been secretly picking people's locks, stealing their most valuable possessions and selling them on eBay for a profit.'

'Grace, please, give it a rest,' said Kitt. 'I know you get

even more hyperactive than usual when you've been stuck in a car all day but—'

'Don't worry,' Grace said, cutting Kitt off. 'I'm willing to keep my peace if you give me my share of the proceeds.'

'Oh, do give over, Grace. You're even more bananas than normal today.'

'Are you trying to pretend there's an innocent explanation for all your reading up on lock-picking?' Grace pushed, though Joe could tell from her tone she knew very well that there was indeed an innocent explanation.

'If I must spell it out for you,' said Kitt. 'You might remember during our time in Whitby a few years ago I was kidnapped and almost thrown in an incinerator.'

'Of course I remember, you never shut up about it,' Grace said, before leaning her head over Joe's headrest and adding, 'All we hear all day is incinerator this, incinerator that.'

'Grace.'

'All right, I get it. I was just trying to lighten the mood. You don't want to be locked in a room somewhere again, unable to get out. I suppose I believe that's the kind of thing a person might want to guard against happening to them twice. Sorry, I didn't mean to bring up a sore subject.'

'I know you didn't, don't worry about it,' Kitt said, the warmth to her voice returning.

Joe wanted to ask more about Whitby and the kidnap and the incinerator but the whole episode had obviously, and understandably, left Kitt with some scars so Joe decided not to try and weasel out any more information on the matter. If Kitt wanted to tell him more about that, or any other brush with danger she may have had, she would do so in her own time. Besides anything else, he wasn't sure how much information he wanted about the unsettling things Kitt had endured in the name of seeking justice for those who couldn't seek it for themselves. His ideas about this profession being like a Raymond Chandler novel at once seemed immature almost to the point of being childish. He hadn't grasped the dangers back then, nor the stakes.

He was starting to now.

'You really think you can pick the lock?' he said instead, impressed that this was yet another skill she seemed to have in her arsenal. He supposed that being a private investigator, you probably had to be prepared for almost anything. Still, it was admirable just how far Kitt had done her best to make sure that she was.

'The truth is, I don't know,' Kitt replied. 'I've not had the opportunity to use the lock-picking information in the field. Perhaps I should be grateful for that. But in the name of trying to help Ralph Holmes, wherever he may be, I'm going to give opening this briefcase my very best shot.'

CHAPTER TEN

This was Joe's first visit to Carlisle and he was surprised by just how picturesque the city was. Like most British cities, it had a high street boasting all the usual brand names one would expect to find but it also had some truly unique architectural flourishes. Not long after passing the welcome sign, they drove straight past the Citadel which, Kitt had informed them, had been commissioned by Henry VIII and was built in 1541. It staggered Joe that a building could survive that many council planning meetings. But then Grace had found an article online that explained some of it had been heavily rebuilt in the 1800s. Still, there was no denying the distinctly medieval aesthetic of the circular towers, illuminated with yellow floodlights, which once operated as a fortress, later as a prison.

From there, they had driven over the Eden River to The Queen Mary Hotel in Marlborough Gardens. According to Kitt, Mary Queen of Scots had been held captive in a tower at the nearby Carlisle Castle. The buildings in this area of town may not have been medieval fortresses, but they were impressive in their own right. Big, detached red-brick affairs, each with their own keenly pruned gardens. The streets were wide and lined with Victorian-style lamp posts. On hearing Kitt explain the relationship between Mary Queen of Scots and Carlisle on the drive to the hotel, Joe had wondered what kind of establishment would choose emancipation as a theme. On arrival, he saw with his own eyes that it was thankfully nothing more than a historic reference. The hotel was the polar opposite of prison-like Lowland View bed and breakfast outside and in and mercifully, given they had Rolo in tow, it was also dog-friendly.

A strange feeling came over Joe on entering the hotel. Somehow it felt to him that they had re-entered civilization after their cold, windy stint out on the isolated coastline. The doorway to the hotel was marked by two cylindrical pillars which, just like the rest of the exterior, had been painted white. Joe had marvelled at how spotless the stone had looked. But perhaps it was only natural to marvel at such details after being stuck in the airless death trap run by Julius Yeats.

Inside, Joe was almost overjoyed to inhale the scent of lemon-fresh sanitizer and a waft of roasting beef that filtered through from the restaurant. He had wondered if he'd ever get the stench of The Lowland View B&B out of his lungs but the fragrant smells of their own hotel made those unfortunate experiences little more than a fading memory.

At the smell of food all three of them, four counting Rolo, had decided a meal was in order. Kitt, Joe and Grace had all had a sandwich in the car on the way over but that felt a long time ago. Thus, the second they'd checked into their rooms, and Joe had settled the dog in his, they had dined in the hotel bar. After the long afternoon they'd had trying to ascertain whether Carly had any need to be concerned about her uncle, all three of them had devoured their meal and spoke sparingly between mouthfuls.

The hotel had provided a bed, a bowl and some food for Rolo but being a complete soft touch with animals, Joe made sure he wrapped some of his chicken in a serviette for the hound, after carefully removing the bones. It seemed a good idea to do all he could to encourage the dog to trust him, at least until he was able to purchase a lead for the beast and hopefully better control him. If past experience was anything to go by, feeding a dog roasted meats was a sure-fire way to get their obedience, if not their trust.

Once everyone, including the dog, had been fed, they had reconvened in Kitt and Grace's room and Kitt had got straight on with the task of opening the briefcase by any means necessary.

'How's the lock-picking going, Kitt?' Grace asked while Joe held his breath, waiting for Kitt's response. He was lying on Grace's bed with Rolo by his side, struggling to keep his eyes open. The beds at this hotel were the kind you sank into. As if the bed was hugging you and didn't want to let you go. Or did Joe just feel that way because he was so tired? The drive, and everything that had transpired that afternoon, had really taken it out of him. So much had happened in such a short space of time and yet the afternoon had felt almost never-ending while it was happening.

'For goodness' sake, Grace,' Kitt snapped from her chair over at the dressing table. 'Can't you find something else to do rather than ask me that?'

Grace, who was sitting on the other side of Rolo, made a show of thinking quite deeply on that question. 'Uuuuum . . . no.'

'If you're going to ask me every thirty seconds how things are going, I'm never going to be able to concentrate long enough to make any progress,' Kitt chuntered.

'Noted,' Grace said while Kitt rolled her eyes. No doubt wondering how long Grace would manage to keep her peace before asking again.

Joe kept his peace, not wanting to distract Kitt from her task. He imagined he wasn't going to get any sleep until that briefcase was open so the quicker that happened, the better. Idly, he stared up at the cream-painted ceiling. Each room was fitted with a small chandelier which, though not to Joe's taste, was much more welcoming than the bare bulb in the room where Ralph Holmes had supposedly stayed.

And the only thing Joe could smell here was the soapy scent of fresh-laundered towels.

Grace flopped back against a pillow. 'This is taking for ever.'

'I've only been at it for six minutes, give me a chance,' Kitt said. Joe looked over to where she was sitting to see her grappling with a straightened-out paperclip. Could getting into a case really be that easy? Well, she hadn't had any luck yet but like she said, it took concentration and Grace was being as distracting as usual. Perhaps if Joe distracted Grace, Kitt might have a fighting chance of solving the problem that bit quicker.

'So, Grace,' Joe said, hoping that in singling her out he wasn't being too obvious. 'How do we handle it if we find something unnerving inside this case?'

'You mean, like a severed head?' said Grace.

Joe tried to keep a straight face as he spoke again. 'I don't think that case is quite big enough to hold something like that.'

A wicked little smirk formed on Grace's lips. 'That's because you're working on the basis that the severed head is in one piece.'

'Grace, please,' Kitt said without looking up from the briefcase.

'I was thinking more like if we found something that incriminated Holmes,' said Joe, again trying to steer Grace's attentions in a more useful direction. 'How do we deal with it, in terms of breaking it to Carly?'

'There's no easy way of breaking news like that,' said Grace, adopting a far more serious expression than Joe had ever thought her capable of. 'It depends on what we find. I like to think she's smart enough to know we might find things out about her uncle that could prove hurtful. But knowing that intellectually is different from hearing the truth in real time. So, if there is something in there that incriminates Ralph Holmes, maybe points to a reason why someone might make him disappear, we'll need to be as sensitive as we can when we tell Carly about it.'

'I can't help wondering if we'll find something damning in there about Julius Yeats. He's by far the shadiest person we've met here so far.'

Quick as a flash, Grace said, 'I'm not sure he would have handed over the briefcase and the dog for a measly fifty quid if he had something to do with Holmes's disappearance, like.'

'Bloody thing's probably full of promotional fliers for The Lowland View bed and breakfast. That's the kind of stunt Yeats would pull,' Kitt muttered under her breath, while continuing to wrestle with the paperclip. Seemingly, she was still keeping one ear on the conversation. 'He probably had the key, emptied the thing of any valuables – or evidence of anything that might incriminate him or his establishment – and then threw the key away. I wouldn't put it past him. I'm not sure I'd put anything past him.'

'I know what you mean,' said Grace. 'But then again, I suppose if the police had rocked up looking for Holmes, Yeats could have ingratiated himself with them by providing the briefcase, even if it was empty. Sounds like the kind of weaselly thing a man like him would do.'

'He's definitely someone I could imagine being a small-time crook, the way he swindled you out of that money,' said Joe. 'I suppose the big question is whether or not he'd ever graduate to anything more sinister than that.'

'He didn't really strike me as someone with a lot of back-bone,' said Grace. 'And committing a serious crime – one in which people get hurt or worse – takes a certain amount of grit. One thing I will say, it was a bit weird how he assumed we were the police when we showed up.'

'Yeah, that's true. Especially when we hadn't told him what we were there for,' Joe agreed. 'If we'd said, we're looking for this missing person, like we did with Donna at the pub, then it would have been reasonable for him to ask if we were linked with the authorities. You'd expect officers to be looking for someone in a situation like that.'

'But all we did was ask for the owner,' said Grace. 'For all he knew we could have just been potential guests enquiring about a big group booking or asking for help because our car had been boxed in in the car park by another vehicle. But he didn't assume it was something small like that. He immediately assumed we were there on official police business.'

'A fishy response for sure,' Kitt said, though it was obvious by her tone that most of her concentration was still focused on the lock.

'Donna did say that Yeats isn't the kind of person she'd want to get on the wrong side of,' said Grace. 'I wonder if she was trying to tip us off about something he was up to without actually saying it out loud in front of all the regulars she had in. You said yourself, Kitt, that the B&B could be a front for something else.'

'Yes,' Kitt said. 'A drug smuggling operation or money laundering immediately spring to mind. He certainly didn't want the police keeping an eye on the property, which doesn't exactly give you confidence in his innocence.'

'I suppose it could be either of those things,' said Grace. 'Or something else in the same sort of crime bracket. The thing about Donna's warning that really rattles me is that she's a pub landlady. You've got to be pretty tough to do that job, you know. Especially out there, in an isolated area. There aren't any nearby police stations to call if you're having trouble with someone who's had a pint too many. I imagine she lets people know who's boss as soon as she can. But despite all that she is wary of Yeats.'

'Just thinking about Yeats and the place he runs gives me the shivers,' said Joe. 'It's got that air about it, you know, that some really dark stuff has gone down there over the years.'

'I think that's true of most commercial accommodation,' said Kitt.

'Really?' said Joe. The darker events that might transpire in any given hotel room had never really crossed his mind when he and Sarah had been on honeymoon in the Seychelles, or on any of the many other little getaways they'd managed in the time they'd been together.

'Law of averages,' Kitt said, still distracted by the task of opening the briefcase. 'Any given hotel room probably has new residents in it roughly every three nights. That's a hundred different groups of people a year, at least. In each room. I would say at least some of those people had to be up to no good. There's no real arguing with the numbers.'

'You don't want to get Kitt started on topics like this,' Grace said. 'She's too well-read, if you ask me.'

'No such thing!' Kitt called over, but Grace wasn't going to be deterred from making her point.

'There are some things you don't need to think about when you rest your head on a pillow at night and how many people have stayed in your room and what they might have got up to is one of them. I think in Yeats's case, though, his B&B is more likely to attract the wrong crowd than most. The only logical reason he'd be worried that we were the police is if he was running some kind of racket himself and was making sure he didn't accidentally say something to get himself caught.'

'Maybe,' Joe said, but in his mind another story was

forming about Ralph Holmes. What if he really did book into The Lowland B&B not knowing what kind of place it was? And to keep the peace on his holiday he just stuck it out. But then, one day – or night – he saw something he shouldn't. Maybe the owner was involved, or maybe he just witnessed them turning a blind eye. And whoever it was who perpetrated the act decided to make sure he didn't tell anyone else. It seemed to Joe that Yeats would do almost anything for fifty quid. Including keeping his mouth shut if someone he was afraid of told him to. Maybe it was just the creepy atmosphere of the boarding house that had got to him but Joe couldn't shake the feeling that Yeats was somehow involved in the disappearance of Ralph Holmes. Even if it was just that he knew more than he was letting on. If he was withholding something crucial, like a reason or motive someone might make Ralph Holmes disappear, he was getting in the way of them helping both Holmes and Carly.

'Oh . . . oh!' Kitt exclaimed, before going very quiet. She looked over at Joe and Grace. It seemed to Joe that she barely dared utter her next words. 'I – I think I've got it,' she added, her voice trembling with the same anticipation Joe now felt.

Slowly, Joe and Grace stood up from the bed and moved closer to where Kitt was sitting. Taking a deep breath, Kitt lifted the lid on the briefcase.

'Oh ... my ... God,' said Grace, as she looked at its contents, her tone betraying her disbelief.

Joe for his part could only stand speechless over what he was looking at. His mouth hanging open. His throat drying out as he contemplated all of the possible implications.

CHAPTER ELEVEN

Though none of them had put gloves on to have a root around quite yet, just looking into the briefcase from a few paces away was enough to confirm this was a big discovery. Inside, Joe could see wads of cash, just as Grace had wished for earlier. But the money was in various different currencies, each currency packed in a clear plastic bag.

Examining the contents closer after the initial shock of seeing so much money in there, Joe noticed a photograph of a man. Not Holmes. Someone else. The subject had short grey hair cut very close to his head and wore a long, double-breasted camel coat. It struck Joe as odd that there was a physical photograph in the briefcase. Almost nobody printed photographs these days. Nearly all images were exchanged digitally. Was this man a friend or foe to Holmes? Assuming, of course, that they could take Yeats's word for the fact that this suitcase did in fact belong to him.

While pondering this, Joe let his eyes roam further over

the contents. He noticed a small, pocket-sized notebook with the words *St Michael* scrawled on the top page in pencil. Nestled next to that were several passports for several different countries and, perhaps most worryingly of all, there was a small handgun resting next to them.

Slowly, Kitt put on plastic gloves and opened the passports in turn. All of them had a picture of Ralph Holmes inside them. Some of them, however, had alternative names printed inside. Alan McKendry. Keith Driver. James Piper.

Aliases for Carly's uncle. The man they had known as Ralph Holmes. Kitt dropped the last passport back into the case and then slammed the top of it shut as though that would somehow make what they had seen in there disappear.

'Oh my God,' she said, standing up and taking three paces. 'Oh my God.'

'Stop saying that,' said Grace.

'You said it first,' said Kitt.

'I know that. That's my job when we make an unexpected discovery. But when you say it, it freaks me out. You don't say things like that in these situations. You look unruffled and then talk about something you read in a book once so that we all get so bored we forget about the possible danger we're in. That's the unwritten rule.'

Kitt stopped pacing and glared at Grace. 'Thank you for that. As it happens, I have read enough to know that there are two likely things the contents of that case suggest about Ralph Holmes. Neither of them exactly comforting.'

'I'm listening,' said Grace.

'The first possibility is that he's involved in organized, international crime in some way,' said Kitt.

'As in, committing crimes across borders? Joining forces with criminals overseas?' said Joe.

'It wouldn't be the first time we'd brushed up against that kind of person,' Kitt said with a nod. 'The most common types of operations are usually to do with drugs or money laundering but if he is involved with some kind of international racket, it's impossible to know exactly what he might have been doing, and how he was doing it, without more context. It could be something particularly grim, or grave. Nothing can be dismissed at this stage.'

'Organized crime gives me the creeps,' said Grace. 'Some of these gangs and groups are more meticulous than you'd believe. They'll go to extreme lengths to protect their operations. There's usually a very convoluted chain that prevents anyone at the top, anyone who is really calling the shots, ever getting caught by the police. So it just continues on for years with the same ring leaders and different patsies. If that is how Ralph Holmes is making his money, though, I'd say we are looking at one heartbroken client.'

Joe's thoughts immediately leapt to the look of desperation when Carly had told them about her uncle's disappearance. She had been convinced that her uncle was in trouble of some kind and that he needed her help. But she'd talked about him owing money to the wrong people. She'd never suggested anything more sinister than that. How would she react if they uncovered some horrible truth about how her uncle made his money? Money laundering and drug dealing were bad enough but organized crime groups were sometimes involved in human trafficking too. Would Carly still want to help her uncle if he'd done something unforgiveable? Would Kitt for that matter?

'What about the second possibility you mentioned?' said Grace.

'Spy.' Joe said the word before Kitt could, though he could barely believe it was coming out of his mouth.

Kitt pressed her lips together before speaking as though trying to digest the prospect herself. 'Espionage of some nature could be involved here. Individuals involved in that kind of work have need of things like foreign passports and currencies. Not to mention the gun.'

'You mean, he could have been working for the British government when he disappeared?' said Grace.

'Unfortunately,' Kitt said, 'we can't assume who he was working for. With Holmes missing, there's no way of ascertaining if he was working for the British government . . . or someone else.'

'Someone else . . . like who?' said Grace, her eyes widening. 'You mean, a foreign country? Spying on Britain and helping someone who might want to compromise our security?'

'We can't rule it out, not yet,' Kitt said. 'Britain has had frosty political relationships with a number of countries for years. From what I know, sometimes these countries send their own agents across seas to infiltrate our systems. In other circumstances, they try to convert British people already living and working in the system. Bribing them or otherwise incentivizing them to provide information that could prove damaging to the government. Ralph Holmes could be working for anyone and there's no point speculating who at this point. We just have to leave it on the table as an option and tread very, very carefully.'

'So, what do we do now?' Joe said, still in disbelief at how quickly things had become more serious than he ever imagined they could be. Opening that briefcase had changed everything for them.

Kitt took a deep breath and closed her eyes for a moment. When she opened them, she seemed somehow more in control. 'The first thing we need to do is secure our own records. We need to take photographs of the contents of this briefcase. We need to have photographic evidence that this case once existed and was in our possession in case it's important later because one way or another, we're not going to be able to hold on to it.'

'Are you going to pass it on to the police?' said Grace.

'I think we have to,' Kitt said. 'Even though that is highly likely to make working our case more difficult. The truth is, anything this serious can't be kept from the authorities. And for all we know, they already have some intelligence that will help them work out what this briefcase means and how it relates to Holmes. Before I get anyone local involved, however, I'll call Mal and see who he thinks we should speak to and how we should go about it.'

'OK, that makes sense. But then what?' said Grace. 'Where does it leave our search for Ralph Holmes?'

'The same place it was before, except now we've got a possible reason why he's missing. Carly is paying us to find her uncle so regardless of where it leads us, that's what we've got to try and do,' said Kitt.

'Do you think Carly knows anything about this?' said Joe, casting his mind back to the initial meeting they had with her.

Kitt shook her head. 'She didn't give any indication of it. Other than saying she didn't know how her uncle made his money.'

'If I was in her position, my first thought would be that he might be involved with something that wasn't totally above board – shady investments or something,' said Grace. 'I don't think I'd even contemplate the idea that my own uncle was some kind of James Bond figure. God, can you imagine your uncle being James Bond?'

'Or a Bond villain,' said Joe, unable to stop himself from dwelling on the idea that Ralph Holmes could be an enemy of the UK government, spying for another country that means them harm.

'That idea is certainly going to put a different complexion on family dinners at my parents' house,' said Grace.

'Funny, isn't it?' said Kitt. 'We know objectively that espionage happens every day. That there are government agencies working in intelligence, monitoring threats to national security. But it still seems like a surreal idea that these people operate in society alongside us. That we might brush shoulders with them without even knowing about it.'

'Assuming Ralph is a spy, and not a criminal,' said Joe, 'what on earth do you think brought him up here? I don't really have a solid explanation as to why but I just don't picture a place like this as a hotbed of international espionage.'

'I don't know much about why spies go where they go, or do what they do,' said Grace, 'but I did read online that there are a few naval bases in the area. Maybe it has something to do with that?'

'Quite possibly,' said Kitt. 'There's the nuclear plant at Sellafield, of course, but that hasn't produced nuclear energy for decades. Last I read about it, they were slowly shutting the place down piece by piece . . . But, of course, the campus is huge. Thousands of buildings.'

'You think the government might be working on something top secret there?' said Joe. 'Using the decommissioning of the plant to cover up something else?'

Kitt chuckled. 'I can't say my ideas were that grand, though I suppose it's not impossible. I was mostly thinking about all the sensitive data that might be lying around a place like that. Some of those buildings probably still contain classified documents or information.'

'And you think a spy working for another country might try and access that information?' said Joe.

Kitt shrugged. 'I really don't know. I just don't think it's an idea we can rule out until we know more. Anyway, I must get on the phone to Mal about this and see what he thinks we should do.'

'What are we going to do about updating Carly?' said Grace. 'The discovery of the briefcase feels like something we should let her know about. Maybe it will jog something in her memory. Something that will help us with finding Holmes.'

'First, I'll check Mal thinks that's a good idea. The odds are he'll have more of an idea about how government agencies work than we do. But assuming he can't see a flaw in the logic, we will ring Carly and let her know we've found a briefcase we believe belongs to her uncle. When you talk to her, describe the contents but don't be drawn on what they might mean. Tell her it's too early to say, because to be honest, it is. The last thing we need is to have her worrying that her uncle might be involved in some kind of crime ring or spying for, or on, the UK government when, in fact, nothing is confirmed yet.'

'You're sure now's the right time to tell her about the briefcase?' said Joe. 'Should we not wait till we know more?'

'Probably not an option,' said Kitt. 'As soon as the police

see the contents of that briefcase, I'd imagine they'll start to pay a bit more attention to this case. And the likelihood is they'll have some questions for Carly. Better that we call her and let her know that the police are likely to engage now than leave her worrying that we're her only hope in finding her uncle.'

'I suppose that makes sense,' Joe said. He took a deep breath, trying to take everything in. His first case as an amateur private investigator and this is where it had led, either an international crime ring or international espionage. The thought of grappling with that level of investigation when he had really just started learning the ropes both frightened and excited him all at the same time. On the one hand, there were few things he'd love more than to be part of a team that brought down an international crime ring or stopped an enemy spy from gleaning information that could threaten national security. There's no doubt that in doing so he'd have made a real contribution to making society a better place. It's a story he'd dine out on for the rest of his life. Likely he would need to as his life was unlikely to ever get more exciting than this.

On the other hand, though, he couldn't help but think about Carly. From everything she'd told them, she thought of Holmes as a kindly uncle. One she cared enough about to hire a private investigator even when the police told her there was nothing to be done. Holmes might still come out of this looking quite well, of course. He might not be involved with international crime, or be working for a foreign government. There was still a chance he could have been serving his country, working for a UK agency and completing a patriotic mission when he disappeared.

And yet, there was an unsettled feeling in the pit of Joe's stomach. One that told him that when it came to Ralph Holmes, there were yet more dark secrets to unravel.

'Hi, Mal,' he heard Kitt say over the phone. 'I'm sorry to call so late, love, I know you're knackered from working on the fraud case but, look, something's happened. I mean, we've found something unsettling, and we're going to need your help.'

CHAPTER TWELVE

'Anything else you can tell us about how you came upon this briefcase?' Detective Inspector Cobb asked several hours later. It was nearing one in the morning and even in spite of all they had found in the case, the heady possibilities the contents conjured, Joe was struggling to keep his eyes open. He rubbed them for what must have been the tenth time in the last quarter of an hour. Blinking hard after doing so in an attempt to refocus on the scene that was playing out in Kitt's hotel room.

The detective from Cumberland police headquarters had arrived at the Queen Mary Hotel just after Halloran had an hour or so ago. After talking to Kitt on the phone, Halloran had become quite worried about the scale of the case they were working and had driven across the Pennines to make sure any interactions they had with the police were properly handled.

Kitt, Grace and Joe had spent the time awaiting the arrival

of both Halloran and the local police photographing the contents of the briefcase and, while wearing gloves, had turned each item over to make sure they weren't missing any obvious clues.

The only thing that hadn't been evident from their initial assessment of the briefcase was some markings on the back of the photograph featuring the man in the camel coat. It seemed someone had been keeping some kind of tally. Across the bottom of the reverse of the photograph, there were twelve strikes in the tally. Across the top, the tally had been written in two blocks. The first totalling twelve and the second ten. The trio had spent quite some minutes trying to come up with some idea about what the person who made these markings – presumably Holmes – could have been counting but without any context, they hadn't settled on anything that sounded remotely plausible. Grace, in her usual macabre vein, suggested that Holmes may have been totalling the number of people he'd shot with the enclosed pistol but, when pressed, couldn't come up with a convincing reason why he might do that.

'I think we've covered everything,' said Kitt, in answer to Cobb's question. 'Though of course if I think of anything else, I'll report it immediately. I . . . I don't think Mr Yeats knew what he had in his possession. Otherwise, I doubt he would have handed it over to us. But I suppose you never know. It might be worth talking to him again. He might be more keen to cooperate with a police officer than he was with us.'

'Sadly, I wouldn't hold your breath on that,' Cobb said, pursing his lips, the lines around his eyes growing deeper at the mention of Yeats. 'It's funny how often Mr Yeats's name comes up in our enquiries and yet somehow there's never a shred of evidence that he's done anything untoward.'

'Got a few like that on our patch,' Halloran said. 'I know how it goes. Like Kitt, I doubt he'd have handed that briefcase over if he'd known there was money in it from the sound of his . . . shall we be kind and call them antics?'

'Why not, I'm in a charitable mood,' Cobb's partner Jessops piped up. She was a little taller than Cobb and a little quieter. At least, she had taken the back seat while Cobb had questioned them all about how the briefcase had been acquired.

'Maybe if you lean on him hard enough, you'll get lucky and he'll let something slip,' Halloran said, a smile peeking through his beard at Jessops' comment.

'Maybe,' Jessops said. 'But that man could worm his way out of anything.'

'We'll see what he has to say for himself,' said Cobb. 'You keeping the dog for now?' The officer glanced over at Rolo, who lay mournfully on the maroon carpet. His chin hard against the floor and his big brown eyes looking up at the humans who, perhaps on some level he knew would decide his ultimate fate.

'I like dogs,' Halloran said, before walking over to where Rolo was lying. He crouched down to give the hound a stroke behind the ears and Rolo responded by leaning hard into Halloran's hand.

Kitt rolled her eyes. 'Iago can't hear you from this distance, Mal.'

'You don't know what that cat's capable of,' Halloran muttered under his breath, while Rolo sat up and pawed at Halloran's coat for more fuss.

'I'd like to hold on to him at least for now, only if that's all right,' said Joe. The house had felt so empty since Sarah died. Objectively, he understood that if Holmes wanted his dog back when they found him, he'd have to say goodbye to the pooch. But secretly, Joe had already been imagining that by some twist he'd get to keep Rolo for himself. And he'd have some company, without the difficult entanglements a new roommate or romantic interest might create. 'That is, if you don't need him for evidence or anything. I don't really know how all this works, I'm just with Kitt's team for work shadowing, you see.'

'Holmes has been missing four days now,' said Cobb. 'Even if the dog was present when he disappeared, or when something else happened to him, four days is long enough that any forensic evidence on his coat or paws would be long gone. Especially if he's been kept in The Lowland View bed and breakfast. So, if you're happy to look after him for now, well, it's one less dog in the pound.'

Instinctively, Joe walked over to the dog and joined Halloran in giving him a stroke or two. The poor dog had surely been through enough without being sent off to the pound. He scratched the dog under the collar. The name plate medallion around his neck jangled as he did so.

'It's no trouble at all to look after him, even if we end up going back home. He can stay with me in Huddersfield until, well, until he's needed elsewhere,' said Joe.

'Is there anything we can do to help regarding this matter, Inspector Cobb?' said Kitt. 'We've been hired to find Holmes, as you know, so we are at your disposal if there's something you'd be happy to have a civilian check into.'

'I've worked several cases where Kitt's provided useful intelligence,' Halloran chimed in. 'She can be an asset if there's information known to the public you want her to look into further.'

'Much as we appreciate the offer,' Cobb said, throwing a sideways glance at Jessops, 'the contents of that briefcase suggest that this could be really serious business. Which means we'll have to keep everything strictly compartmentalized, I'm afraid.'

'I understand,' Halloran said with a nod.

'We are still beholden to our client, of course,' said Kitt. 'So we'll continue to make enquiries about Holmes in the Port Carlisle area. If we find anything concrete, we'll pass it on to you.'

'That's very generous,' Inspector Cobb said, 'but given

we've got police resources at our disposal, the odds are we'll turn something up before you do.'

The gentle smile that had been resting on Kitt's lips disappeared at this. Grace shot Joe a look of mock horror to indicate that Kitt would not appreciate a comment like that. Cobb, however, wasn't going to hang around long enough to notice that Kitt had been put out by what he'd said.

'Thank you again for bringing this matter to our attention,' said Cobb, while giving Jessops the nod that it was time for them to get going. 'We appreciate all the information you've given us and will be in touch if there's anything else.'

The briefcase swung from Cobb's gloved hand as the pair made their way towards the door and left the room.

The second the door was shut, Kitt's tirade began.

'Turn something up before we do, indeed—'

'Now, pet. Come on. Cases like these are their full-time job,' said Halloran. 'They're not used to having civilians do anything much other than report things to them.'

'It's *my* part-time job,' said Kitt. 'I do have some experience. It's not like I've never solved a case. Our work has been well-publicized in the media.'

'Thanks to our first-class PR department,' Grace said, pointing a thumb at herself.

But Kitt was too irritated to notice Grace's attempt at mild humour. 'To be brushed off like that, like I'm nothing but a raving amateur. I can do without it. They wouldn't even have that briefcase if we hadn't followed up on a case the police deemed not worthy of their time. It really grates my cheese when they do things like this.'

'I know,' Halloran said with a smile that was clearly designed to try and draw a smile from Kitt. 'You don't have to tell me how good you are at investigating. I've been watching you for years . . . very closely.'

In spite of herself Kitt did smile at this. 'Oh, give over, Mal. Honestly. You'll give Grace enough ammunition for months to come on the teasing front.'

'Oh, I've already got plenty of that,' said Grace. 'Halloran can't possibly drive back to York tonight. It's too far.'

'I don't say this often, but Grace is right,' said Kitt. 'I can text Marie next door in the morning and ask her to feed Iago.'

'Which means the three of us will have to stay in this room like one big happy family,' Grace said before turning to Halloran. 'Are you my new dad?'

'Grace!' Kitt said, shaking her head. 'In what context am I your mother?'

'Mmm. I'll get back to you on that,' Grace said, and before she could say anything else, Kitt jumped in.

'I'm sure we can find an extra room for you somewhere in the hotel,' she said to Grace. 'That way I'll actually get some sleep tonight and tomorrow we can set off fresh on the trail of Ralph Holmes.'

'But I thought you told Cobb everything,' Halloran said.

'He'll be following up on what you've said, so is it really worth getting straight back on it?'

'I need to sleep on it. All of it. Evie was talking about coming up to visit us tomorrow and maybe that will provide a bit of welcome distraction, you know. Give me enough mental space from it all for something new to come to mind. We can't just sit around when we've got a client counting on us, though,' said Kitt. 'We've got photographs of everything in that briefcase so we've got all the information the police have. I'm sure it won't be so difficult to notice something they haven't before they do and beat them to the punch . . . Oh, er, no offence, Mal.'

'None taken, I suppose,' Halloran said with a grudging smile. 'But you're going to have to be very careful about any next steps. The contents of that briefcase . . . the best-case scenario is that you've stumbled across something that belongs to a British intelligence operative. But even that could have dangerous consequences.'

'In what way?' said Joe, frowning.

'I know what Halloran's getting at,' said Kitt. 'Why would he leave it? The briefcase, why would he just leave it in a boarding house like that when it contains currency, identification and a weapon?'

'He wouldn't,' said Grace. 'You would never leave something like that behind. Holmes's photo was on each and every one of those passports. If he was a British agent, which as Halloran says is a best-case scenario, he wouldn't just leave something like that lying around for a possible enemy to find. Especially in a case with a lock that can be picked.'

'Yes, that's a good point,' said Joe. 'If you do work for a government agency, why would you be carrying such a low-tech briefcase? Wouldn't they be more likely to use some high-powered combination lock? Or a biometric lock or something? Or have I just seen too many Tom Cruise films?'

'I know that seems more likely,' said Halloran. 'But I can only go on how it works for undercover coppers. You are trying to blend in. Trying to make it seem like it's no big deal that you're walking down the street holding a briefcase with classified contents inside. As such, the costume has to match. Has to be inconspicuous. If there was some kind of high-tech lock on that thing, anyone who saw Holmes on a bus or a train or simply sitting in the park with it waiting for a meet might get suspicious about what was in the case.'

'But nobody would look twice at someone carrying an old-fangled manual lock briefcase,' said Kitt.

'Exactly,' said Halloran.

'But going back to what you said before,' said Joe. 'The fact that you wouldn't willingly leave a briefcase like that in a room for an enemy to find, are you trying to say you think something terrible happened to Ralph Holmes?'

'If he's a British agent, and not a crime ring leader, then yes,' said Halloran. 'I'd say the most likely scenario in that event would be that he had either been captured by an enemy agent or murdered by one.'

Murdered.

Joe gave himself a moment to let that word sink in. How right Carly had been to worry about her uncle. To press the issue even though the police had sent her away.

'If that is the case, Carly was likely right about Holmes leaving that voicemail under duress,' said Joe.

'It looks like it,' said Kitt.

'But this is exactly why even the best-case scenario is a terrible scenario for you,' Halloran continued, determined to make his point. 'If Holmes has been captured or murdered by an enemy agent, the people who are holding him or have killed him are the most dangerous you can imagine. Most of them are field-trained assassins. And if they find out that you are on the trail of Ralph Holmes, well, I see no reason why they won't make it their business to tie up loose ends.'

'You mean . . .' Grace started to speak but clearly couldn't bring herself to finish the sentence.

'I mean,' Halloran said, slowly, deliberately, 'if they find out that you are looking for Holmes and trying to bring to light what happened to him, you could very well be their next target.'

CHAPTER THIRTEEN

After receiving a phone call from Grace the night before regarding the briefcase they'd found, Carly had driven straight up to Carlisle to join Kitt, Joe, Halloran and Grace at the hotel breakfast table the following morning. She'd set off even before the crack of dawn from a friend's house in Derby so she could speak to Kitt in person about what they had discovered so far. Quite understandably, according to Grace, Carly had been more than a little bit disturbed about the contents of the briefcase and no matter how Grace had tried to fob her off with generic phrases such as 'we can't draw any conclusions yet', Carly hadn't seemed all that convinced by this tack.

'Have the police been in touch with you?' asked Kitt, once Carly had poured herself a cup of tea. Joe could tell she'd left her friend's house in a rush because her blonde, bobbed hair, which had been meticulously straightened when she'd paid her visit to Hartley and Edwards Investigations, rested in gentle, somewhat unkempt waves.

'They haven't, not yet,' said Carly, grabbing a slice of toast and buttering it. 'I was a bit surprised by that. I mean, from what you say they only left the hotel in the early hours of the morning but I was sort of expecting a call first thing. Not because I think my case should be sitting at the top of the pile or anything. Just because what you found . . . well, to say it sounded serious is a bit of an understatement. Is it wrong for me to assume they'd be all over something like that?'

Carly looked over to Halloran as she said this. Kitt had already introduced him as her partner and made Carly aware he was an off-duty detective inspector and she'd seemed rather pleased to have someone who was experienced in law enforcement sitting at the table.

'I would have expected them to be in touch with you as soon as possible,' said Halloran. 'Still, no need to panic about not hearing from them just yet. Lots of things can delay those kinds of communications. Such as waiting for a superior to sign something off or other similar administrative tasks. Quite boring, I know, but it's how we make sure we keep a record of everything.'

'I suspect you'll hear from them soon enough,' said Kitt. 'They wouldn't give much away to us. For all we know they have information we don't and you're not their first point of contact. But I imagine you'll hear from them at some juncture.'

'I'll be keeping a close eye on my phone,' said Carly.

'That's one call I really wouldn't want to miss. I was shocked by what you told me over the phone last night, of course. But I must admit, part of me is also intrigued. There was clearly this whole other side to Ralph that I knew nothing about. What he was doing with all that stuff . . . I really can't even imagine. The most plausible thing I can think of is that he was holding on to those things for someone else. But the passports you found . . . they had my uncle's photograph in them, didn't they?'

Halloran nodded. 'The passport photographs were a match to the photograph you provided to Kitt, I'm afraid.'

Carly nodded and a bitter smile crept over her lips. Tears formed and she looked very much like she might cry at any moment.

Nobody at the table seemed to know quite what to say. What did you say to a person facing such unthinkable truths about a family member?

The only thing Joe could think to do was change the subject.

'Rolo's safe and sound at least, you'll be pleased to know,' said Joe.

'Rolo.' Carly frowned as though she wasn't sure what Joe was talking about.

'Yeah . . . your uncle's dog . . . It is his . . . isn't it?' said Joe. 'Don't tell me we've taken him in on false pretences.'

'Yes . . .' Carly said slowly. 'That is the name of Ralph's

dog. But Ralph told me he'd rehomed him a while ago. I – I didn't think he had him any more. Did he bring the dog up here then?'

It had been Kitt's idea not to mention anything about Rolo until they were face to face with Carly again. She had thought it more than a little strange that Carly hadn't mentioned the dog, just as they all had. Kitt wanted to be in a room with Carly when it became known the dog had been found so that she could gauge her physical reactions and make her mind up about Carly once and for all. Joe was pleased that mentioning the dog while Halloran was still with them meant that her reaction would be vetted by two seasoned profilers.

And it seemed she thought the dog was no longer in Ralph's possession. At least that explained why Carly hadn't mentioned the dog before. But what an odd thing for her uncle to say. Before Joe could verbalize this thought, Kitt beat him to it.

'How strange that he said he was rehoming the animal,' said Kitt. 'Why would he tell you something like that when it wasn't true?'

'I – I really don't know,' Carly said. 'Maybe I misunderstood. Maybe he was just putting him in a kennel for a few weeks or something. But no. No, that's not it. I definitely thought he was giving the dog away. Maybe he had second thoughts? People get really attached to their pets. Maybe when it came down to it, he couldn't give the dog up?

Anyway, I am glad he's OK. I had no idea the poor creature had got mixed up in all this.'

'Do you want to take him? Rolo, I mean?' said Joe. 'Or are you happy for me to look after him until we find your uncle?'

Kitt, Grace and Halloran all gave Joe a look that suggested they didn't believe his casual act for a second.

'I've never been much of a dog person,' Carly said. Her distaste at the idea of taking the dog in herself was written across her face. 'Is he a lot of trouble for you?'

'Not at all,' Joe said. 'I love having him around. I'm happy to look after him. He's being well cared for. He had some chicken for dinner last night and he's been sleeping on a chair in my hotel room very soundly.'

Carly chuckled. 'It sounds like it would be cruel to part him from a foster parent like you. I'm grateful to you for looking after him. I'm not sure I have the resources to look after a dog on top of everything else right now. We never had one, me and Dad, so I don't think I'd even know where to start with looking after him.'

'Joe's got it covered, for now at least,' said Kitt. 'While you're here, Carly, I wondered if you would mind us asking you about some of the things we found in the briefcase? Just one or two items in case they mean anything to you?'

'Not at all,' said Carly. 'I was actually going to ask if I could see the photographs you've taken of the contents.'

'Here you go,' Kitt said, passing over her phone. 'If you hit a picture of my cat, Iago, you've scrolled too far.'

'Let me guess, a photo of a moment in which Iago was curled up, asleep on the armchair, looking like butter wouldn't melt,' said Halloran.

'It's so rare he does anything cute, I have to commit these moments to record,' said Kitt. 'Otherwise nobody would believe me.'

Carly smiled at Kitt and Halloran's interplay about the cat and then began scrolling through the pictures. She swiped several times and then must have hit the picture of Iago.

'Is that it?' she said. 'That's all there was in the case?'

'You look disappointed,' said Kitt. Joe could tell by her tone that Kitt was still very much weighing Carly up.

'I was just hoping there'd be something I could help with. Some obvious item or artefact that I recognized, or that maybe I'd see a clue you didn't. Stupid, I know,' said Carly.

'Not at all,' said Kitt. 'I'm sure I'd be just the same in your position.'

'I just didn't see . . . None of those photographs mean anything to me. They're all things that I wouldn't even suspect Ralph of being in possession of.'

'You don't recognize the man in the photograph, then?' said Kitt, changing tack and trying to focus Carly's attention on the finer details. 'The man in the camel coat.'

Carly frowned and scrolled back through the photographs on Kitt's phone. She stopped and stared hard at the screen before shaking her head. 'I'm sorry, he doesn't look familiar. I'm trying to think of the people my uncle has introduced me to over the years, the friends he has. This face wasn't among them as far as I remember.'

'Not to worry,' said Kitt. 'It was a long shot. There's clearly a part of his life he's kept from you and there's a reason why he wouldn't go around introducing you to people who might find themselves in hot water. On the contrary, I suspect he went out of his way to protect you from ever coming into contact with them. Which may be why he left you that voicemail.'

'He has always been very protective of me, even before Dad died,' said Carly. 'I just find it a bit incredible that he has been essentially living some kind of strange double life, and I knew nothing about it.'

'It's always difficult to discover people are not who we thought they were,' Kitt said, her eyes lowering to the table. From little snippets of conversation here and there, Joe got the impression that Kitt had uncovered terrible truths about people she had placed at least some measure of trust in. The life of a private investigator was not an easy one. 'Sorry if this is a bit of a strange or sensitive question,' Kitt continued once she had composed herself again, 'but was your uncle a religious man?'

'Not particularly,' said Carly. 'Why?'

'I just wondered whether St Michael means anything to you, or if it meant anything to your uncle? It was scrawled on a notebook in the briefcase. You've probably seen the photo on my phone.'

'I did see it. It didn't immediately spark anything. St Michael . . .' Carly's eyes narrowed as she mulled the name over. 'No . . . not that I can think of. I'm so sorry, I feel like I'm being no help whatsoever. Which is particularly frustrating because all I want to do is find my uncle, make sure he's OK and then find out what on earth he's been up to.'

'You mustn't beat yourself up,' Kitt said. 'If your uncle has chosen to keep a whole part of his life separate and not tell you a thing about it, then that's really rather out of your control. And it's why you've hired us, to find out what's happening with him.'

'Well, you made a major discovery less than twenty-four hours into the case so I'd say you're doing very well indeed,' said Carly.

'I'm glad you think so, and finding the case may well help us understand why your uncle disappeared but there's still work to do before we get to the truth.'

'In light of what you've discovered, I'll find a hotel in the nearby area and stay a few nights. Not to check up on you, you understand, just in case something else urgent comes up, like the briefcase. Also, if the local police want to question me, they might prefer it if I came into the station and I just want to feel like I'm doing everything in my power to get my uncle back as quickly as possible.'

Joe glanced at Kitt and Halloran out of the corner of his eye. They were nodding but from the conversations they'd had the night before he knew, in his heart, that Carly probably wouldn't get her uncle back. At least not alive. He winced at the thought. Her face was still so full of hope. How heartbroken she would be if their worst fears were confirmed.

'I've been thinking,' said Grace.

'Always an ominous start to a sentence,' said Kitt.

Grace shook her head at Kitt but continued. 'It's something that I've remembered from the maps of the area I was browsing when I was looking into the criminal history at Anthorn and Bowness-on-Solway, et cetera. The name St Michael appeared on those maps.'

'Did it? Where?' said Kitt, the lift in her voice betraying her excitement at this revelation.

'Burgh by Sands,' said Grace. 'Do you remember it? The little village we passed through before we reached Port Carlisle, the church there was called St Michael's.'

'That's barely any distance at all from where Holmes was staying,' said Kitt. 'Do you think he had some business there?'

'If I had to guess given the contents of the briefcase,' said Halloran, 'I'd say the most likely scenario is that Ralph was going to meet someone at the church. I don't know exactly what the purpose of the meeting might have been. But given the multiple aliases and the fact that St Michael – if it does refer to the church – is the only place mentioned by name, that seems like the most probable explanation if you ask me.'

'Perhaps that's where he went on Wednesday night,' said Joe. 'When Yeats said he saw him leave the boarding house.'

Slowly, Kitt nodded. 'That's when the missing time began. Between Wednesday evening and the voicemail he left for Carly on the Friday. Assuming you're speculating along the right lines, maybe that meeting didn't go at all as Carly's uncle planned.'

CHAPTER FOURTEEN

'Mind the grass now!' a lady wearing floral gardening gloves called over to Joe, Kitt and Grace as they made their way across the churchyard at St Michael's Church in Burgh by Sands.

After breakfast, Halloran had had to drive straight back to York to get on with the fraud case he was working on. Carly had wanted to join them in their visit to St Michael's but Kitt had thankfully convinced her to concentrate on finding accommodation nearby and leave the official investigating to them. Given that they had no idea what they might uncover at the church, Joe was relieved when Carly agreed to this. Granted, if they found something distressing, they would still have to break the news to her but they could do so gently and in a quiet setting. If she had insisted on following them to the church, they would have had no control whatsoever over how their client received news about her uncle.

On top of all this, Kitt had had a text message from Evie to say that she was heading over on the train and would catch up with them at the end of the day for a drink or two.

The second Grace had been reinstalled back in Kitt's room, they'd driven out to the firth. It was a misty October morning. The sun was trying to break through the woolly cloud, but without any success.

Joe couldn't help but think what a pity that was, as they walked across the cemetery. He would have welcomed the warmth of the sun on his face just then. Instead, Joe tried to keep the cheerier evening ahead of them in mind. Listening to Evie talk about her various vintage finds and basking in the glow of banter exchanged between friends. Though he didn't share a history with Kitt, Evie or Grace, they were good company. And thinking about that certainly beat speculating over what they might uncover next about Ralph Holmes.

'We wouldn't dream of cutting across the cemetery,' Kitt called back to the woman who had shouted over to them. 'I promise you that.'

'Sorry,' the woman said, digging her trowel into the soil and wiping her hands on her apron. 'I don't mean to sound like a dragon about it, but not everyone's as conscientious, you know. And it takes some maintaining, this place does. Honestly, you wouldn't believe how much.'

'I've done a bit of community gardening in my time,' Kitt said. 'I can imagine it takes a fair bit of work. There's really no need to explain yourself.'

Joe was secretly wondering why the woman had called out to them like that when for all she knew, they could be coming to pay their respects to a loved one who was buried in the cemetery. It seemed a bit insensitive to shout at them about grass under such circumstances but, given they'd likely need her help, Joe thought the best course of action was to keep quiet about it.

'Here to see our bells, are you?' said the woman. She had dark beady eyes and she looked from Joe to Kitt, to Grace in quick succession. Trying to gauge what their business here might be.

'Bells,' Kitt repeated.

'The originals were stolen from our church by Scottish raiders in 1626,' the woman said, clearly reciting a speech she'd given many times over before. 'But then the thieves had to throw them in the firth because they were weighing them down. They couldn't have got home otherwise. People round here were so outraged from the loss that they went and stole bells from Scottish churches. We've still got the stolen goods all these years later.'

'Even the churches round here are crooked,' Grace said, a little aghast by the story.

'What did you say?' the woman said. Joe couldn't tell whether she had heard what Grace had said and was goading her to repeat it or if she was genuinely hard of hearing. Either way, Grace thought better of saying it again.

'Oh, nothing, that's quite a story,' she said, while shooting a look at Kitt.

'That does sound like very interesting history,' Kitt said, and it was obvious by her longing looks at the church building that she was quite tempted to get sidetracked into looking at the bells. 'But we are actually here for a different reason. My name is Kitt Hartley. These are my associates, Grace Edwards and Johan Golding.'

Joe deduced from this formal introduction that Kitt wanted this woman to get the air of serious business, and it worked. She at once stood up a little straighter and looked Kitt up and down, examining her far more closely than she had before.

'Jemima Quint,' the woman said. 'I'm a volunteer here at the church. Have been for over a decade now. Is there something I can help you with?'

'I do hope so,' said Kitt. 'We're looking for this man. Have you seen him?'

Kitt turned her phone to the woman so she could look at the picture of Ralph Holmes, just as Donna and Yeats had before her.

Joe looked carefully at Jemima's face as she studied the picture. He wasn't really sure what he was looking for. Some obvious tell perhaps that Jemima did recognize Ralph but none presented itself.

'I'm afraid I haven't seen him. Is he local to the area? I know most people who live round here,' said Jemima.

'He's not. As far as we know he was visiting the area on holiday. But he's gone missing.'

Jemima looked sharply at Kitt then. 'Is he trouble?'

How to answer a question like that! The truth was, they had no idea if Holmes himself was trouble. If he was dangerous. If they should warn Jemima to be careful. Or if indeed Holmes was in trouble himself and was in need of their help. Halloran had seemed to think that the theory he might be working for a British agency was a best-case scenario and even that posed quite the risk to their health.

'Not that we know of,' was all Kitt said. It was all she could have really said under the circumstances. 'But as with anyone you don't know, I wouldn't approach him if you see him. Instead, you could ring me and let me know.' Kitt gave Jemima a card from her pocket. 'A relative of his has hired us to find him. She's understandably worried. There was some suggestion he might have visited this church on Wednesday evening. Which is why we thought we'd just check in and see if you'd caught sight of him.'

Kitt looked back at the gate they'd entered through. 'Are these gates locked at night, Jemima?'

'Not until ten p.m.,' she replied. 'But after that, yes, the gates are locked and the church is locked up every night. We used to leave them open. You know, for the homeless or anyone else who needed a roof over their head at night. But too many vandals. It was costing us so much money to do the repairs we just couldn't justify it any more. Breaks your heart, it does, that someone would put a brick through a stained-glass window.'

'I'm with you on that,' said Kitt. 'Tragic and unnecessary destruction. So last Wednesday, a week ago today, were you here at the church as you are now?'

'Now, let's see . . . yes, as a matter of fact I was. But I'm not here all hours. We don't think it's fair to ask volunteers to do that. I tend to pop off at dusk for my tea and then come back at ten to lock the gates.'

'When you came back to lock up, did you notice anything unusual?' said Kitt.

'Like what?' Jemima said with a shake of her head.

'Anything at all. Anything out of place. Any strange sounds,' Kitt pushed.

'I'd have jumped out my skin if I had,' said Jemima. 'I've got a nervous disposition and this cemetery is creepy enough in the daytime. No, nowt like that. I wasn't looking for anything, mind, but it all seemed quiet and peaceful to me.'

'OK, well, thank you,' said Kitt. 'I really do appreciate your time.'

'I'm sorry I can't be more help,' Jemima said. 'If I see him, the man you're looking for, I will contact you.'

Kitt nodded. 'We'd appreciate you letting us know if you do see him around. As I say, though, probably best not to approach him as he might get scared off before we can talk to him and let him know his relatives are looking for him.'

'I understand,' said Jemima. 'I'll call you before I do any-thing else. If I see him, that is.'

Satisfied that she'd learned all that she could from Jemima, Kitt turned away then. Joe and Grace followed her as she walked back towards the gates through which they had entered. Kitt was walking at her usual breakneck speed but then, without any warning at all, she stopped suddenly and looked over to her left. She squinted and took a step forward.

'What?' Grace said, when she noticed Kitt had stopped. 'What's the matter? You're creeping me out, standing stock-still like that.'

Joe had to agree with Grace. Kitt's silence and focus was most disconcerting. He followed the direction of her stare but couldn't immediately see what she was looking at. One of the gravestones perhaps? All of which looked ancient to Joe's eyes. The carving on them was barely legible and in parts they were covered by a growth of mossy green. But nothing looked out of place, at least not to Joe.

'Jemima . . .' Kitt called at last.

To her credit the woman didn't waste a moment in ambling over to see what was up. She was quite out of breath by the time she reached them.

'That gravestone there, for William Bateman, laid in 1896,' said Kitt.

'Yes,' Jemima said, 'I know the one you mean. What about it?'

'The soil is disturbed.'

'What?' said Jemima, taking a step in the direction of the gravestone and looking at it more closely. 'Probably wildlife. We do have a lot of pests round here, you know? Part of being so far away from the towns.'

'Looks like one determined squirrel if so,' said Kitt, raising an eyebrow.

Joe examined the earth in front of the gravestone for himself. There was no denying it: Kitt was right. He'd missed it before because he'd been looking at the gravestone rather than the ground itself. Thus, he hadn't noticed that the earth had definitely been disturbed. The question was: why? And by whom?

Joe felt the hairs on the back of his neck stand on end as those queries surfaced in his mind. Some quiet part of him knew there was something off about this whole situation.

'One thing I can tell you,' said Jemima. 'Nobody's been buried here since the Victorian era. There's no reason for anyone to go rootling around the gravesides. We stopped getting people visiting relatives some thirty years ago now. So it's not been disturbed by a member of staff.'

This, at least, explained why Jemima had taken them for tourists visiting the bells rather than mourners earlier. After three decades of not receiving any mourners, you would rather think that you'd seen the last of them. Despite Jemima's claim that nobody had been buried here in over a century, however, there was still no denying the fact the top soil on that grave had been tampered with. And recently. All the other graves were grassed over completely whereas William Bateman's grave had patches of loose grass scattered around everywhere.

'I know it'll mean stepping on the grass but in the interests of ruling out all possibilities in our search for our missing person, do you mind if I take a closer look?' Kitt said to Jemima.

Jemima hesitated a moment but then nodded her ascent.

Carefully, Kitt made her way over to the grave, crouched down and put on a pair of plastic gloves she'd pulled from her satchel. Slowly, she buried her fingers into the soil, digging down with her digits until she seemed to hit something hard. Kitt pressed her lips together and looked over at Grace and Joe.

'What is it?' said Grace, her voice wavering.

Kitt shook her head to indicate she didn't quite know yet. Frowning, she tugged gently on whatever she had hit upon and Joe watched in some horror as from the dark earth she pulled up a human hand.

Instinctively, Joe noticed Kitt recoil a few inches, but she didn't let go of the hand which, Joe was relieved to realize, was attached to a body. It struck him as strange to feel in any way relieved about that. A dead human hand buried in a shallow grave was surely nightmare material whether it was attached to the body or not. But no, some primal intuition was sending the message to his brain that even though this person was no more, it was still a good thing that they had been discovered in one piece.

Jemima jumped back a step and even Kitt caught her breath at the sight of it.

Joe couldn't have blamed her for that, even if this wasn't the first time she was seeing a dead body. There was a terrible paleness to the hand. It had been quite cold on the evenings of late and the only way he could think to describe the pallor is that every drop of cold in the air seemed to have seeped into that limp limb.

Recovered from her surprise, Kitt continued her excavation and reached slightly above where the arm now protruded. She clawed gently at the soil so as not to damage the body she was in the midst of uncovering. How she was able to keep her cool under such circumstances, Joe had no idea. But she kept sweeping away small clumps of earth and within a minute she had uncovered a human face.

Kitt took several deep breaths and looked over at Joe, Grace and Jemima before speaking.

'It's him,' she said, in a mournful tone. 'It's Ralph Holmes . . . It looks like . . . there's a gunshot wound in his chest . . . somebody shot him.'

CHAPTER FIFTEEN

'DI Garner,' the woman in the grey trouser suit said as she held up her identification for Kitt.

Kitt took a look at the ID and then gave a small nod. Joe had been quite surprised when she'd asked to see identification for the officers who had arrived on the scene. He wasn't sure if this was something Halloran had encouraged Kitt to do or if it was something Kitt simply did as a matter of course whenever she was dealing with law enforcement. Either way, Detective Inspector Garner hadn't so much as flinched at the request. She did, however, give Kitt, Grace and Joe a long hard look before speaking again.

'I believe DC Stark and DC Drummond have already taken statements from you when they first arrived to secure the area?' Garner said at last. She wore black-rimmed glasses and looked at Kitt over the top of them as she spoke.

'That's right,' said Kitt. 'We had thought DI Cobb would

come to the scene after the briefcase we uncovered. He was already working on this case, you see.'

Garner raised her dark eyebrows. 'DI Cobb is working on several complicated cases right now and can't be everywhere at once. He has, however, appraised me of the briefcase and its contents. Which you claim you discovered yesterday afternoon at The Lowlands View bed and breakfast.'

Kitt frowned. 'It wasn't a claim. It was a statement of fact.'

The air between Kitt and Garner became suddenly thick and Joe, for his part, didn't really know where to look. Kitt had already been most reluctant to be ushered to the other side of the cordon line. Now she was putting up a fight about the wording being used. Privately, Joe conceded that the word 'claimed' did insinuate they hadn't told DI Cobb the whole truth about the briefcase but he wasn't sure he'd have challenged a high-ranking police officer over the word. Especially not in a high-pressure situation like this one.

Garner didn't directly respond to Kitt's comment. Instead, she asked another question. 'All three of the statements, I'm told, verify that it was you, Ms Hartley, who noticed the disturbed soil on the shallow grave. Is that correct?'

'Yes, that's correct,' Kitt said. There was a wary note in her tone. As though she suspected some kind of trap.

'Have you ever been to this churchyard before today?' Garner pushed.

'No, I have not,' said Kitt. 'We passed the church in the car yesterday. We found the note in the briefcase that read

St Michael, and we put two and two together and thought this might be the last known place Ralph Holmes visited.'

'And while you were here you just happened to notice the soil was disturbed,' said Garner.

Kitt paused, again clearly concerned about what Garner might be getting at. 'We walked past the gravesite on the way out and when I glanced over, some clumps of earth caught my eye. Only because the rest of the cemetery is so well-kept.'

'That's quite a meticulous detail to pick up on,' said Garner, folding her arms over her chest as she spoke.

'Thank you,' said Kitt, deliberately misinterpreting Garner's tone. 'I have worked several high-profile murder cases as a civilian investigator so I like to think I've become a little bit of a Sherlock over the years.'

'Yes, from what I've read about you in DI Cobb's file, dead bodies do rather tend to follow you around, don't they?' said Garner.

Grace looked at Joe, her eyes wide. A sure sign that Kitt wasn't going to take a comment like that lying down.

Kitt took a deep breath, visibly trying to keep herself calm. 'You've got it the wrong way around, DI Garner. The bodies don't follow me, I follow them.'

'Hmm,' Garner said, and Kitt's lips tightened as she did so. 'We'll be conducting forensic tests on the area, of course. Looking for any evidence that tells us how the shooting took place and who might have pulled the trigger.'

Again, Garner looked Kitt up and down.

'We've got your statements now, so you're free to go about your business. We know you're not local to Cumbria but don't go leaving the country until we've got this matter settled,' said Garner.

'No danger of that,' said Kitt. 'I've not got a holiday booked until next June. I'm assuming you'll have drawn some conclusions by then.'

Garner narrowed her eyes at Kitt. 'I think you'd best be on your way, Ms Hartley. We'll take it from here.'

Kitt, of course, wasn't to be so easily fobbed off.

'My partner works as a DI in Yorkshire,' said Kitt. Joe had to give her some credit for waiting so long before playing this card. It was obvious DI Garner was suspicious of her. Possibly all of them. And Kitt could have had the upper hand in the conversation much earlier if she'd explained she lived with a detective inspector. At the very least it might have bought her some goodwill. Perhaps Kitt had wanted Garner to reach the conclusion she should show Kitt basic levels of respect on her own terms. A conclusion Garner obviously wasn't going to come to any time soon. 'Consequently, as you might expect, I'm well-acquainted with protocol. In a missing person's case you usually need someone to identify the body. We were working for a family member of this gentleman. To try and locate him, as you know.'

'Ah, yes,' Garner said, her voice dark, low. 'Holmes's niece.'

'That's right,' Kitt said, her brow furrowing in confusion at the tone Garner had taken. 'Carly Lewis. As we're working with her, we can notify her of her uncle's death. She will be available to identify him. And, in fact, she may wish to see the body anyway. Even if you don't have any need for formal identification in this case. He's her last surviving relative, you see. Or should I say, was.'

DI Garner's ponytail was tied so tight at the back of her head it seemed to make every expression more severe. Again, she looked hard at Kitt before responding. 'If the lady in question wishes to identify the body, she'll need to get in touch with Cumberland police station directly to make arrangements. I'm not sure when she'll be granted access for obvious reasons. The man has a bullet wound to the chest and thus this case will be taken extremely seriously. But she can get in touch with the station and they'll be able to advise her further. If we have any questions for her ourselves, we have her contact details and will be in touch.'

'Thank you,' Kitt said, in a way she had sometimes of thanking a person without sounding even a little bit grateful.

Since it was obvious the trio weren't going to get any more time from the police, they crossed the road away from the cemetery and began walking towards the car.

'Do you think we should call Carly now?' said Joe. 'Tell her to come here, in case looking at the body ends up being an administrative nightmare? She might not want to see the body, and they don't always need the relatives to identify a body when one turns up. But like you said, Ralph was her last living relative and if she does, the last thing she needs is bureaucracy getting in the way. Garner seemed to give the impression it might be some time before she'd be allowed to see him.'

'The thought crossed my mind,' said Kitt. 'But then I tried to put myself in her shoes. If it was someone I loved, who'd been found that way in a shallow grave. Shot. I'm not sure I'd want to visit the crime scene itself. The staff at the morgue have training in making the viewing of a body that bit less terrifying for the person doing it. Here, well, I don't know quite what kind of experience she'd have with that lot running the show. Empathy certainly isn't their strong suit.'

'They carried on like I was the one who had shot Holmes when they were interviewing me,' said Grace. 'Every question had an almost accusatory tone to it.'

'It was no different for me, and Garner made it clear she doesn't quite buy the story that I just happened to notice the soil. Even though I've been investigating crimes for years now,' said Kitt, but then she sighed and shook her head. 'All that said, I have to admit that when Mal catches a case like this he can't afford to take any prisoners either. He has to let everyone in the situation know that he doesn't suffer fools. Being a woman to boot, well, there's a chance that Garner just thinks she's got to be extra forceful to get the message across that she's in charge.'

'Yeah, well, message received,' said Grace. 'Loud and clear.'

'So, what should we do as far as Carly's concerned?' Joe said. 'We were hired to find her uncle and, well, we found him. Just . . . not . . . alive.'

'I feared it might come to this after we found that brief-case,' said Kitt. 'I hoped it wouldn't, of course, but, well, he was obviously involved in something very serious indeed. As for what happens next with our investigation, it's really down to Carly.'

'So, if she wants us to keep investigating, we will, but if not, we're going home?' Joe asked.

'That's about the size of it. She's the client,' said Kitt. 'I know she had her fears that something may have befallen her uncle but perhaps she never got so far as imagining something as terrible as this. She may want to leave the rest of the business to the police. She only called us because they wouldn't take the case in the first place. But as Garner has made abundantly clear, they're very much on the case now.'

Joe nodded. 'We'd better break the news to her in person anyway, I suppose. Hard as it will be. She's going to be devastated.'

'I know, but I think that would be kindest,' said Kitt.

'And what if she doesn't want to leave it to the police?' said Joe.

'Then our job will move from missing persons to murder investigation,' said Kitt, looking hard at Joe's face as she spoke. 'Look, Joe, I don't suppose you really bargained for this when you signed on for some work experience with the agency. I know I insisted on paying you but it's just a basic wage. I wouldn't take it badly at all if you decided that you'd like to come back to us on a quieter week. If we do start investigating the murder, I can only tell you from past experience, it can mean some level of jeopardy. It's difficult to guarantee everyone's safety when there are guns and murderers in the mix and, frankly, I'd never forgive myself if something terrible happened to you.'

Joe smiled, rather touched that Kitt was so concerned for his safety. Even if it was professional concern, it was nice to have someone looking out for him for a change. It'd been a while since he'd had such a luxury. 'I'll admit this is more high-octane than I was expecting, especially given that the last couple of weeks have been mostly admin-based, but I've come too far to turn back now. If Carly wants to continue the investigation, I'll be with you one hundred per cent. I . . . w– what's that?'

'What's what?' Kitt said, immediately turning in the direction in which Joe had been looking. They had just come level with the hedge at the back of the cemetery and tree branches obscured the view. Still, Grace also followed suit, squinting into the trees at the other side of the churchyard.

'Do you see something, in the shadows over there?' said Joe. 'It looks like . . . a figure of some kind. Dressed in black.'

'Oh God, yes,' said Grace. 'That's creepy. What are they doing?'

'I see them,' said Kitt. But the figure must have somehow heard her as a balaclava-covered head looked in their direction and then turned, fleeing.

'Hey!' Joe shouted, giving chase.

'Joe, wait!' Kitt called after him, but Joe wasn't listening. This person, whoever they were, could know something about Ralph Holmes's death. And if they did, even if Carly had to hear that her uncle was dead, at least she'd hear at the same time that they'd tracked down someone who could point them to the killer.

Joe ran down the side of the churchyard beyond the cordon line to just see a black figure whipping around the next corner. Whoever they were, they were certainly fit to run at the pelt they were going. Joe had gone for a light jog three times a week for the last ten years, but he wasn't used to sprinting. He picked up the pace as best he could, the sound of his own panting filling his ears. He tried not to think about what might happen if he actually caught this person, whoever they were. Whether they'd be armed. Whether he could hold his own in a fight when it came down to it. All of these thoughts, as it turned out, became moot. By the time Joe turned the next corner, the country road bordered by farmland and grazing cattle was deserted.

He squinted, looking left, right, behind him while gasping for breath.

Nothing.

No one.

It had all happened so fast, for a moment he wondered if the figure in black had been nothing more than a dream. But deep down he knew that wasn't true. They'd been real enough all right. He'd just lost them.

Joe kicked a stone into the hedge with an angry grunt. Wasn't this case unsettling enough without someone lurking in the shadows, watching the proceedings? Who would do that? And why? Was it as simple as a curious local journalist trying to get their scoop by taking photographs through the hedges? But then why the balaclava? A more likely scenario surfaced in Joe's mind. For some reason that he could not fathom, the killer had returned to the scene of the crime. Could someone be that bold? To go back to a place where they shot someone while the police were combing it for forensic evidence? Or was something else happening altogether that Joe had yet to understand?

CHAPTER SIXTEEN

'How are you doing, if it's not a stupid question?' Joe asked Carly. The pair sat on a bench in Bitts Park while Grace and Kitt were off throwing a ball for an increasingly hyperactive Rolo.

On learning of her uncle's death back in Kitt's hotel room, Carly at once broke down in tears and then felt like she might be sick. When it became clear it was just a bilious feeling and nothing more, Kitt had suggested a walk to the nearby Bitts Park so that Carly could get some fresh air. Joe was impressed by just how fresh the air was. The grass in the park had just been cut and that wonderful green fragrance hung heavy all around them.

Just in case Carly had found herself overcome again, they'd chosen a spot in the park known as The Hollow. A sunken area of parkland protected by the walls of Eden Bridge, that was filled with willow trees and rhododendrons. Had some happier occasion brought them to the park, Joe might have been able to marvel at just how much care the landscapers had taken in making this an almost magical natural space. As it was, he was still trying to get over the guilt of letting that mysterious figure get away from them at the cemetery. They had reported it to DI Garner right away but they had nothing of use to say about the person in question except that they were dressed in black and wearing a balaclava. Garner hadn't seemed all that convinced that there really had been a figure in black but had taken notes on what they had to say anyway.

'I'm over the initial shock, I think,' said Carly. 'But . . .' Her breath caught in her throat as she tried to speak. 'But I . . . I still can't believe this is real. It feels like the most terrible nightmare. That any moment I'm going to wake up and find this was all some ridiculous dream I was having. Except I'm not, am I?'

'I'm afraid not,' said Joe. 'That's what it feels like, I know. When something so terrible befalls you, you can barely believe it. It's like waking up from a bad dream but instead of being flooded with relief that it was all a dream, you are filled with dread because it wasn't. It was all very real.'

'Sounds like you might be speaking from experience there,' said Carly.

Joe started at this. He hadn't realized he'd lapsed so deeply into reflecting on his own life. 'I'm sorry,' he said. 'It wasn't my intention to make this difficult time for you about me.'

Carly shook her head. 'There's really no need to apologize.

It's only natural to draw on your own thoughts and feelings. And I think it helps to know that other people have been through . . . have survived something similar. I'm sorry if you know what this feels like. If you've lost someone you loved.'

Joe forced an unconvincing smile across his lips but then let it fade. 'My wife died, about six months ago now.'

Carly started, and looked at him, sympathy swirling in her deep green eyes.

'Aggressive lymphoma,' Joe said quickly. Though Carly might have been too polite to ask, he knew from past experience that the first question most people wondered about when they'd heard his wife had died was how.

'I – I don't know what to say,' said Carly. 'Except that I'm truly sorry you went through that. And, as you know, I've experienced that pain too. With my father. Although it's not quite the same pain, is it? My father wasn't that old when he died. But he wasn't young like your wife, who I'm assuming was around your age.'

'Two years older. Thirty-two. What you went through may not be exactly the same, but it is comparable. Which is precisely why I wanted to do everything I could to spare you any more pain,' said Joe. 'And why it's bloody wrong that you should have to go through this on top of everything else. How is that fair?'

Joe took a deep breath and tried to steady himself when he realized how loud his voice had become. The anger that simmered over what had befallen him six months ago sometimes boiled over, particularly when injustice reared its head. He still hadn't come to terms with the fact that someone as young and good as Sarah could be the indiscriminate victim of a disease. There was no logic to it. No reason.

'It's not,' Carly said, with tears in her eyes. 'There's nothing fair about it. Anyone who says so has read too many Facebook memes. But then again, I stopped expecting fair a long time ago. Now ... I just have to find a way of dealing with the fact that I'm ... I'm' – she had to take a minute to compose herself before she could choke out the last word – 'alone.'

On finally finishing the sentence, Carly's tears started to fall. Had Carly been a friend, Joe would have put an arm around her but she was a client and the truth was, he didn't know her that well and didn't want to intrude on her personal space. Instead, he tried to think of something to say. Something that would comfort her the way his arm might around her shoulder.

'God, I know what it's like to feel alone.' He sighed. 'The only way I've managed to get through it is to remind myself that there are seven billion people on this planet. Seven billion. I think, on balance, it's quite difficult to be truly alone in this world. Though we might feel lonely. I certainly have and perhaps you will. But I suppose it's about remembering that there are people you can reach out to, even if it's uncomfortable. They may not be blood family but maybe they'll be a different kind of family.'

Joe's gaze wandered over to Kitt and Grace, who were fussing and playing with Rolo. The dog had done his level best to get as filthy as possible, Joe noted. He was covered in grass cuttings and his paws were thick with mud. Kitt and Grace were chuckling at the dog's antics as he tore after a tennis ball they'd bought him from a local corner shop. Joe hadn't been with Hartley and Edwards Investigations any time at all and there was no real reason why he would continue working with them after his work shadowing period was up. Yet, they were undoubtedly a support system he'd never want to be without. They had taken pains to make him feel at home in their offices. They'd welcomed him into their fold. They'd helped him remember how to feel at ease in other people's company. And for that, he'd always be grateful.

'Damn it,' Carly said, snapping Joe out of his thoughts. 'I can't find a way to argue against your logic there.'

Though her tears were still falling, a small smile formed on her lips. A little mark of gratitude for his attempt to help her see that even with her uncle gone, she wasn't alone.

Without warning, Rolo took it upon himself to charge back towards Joe at that point. He put two heavy paws up on Joe's knee and seemed to take an inordinate amount of pleasure in muddying his jeans. Rolo was such a big dog that the mere force of the gesture knocked Joe backwards against the bench. He prised the dog's paws off his knees and let them fall to the ground before ruffling the fur on top of the hound's head to make it clear that even though Joe could do without the mutt's paw prints on his Wranglers, he was still very fond of him.

'Maybe you could take Rolo?' said Joe, his heart sinking a little at the thought of handing the hound over. 'He did belong to your uncle after all.'

Carly looked at the dog for a moment and then at Joe. 'No,' she said. 'He seems really happy with you. As I said, I'm not really a dog person. I think dogs can sense that and if he's happier being with you, it'd be cruel to take him away. Maybe I'll get a hamster, or something . . . a little more low maintenance.'

Joe chuckled at the idea that a hamster might be lower maintenance than a dog. Every hamster he'd crossed paths with had been an expert escape artist. He'd spent more time looking for his pet hamsters as a kid than he had stroking them.

'How are we getting on over here?' said Kitt when she and Grace made it back to where they were sitting. 'Has the nausea passed?'

'It has,' said Carly. 'I've never felt anything like it.'

'It's very common,' said Kitt. 'And you might yet get more strange sensations – physical and psychological – over the coming weeks so you'll need to take it easy.'

'The police will also probably be able to recommend a bereavement service,' said Grace. 'I'd ask about it if and when you talk to them if I were you. Best to have all the support you can get at a time like this.'

Carly nodded. 'You've all been very kind, which is why it's so difficult to say what I have to say next.'

Kitt smiled. 'You don't want us to investigate any further?'

Carly looked at Joe, Grace and Kitt in turn and then nodded. 'I'm sorry. I know you've only been out here . . . well, not much more than twenty-four hours and it's a bit of a trek from York. A long way to come for a day's work. And that there's still the strange mystery of the briefcase you found and the figure in black from the cemetery to identify but it's . . . all this . . . it's not something I expected. Not something I could even have conceived of when I came to you on Monday. I thought maybe you'd uncover that my uncle was hiding out somewhere from someone who wished him harm. But now . . .' Again, Carly lost her composure but managed to regain it relatively quickly. 'Now that his body has been found, I think it's better if the police handle it. They're trained to do so and you've made them see there really was a case to follow up on. So . . .'

'Carly,' said Kitt, holding up a hand. 'You really don't have to say any more. You asked us to investigate, we did and now the police can handle it. We've got a friend to meet for a drink shortly but then we'll get our things packed up and head back to York.'

'I appreciate you being so understanding,' Carly said. 'Obviously, you've got my deposit but I'll settle the rest of the bill as soon as you send it to me.'

Kitt waved a dismissive hand. 'No rush with that with all you've got going on.'

'That's good of you. Do – do you think it's too soon for me to go to the police station and ask about seeing my uncle's body?' Carly said, before biting her lip.

Kitt looked at her watch. 'Let's see now. They've been at the scene for about five hours, give or take. Considering you're the last living relative of the deceased I'm a bit surprised you haven't had a call from them already, if I'm honest. Under the circumstances, I think it's perfectly reasonable to show your face down at the station, explain who you are and that you want to see your uncle. If you also explain that you don't live locally and will have to get home at some point, that might speed things up.'

'Thanks,' said Carly. 'I think I'll go and do that now. Then, when they're done with his personal effects, at least they'll know who to send them on to so I'll . . . I'll have something to remember him by.'

'Would you like any of us to come to the station with you?' said Kitt. 'No charge, we just want to make sure you're OK. It is quite soon to go off doing administrative tasks when you've only just found out about your uncle's passing.'

Carly smiled. 'That's very kind but I think I'll feel better to be doing something, anything than sitting around and waiting. And I don't know why, I just feel this is something I have to do by myself.'

Kitt nodded as Carly stood and said her goodbyes. Kitt

gazed after her as she walked towards the steps that led up to Eden Bridge.

'What a tragic end to the story,' she said, plonking herself down on the bench next to Joe. 'Obviously, I did fear the worst but I was hoping for the best too.'

'We all were,' said Joe.

'So, does this mean we're going home?' said Grace.

'It does that,' said Kitt.

'Shame,' said Grace, 'I was hoping to pay a visit to the travelling fairground at Silloth.'

Kitt frowned. 'I'm not sure when you thought we were going to fit that in.'

'A girl can dream,' said Grace.

Both Joe and Kitt turned towards Grace, detecting something lacklustre, dare they even say quiet about her tone.

'Are you holding up all right, Grace?' said Kitt. 'You don't seem quite yourself. And I know we've had a bit of a shock today.'

Grace opened her mouth but then seemed to think better of it. A few moments passed before she did in fact speak. 'I know everything we've uncovered on this case is enough to bring out the paranoia in anyone but I can't get that figure in black out of my head.'

'In what sense?' said Kitt.

'This morning, when we were packing up the car to go to St Michael's, I can't put my finger on it but I had this . . . this feeling,' said Grace.

'What kind of feeling?' said Joe.

'It felt like someone was watching me, watching us,' said Grace. 'Whenever I'd look around to see if there was anything to it, I couldn't see anyone around. But what if I just didn't catch them at it? What if that figure, whoever they are, was watching us and followed us to St Michael's Church?'

'Why would someone do that?' said Kitt. 'Moreover, who would really know to do that? That we were looking into Ralph Holmes's murder?'

'Donna at the pub could have told someone,' said Grace. 'The wrong someone. Or Yeats could have followed us back to our hotel yesterday afternoon. He's creepy enough, I wouldn't put it past him.'

'Wouldn't we have noticed?' said Kitt.

'I don't know, would we?' said Grace. 'We didn't know what was in the briefcase then. We didn't know there was some bigger conspiracy going on. We still don't know why Holmes was carrying a briefcase like that or what happened to him on that lost Thursday.'

'And you think someone was following us to . . . what? See what we knew about those things?'

'Possibly,' said Grace. 'It just seems too much of a coincidence, you know. That I feel like someone is watching us and then a mysterious figure in a balaclava turns up at the cemetery where we find Ralph Holmes buried. All I can say is, until I'm safely back on Yorkshire soil I'm going to be looking over my shoulder.'

CHAPTER SEVENTEEN

Joe was just packing the last few things into his suitcase back at The Queen Mary Hotel when there was a loud, hurried knock at his door. It took him a moment to get across the room and in that time the person knocking had started banging frantically with their fists.

This in turn stirred Rolo from his sleep, and he ran towards the door, barking and growling.

Joe did what he could to calm the dog, dashed the last few feet towards the door and opened it to find Carly standing on the other side, her eyes red raw from crying, her face blotchy.

'Carly . . .' Joe began, but before he could say anything else she knocked on Kitt's door, which was opposite his, in much the same manner she had his. Even though she was clearly nigh on frantic, she'd still had the wherewithal to remember her way back to their rooms.

The moment Kitt, Grace and Evie appeared at the door

Carly spluttered out, 'You're back on the case. If you'll take it, that is.'

Joe looked at Carly, then at Kitt and Grace in turn. Evie, for her part, had been left open-mouthed at the sudden interruption to what had been a reasonably quiet and merry evening. Evie had, as promised, met them for drinks in Carlisle. Kitt had persuaded Grace that they would keep a close eye on the road behind them on the way home to make sure nobody followed them across the Pennines and since they were all travelling that direction anyway, Joe had offered to drive Evie back to York too so she didn't have to grapple with her shopping bags on the train.

'Sorry,' Evie said, as though it was somehow her fault that Carly had come banging at their door without any prior warning. 'I can make myself scarce if you like. I'm a friend of Kitt's but it sounds like you might want a bit of privacy.'

'Oh, I'm past caring about privacy,' said Carly, swiping tears off her face only for more to fall and replace them at once. 'The whole world needs to know about what's happened to me this afternoon. The whole world. Otherwise, they'll get away with it.'

Much as Joe knew Carly had been through an incredible amount in the last twenty-four hours her wild gestures took him back somewhat. When Carly had left them in the park, she had been sombre but seemed to be starting to accept what had happened to her uncle. Now she was practically raving. What on earth had happened at the police station to provoke this kind of reaction?

'Why don't you come inside?' said Kitt, in a calm, quiet voice. 'You can tell us all about it once you've sat down and collected yourself. You look like you've had a terrible shock.'

Carly did as she was instructed and followed Grace and Evie into the room opposite. Kitt waved Joe in.

'Stay, boy,' Joe said to Rolo, giving him a little reassuring pat before closing his bedroom door. He wasn't sure exactly what was going on with Carly but he doubted she needed the distraction of Rolo bounding around the place.

Once the dog was secure, Joe crossed the corridor over to Kitt's room and shut the door behind them.

'It was awful,' said Carly. 'It's just the worst thing. I can't even get my head round it. I don't know what to do. I . . . I . . . I . . .'

'Now then,' said Kitt, taking full control of the situation. 'Sit down, take a deep breath and tell us one step at a time what's happened. Take as long as you like over it, we're not going anywhere.'

Carly forced a smile in Kitt's direction even though it was followed by more tears. Slowly, she did as Kitt instructed and sank down on to the bed. 'Ugh, I'm so sick of crying,' she said, drying her eyes and making a visible effort to control herself. She took another few deep breaths before speaking again. 'I went to the police station as you instructed to discuss identifying my uncle's body and to pick up any belongings he might have had on his person when he was . . . when he was . . .' Carly couldn't bring herself to finish the sentence and Joe understood why. It was hard enough telling people that he was a widower and his wife had died of an illness. He'd never been able to imagine what it must be like to have to tell other people that someone you loved had been murdered. That they'd gone out of this world in such a cold, brutal fashion. There was no justice in illness any more than there was in murder. Disease could be just as arbitrary. But at least disease was a natural part of life. And in many circumstances, people dying of an illness had time to try and process it. To say their goodbyes. Murder victims never got a chance to do any of that and this was something that, Joe guessed, was one of many things Carly would much rather not think about just now.

'And what happened when you got to the police station?' said Kitt, gently trying to move Carly on from the terrible thought of her uncle being shot in cold blood and buried in a shallow grave where the killer no doubt hoped he'd remain undiscovered.

'They asked me to take a seat, which I did. I thought, on that basis, they knew what they were doing. But an hour passed. Two. Three. I tried to keep my queries to a minimum as they had said it would take some time. But when it got to three hours, I did go up to the desk and ask what was taking so long.'

'What did they say?' said Grace. 'It does seem a weirdly long time to keep you waiting.'

'They said . . . they said they'd asked all of the senior officers about my query but . . . but . . . ' Carly started to lose her composure again but managed to regain it. 'They had no record of my uncle. No record of his body. No record of his murder. No record of the officers you said you'd spoken to.'

Kitt's eyes widened and it took her a moment to compose a sentence. 'You're telling me that there is no DI Garner? No DC Drummond? No DC Stark?'

'I gave them all three names. I explained that they'd taken statements from you earlier that day. But they said, though they'd wanted to confirm their suspicions with senior colleagues before confirming it to me, nobody by those names had ever worked with Cumberland police station,' said Carly. 'I didn't understand, of course. I knew you wouldn't have just made all that up. But they wouldn't engage with me about it.'

'But . . .' – Kitt paused, obviously in as much shock as Joe, Grace and Evie were about this revelation – 'what about the briefcase we found? Did they say anything about that?'

Carly shook her head. 'All they said was that DI Cobb had already closed that case. And they wouldn't let me talk to him about it. I've seen the photos you took of the contents. I know it existed. And I know there'd be no reason for the police to just close a file on something like that.'

'Closed . . . That's mad,' said Grace, shaking her head. 'DI

Cobb was stood in this room, just last night, telling us how he'd handle it from here. He seemed to think it was serious. They can't have got to the bottom of it all so quickly, can they? Why would he just close the case?'

'I wasn't given a reason. They wouldn't tell me anything,' Carly said. 'And of course, the more they shut me down, the angrier I got. I think they were on the brink of arresting me for disturbing the peace. I'm not sure if you can still get arrested for that but I'd be the first to admit I was out of control in there. I felt like I wanted to climb up the walls, I was so frustrated.'

'That's understandable,' said Kitt. 'I can barely believe what you've been told myself. After hearing about the death of your uncle earlier in the day, the last thing you needed was something like this.'

'What does this mean?' said Joe, rubbing a hand across his face. 'Are Garner, Drummond and Stark from a different station and we just didn't realize it?'

Kitt shook her head. 'Cumberland station was definitely the name they gave us. I'll have to speak to Halloran before we jump to any conclusions but, let's be honest, this whole thing is very strange indeed. If I didn't know better, I'd say this was some kind of cover-up.'

'I have to admit, that was my first thought,' said Carly in a wavering voice. 'In fact, it scared me how quickly that idea surfaced in my head. But that's how it felt when I was in there, you know? Like they were trying to deny my uncle ever even existed. There's a briefcase in their evidence room containing passports with his photograph in them, for heaven's sake. Undeniable proof of his existence. But . . . this is the police we're talking about. Why would they – or anyone else for that matter – cover up the death of my uncle?'

Kitt pressed her lips together and shook her head. 'We can't know anything for sure. But it's quite possible that the briefcase we found contained evidence of some kind of activity that someone didn't want to come to light. Or that your uncle was involved with something that also involved the briefcase and the police, or someone higher up, and they don't want anyone to know about it.'

Kitt paused before speaking again.

'As you can tell, vague theories are the best I have to offer you at present. I really can't quite believe that the police are behaving this way about the matter.'

'I could ask Charley, my wife, about this kind of thing, if it's of help to you?' Evie said. Given that she was not part of the investigative team, Evie had kept her peace while Carly had explained her experience at the police station. But anyone seeing Carly like this would want to do something to help. It was the most unthinkably scary prospect. That a loved one could die and the police wouldn't even acknowledge receiving the body. 'My wife is a detective sergeant,' Evie clarified. 'She works with Halloran. I'm sure between them they must have brushed up against something like this before. They might know who – or what level of officer – will have given the order to deny your uncle's body was ever delivered to them.'

Carly managed to half-smile at Evie. 'I'm grateful for any help from any source. I'm at a complete loss as to what to do. How can I have a funeral for my uncle if nobody will admit where his body is? And how are we supposed to get to the bottom of what happened to him?'

'If Charley knows anything about situations like this, I know she'll tell me, given the circumstances,' said Evie. 'She knows as much as I do the damage these kinds of situations can do.'

'Thanks, Evie, we can use all the help we can get,' Kitt said before turning her attentions back to Carly. 'I think that whoever is behind this order, to deny that your uncle was found dead, is in the business of making sure we never do find out what happened to him. And that prospect, the notion that someone would go to these lengths to cover something up, scares me more than I can say.'

A quiet fell across the room as they all contemplated the possible implications of the police denying Ralph Holmes had been found murdered that afternoon. Joe had seen it with his own eyes. Had seen Kitt pull a limp hand from the cold, damp earth. He'd been interviewed about this by police officers – or people claiming to be police officers. As Kitt had said, Ralph Holmes's murder must point to something truly heinous for the police to cover this up. And if they were willing to make a body disappear – whoever they were – it wasn't difficult to contemplate the idea that they had been following and watching Joe, Kitt and Grace ever since they had discovered that briefcase at The Lowlands View bed and breakfast.

Before now, Joe had hoped Grace was just feeling a little bit on edge after the discovery of Holmes's body. But between this obvious cover-up, the strange figure who had been spying at the cemetery and the odd feeling Grace had been having, the sense of being watched, perhaps they had accidentally become embroiled in a conspiracy far more complicated than they had realized.

'I don't know what my uncle was up to when he was killed,' Carly said, breaking the silence. 'For all I know it could have been something terrible. But all I can tell you is he was never anything other than wonderful to me. And I don't think he deserved to go out this way.'

'Does anyone?' said Kitt. 'Regardless of what they may have done, does anyone deserve to be shot and buried, as your uncle was, in a shallow grave?'

Carly shook her head. 'I don't think so. What happened to him . . . I can't figure it out but it's just all wrong. Nothing that you've uncovered since you came up here fits in with the man I know.'

Kitt put a hand on Carly's shoulder. 'I wouldn't be doing my job if I didn't tell you this, but I think continuing the investigation might be dangerous. Not just for us, but possibly for you. You are Holmes's last living relative. The only one who's going to go looking for him. The police are aware of that, which means the people who covered up your uncle's death are also likely aware of that. You could become a target yourself if we keep digging on this.'

Slowly, Carly nodded. 'I know. But what am I supposed to do? I can't just walk away. If I do, I'll have to live with the fact that I did for the rest of my life. I want to find out what has happened here. I know it might prove dangerous for you, so of course I won't force you. But if you think there's even the slightest chance that you can get to the bottom of what happened to my uncle, I'll double your fee. Regardless of how dangerous it might be. I just have to know what happened to him.'

CHAPTER EIGHTEEN

'All right, love,' Kitt said over the phone to Halloran as she walked back into the hotel bedroom from the bathroom. 'I'll try not to bother you for the next twenty-four hours. Stay safe.'

'Finished making all your lovey-dovey sounds with Halloran?' Grace said, flashing a cheeky smile.

'For now,' Kitt said, tartly, raising an eyebrow at Grace.

'What did he say about all this business with DI Cobb and DI Garner?' said Joe. He could see Kitt and Grace were about to launch into a full-blown banter tournament and he couldn't control his curiosity any longer over all that Carly had relayed to them a little over an hour ago. Kitt had advised Carly to go back to her hotel in the centre of town while they strategized about what legitimate next moves they might be able to make to get to the truth of the situation. Evie, on realizing she wasn't going to be getting a lift back to Yorkshire tonight, hopped on the next train towards York, leaving her bags with them to ferry in the car whenever they did make it back across the Pennines.

Understandably, once all that was settled, Kitt wanted to talk to Halloran about the situation before anything else was decided but Joe wasn't going to let Grace's playful streak take hold now that there were more than likely answers to be had.

Kitt took a deep breath before answering. 'Mal doesn't know for sure – he's not connected with Cumberland station and has no business ringing them for information on behalf of his girlfriend – but he suspects someone very high up the food chain has ordered them to deny that they are holding Holmes's body.'

'Would the police really do that?' said Joe.

'One only has to read the headlines to know that a lot of things go on in the police force as a whole,' Kitt said. 'Some of it terrifying. But Mal did say he hadn't heard of anything like this happening before. He did say a few things didn't add up about how the investigation was being run. There were no media appeals for information, which in a case like this are standard procedure. There was no crime scene guard on post at the churchyard either. Of course, if the people we spoke to weren't real police officers then that explains why some of these procedures weren't followed. But Halloran says he certainly hasn't been involved with anything like this in the past.'

'Ah, but would he tell you even if he had?' said Grace.

'It's a fair point,' said Kitt. 'I can't be sure about that because he's got orders to follow. But Halloran says although government agencies do work closely with the police, particularly some sections like counter-terrorism, he cannot imagine a reason why they would deny having Holmes's body. The only conclusion that he could come to is that this story was somehow for public safety. That something about the body, though he had no idea what it could be, posed a threat so serious that their only tack, given how few people knew about its discovery, was denial. But he's the first to admit this still doesn't make any sense to him. We were there at the scene. Officers were there at the scene. Why not just explain to Carly that she couldn't have access to it just now but reassure her that her uncle's body was safe? Why deny ever having the body? Or that DI Garner exists when all three of us spoke to her just hours ago? And it's not just Mal, by the way. Evie must have asked Charley about the situation the second she got back to York because I've just had a text from her to say she'd never heard of anything so bizarre either.'

'So that's two experienced police officers both insisting they've never encountered such an odd state of affairs. Something really disturbing is going on here,' Joe said. 'Like you said, we talked to Garner. We know she exists. She showed you her ID. We found the body. I suppose they might think they've got plausible deniability so long as only we knew about it but what if we went to the press? Why are they sure that we won't whip up a media storm about this missing body?'

'I don't know,' said Kitt. 'It's clearly a cover story for something. But it's completely disproportionate given the situation, i.e. that Carly was simply trying to say goodbye to her dead uncle. Whatever their reasons for making up this wild distortion of the truth, both Halloran and I agree that this whole situation has gone too far. To the point of cruelty when it comes to poor Carly. Denying that her uncle's body was even found . . . I mean, I understand that there are things that go on in this country that only counter-intelligence officers and the like will ever know about, and perhaps, given the contents of the briefcase, that's what's happening here, but shouldn't those closest be offered a better cover story than blunt denial?'

'It's off and no doubt about it,' said Grace. 'It's making me feel a bit queasy, actually. Surely they could get Carly to sign some kind of NDA and just let her know what happened to her uncle?'

'That's what I said to Mal,' said Kitt. 'If they had offered her closure and even if she hadn't been able to tell us a thing about it, I'd have set off back home straight away safe in the knowledge that she could move on from this chapter in her life.'

'But she's been left hanging,' said Grace. 'No explanation whatsoever. If I think about it too much, it boils my blood, it really does. When they told her that, at the police station, denied all knowledge of the body, she must have had a moment when she questioned her own sanity – or even our agenda.'

'I can't imagine the scene,' said Kitt. 'She said she got angry, and who could blame her? I think I'd end up locked up in a cell if it was me in that situation.'

'So, what can we do?' said Joe. 'And how do we go about it?'

'That's the central question,' said Kitt. 'It's all very well solving a murder when you've got a list of possible suspects to work through. It's a simple process of elimination. You gather your information on them one by one until there's only one candidate – or collaborative group – left standing.'

'But we've been lacking any prime suspects from the start,' said Grace. 'Yeats is as dodgy as they come but he strikes me as too spineless to actually end somebody's life. And the guys down at Donna's pub were listening in to what we were saying but it was probably just local curiosity.'

'The reason we haven't had a viable suspect list is because we haven't been up against a single perpetrator,' said Kitt. 'We're up against an invisible force. An agency of some nature who are willing to lie and misdirect to protect . . . I don't know what. Whatever it is they're protecting.'

'Do you think this agency, whoever they are, have covered up Holmes's death because he was working for them or because he was working for someone else?' said Joe.

'Impossible to say,' said Kitt. 'We still don't know who

Holmes was loyal to but I think, given the strange nature of this cover-up, that it's more likely he was working for some kind of agency, rather than being a participant in some kind of international crime ring.'

'Did Halloran have any suggestions about how we go about furthering the investigation?' said Grace.

'Carefully,' said Kitt with a wry smile. 'That was his main piece of advice and the part he really wanted to be sure I'd taken on board. As you might imagine, given his protective sensibilities, he's less than thrilled that we're continuing the case at all.'

'Yep,' said Grace. 'That sounds about right for Halloran.'

'He's too busy with this fraud case to come back over and support us so we are going to have to work to our own strengths,' said Kitt. 'We need to start by re-examining every piece of evidence in that briefcase we found, via the photos we took. We need to assume nothing as we do so. Keep as open a mind as possible. If we do that, we're likely to generate another lead we can follow.'

'We still haven't figured out what role the man in the photograph played in all this,' said Joe.

'The man in the camel coat,' said Grace in a deep, foreboding voice. 'Sounds like the title for a spy novel.'

'For all we know, that's a picture of the man who killed Holmes,' said Joe.

'I know,' said Kitt, picking up her phone to once again look at the photograph. 'He seems to be the missing link.

Or at least one of them. I have wondered whether we've made too many assumptions about Holmes's movements. Yes, we found him buried at St Michael's, but we know he couldn't have been killed there on the Wednesday evening because he left Carly that voicemail on the Friday. This means he must have been killed at a later date and buried in the churchyard.'

'So, maybe he didn't have a meeting at St Michael's at all, like we assumed?' said Grace.

'Well, he didn't go back to his room for his dog so we know something happened on that Wednesday night, and maybe this man in the photograph had something to do with it. Or maybe Holmes went to meet this man on that Thursday we can't account for. But, of course, even if he did, that doesn't mean that . . .'

Kitt trailed off. Grace and Joe looked hard at her, trying to determine what had caused her unexpected silence.

'What?' said Grace when Kitt didn't immediately explain herself. 'You know it creeps me out when you cut off mid-sentence like that.'

'Sorry,' Kitt said, starting as though she had forgotten they were even in the room with her. 'I just can't believe I didn't see it sooner.' She peered harder at her phone and swiped her fingers over the screen to zoom in even further.

'See what?' asked Grace.

'There's a statue in the background of this photograph. It looks . . . vaguely familiar to me.'

'How can you tell anything about the location from that photo?' said Grace, looking at it again for herself on her own phone.

'It's small, you have to really zoom in to see it. But there is a statue in the background. Oh, why does the damn thing look so familiar?'

'Let me have a look,' said Joe. Kitt turned the zoomed-in photograph to him and the moment she did so, Joe had no idea why he'd asked to see the statue. He wasn't an art affi- cionado. Far from it. It was a woman, that much he could make out even though the image was a bit pixellated at this size. And it had been chiselled from white marble.

'Sorry, I don't think I'm going to be much help with that,' Joe conceded.

Kitt, offering a commiseratory smile, looked at the pic- ture again. 'I've just got to think. What have I been reading about statues in the last month or two?'

'Knowing you, that's going to take some time,' said Grace.

'You're not helping,' said Kitt, staring hard at the pho- tograph. 'Try searching Google for me, Grace, for Venus statue, goddess of love ... Try putting the words latest or new in there too otherwise we're just going to end up with articles about Antioch's *de Milo*.'

'Right,' Grace said, clearly only having understood half of what Kitt just said. Joe wasn't clear on all of it either. It was quite unusual to come across a person as clued up about drug rings as they were fine art and secretly Joe found himself a little envious of Kitt's breadth of knowledge.

'Oh!' said Grace. 'There's a specially commissioned version of it that has just been unveiled.'

'That's ringing some bells,' said Kitt. 'Didn't it take the artist twenty years to complete or something like that?'

Grace scrolled down on her phone to check Kitt's information. 'That's the one. It's being displayed at the Institute of Art in Edinburgh.'

'Which means,' Kitt said, 'we now know where this photograph was taken and where we might find the man in the camel coat.'

In that moment, Joe was certain he had never heard happier news than that. With Holmes's body missing, the briefcase confiscated and the local police pretending that there was no case to be answered, things had never felt so hopeless. St Michael and the photograph had been their only two clues and they'd already exhausted one of them. Perhaps the location in which the photograph had been taken was important in some way. Whatever the situation, having something to work from was better than having absolutely nothing at all.

'The only reason I can think a British intelligence officer, or someone who works with them, might be in a cultural institution like that is that it would make a good meeting place,' said Joe.

'Lots of background noise,' Grace said with a nod. 'It

would be difficult for anyone to overhear or record your conversations. And it's an innocuous place to be seen. Not like
some dodgy backstreet warehouse where people might so
obviously be up to no good. It doesn't raise any suspicions.'

'Wasn't there something on the back of that photograph?'
said Joe.

'There was,' said Kitt. 'A sort of tally. Two sets at the top
and one at the bottom.'

'OK. Let's start at the top of the photograph,' said Joe.
'Those numbers tallied twelve and ten if I remember cor-
rectly?'

'That's right,' said Kitt. 'I just don't know what they could
have been totalling up. Unless . . .'

Kitt paused again, tilting her head as she looked at the
photograph of the tallies on the back of the photograph.

'Unless . . . ?' Grace said. 'Kitt, you're doing it again.'

'Sorry,' said Kitt. 'The cogs do take a bit of time to whir, you
know? Unless it isn't a total. Unless that's just a code designed
to throw anyone else who might see it off the scent.'

'You mean, we should just read the numbers as twelve
and ten,' said Joe.

'Twelfth of October,' said Kitt.

'That's . . . tomorrow,' said Grace. 'Do you think that could
be it? That it's just code for a date?'

'I don't know but the problem is, I don't have enough
information to guess at what else the figures might be,'
said Kitt. 'We obviously know that Holmes wasn't here on

holiday as he'd told Carly. He'd come up for some serious business and perhaps that entailed a meeting. At this place. With this man.'

'I think you might be right,' said Grace. 'We know Holmes left the boarding house on Wednesday evening and wasn't seen again. But we don't know what happened after that, only that his body ended up at St Michael's.'

'So his movements on that Wednesday and Thursday are still a mystery, as are his reasons for visiting St Michael's in the first place,' Kitt said with a sigh.

'Yes,' said Grace. 'But at least we know he went to the boarding house at some point on the Wednesday. It's that missing Thursday, that's the most infuriating detail we're lacking. But whatever was going on during that time, maybe he was supposed to meet with this man the following week to either report back or exchange information.'

'It's a working theory,' said Kitt. 'Which is the best we can probably hope for at the moment.'

'So, you think the man in the camel coat was some kind of contact for Holmes?' said Joe.

Kitt shook her head. 'I've no idea. He might have been. He might have been an enemy agent Holmes intended to take down. There's only one real way to know for sure.'

Joe raised his eyebrows as it dawned on him what Kitt was suggesting. 'The other number on the photograph is twelve. Which is probably a meeting time. You're suggesting that we attend the meeting.'

'In a way,' said Kitt. 'I'm not suggesting that we pretend Holmes sent us or something. But perhaps we'll be able to talk to this man in more detail, somehow get some information out of him that will tell us more about Holmes and what happened to him. Or who this agency, this higher up entity that seems to be calling the shots here, even is.'

'But we – we can't do that,' said Grace. 'Look, I'm usually the first one to suggest doing something adventurous. It's pretty much my job around here otherwise Kitt would be stuck indoors all year with her books. But we don't even know who this person is. He could be an international crime lord for all we know. Or a trained assassin. Or . . . well, I don't know what's worse than a trained assassin actually, but it could be something even worse than that. Whoever is behind Holmes's death, they were powerful and organized enough to intercept the body and make it disappear even after we discovered it. I'm sure they'd have no trouble making us disappear too if they wanted to.'

Kitt sighed. 'I understand. I don't expect you to come with me on this one. You are right in all you say, Grace . . . shocked as I am that you're the voice of reason in this situation.'

Grace pressed a hand against her chest as though the insinuation she was ever anything except sober and reasonable was the worst kind of slander.

'But the truth is,' Kitt said, ignoring Grace's gesture, 'that this is the only lead we have on finding out what really happened to Holmes. And you saw how distressed Carly was. Halloran has no idea why they'd do it, and neither do I. But it's obvious they're not going to tell her a damn thing about her uncle unless we find a way of forcing their hand. So, though Halloran will throw an absolute fit when he finds out about it, I'm going to Edinburgh to meet this man. It's not as though we can go to the police after what happened to the briefcase and the body we found. For all we know they've already figured out where this photograph was taken for themselves and apprehended the subject. But in case they haven't, in case there's a chance he shows up and knows the answers we are looking for, I have to go.'

Grace nodded. 'Well, Edinburgh has a lot of bookshops. I can't exactly let you go there unsupervised. But part of the reason I'm taking this so seriously is that I looked at the updates on the local newspaper websites this evening. Murder in any community, but particularly a small one like this, is always big news for the local papers. Not one of them have covered it. It's almost as if they've been instructed not to. You asked earlier why they're not worried about us going to the press. I think that's why. I think somehow, I don't know how, they have the power to silence them.'

Grace paused then and Joe was sure he'd never seen her look so serious.

'I'm scared, Kitt,' she said, when she did at last speak again. 'I'm not going to lie about that. But I'm not letting you go to Edinburgh by yourself either. If you're going, I'm in.'

'Me too,' said Joe. 'And don't forget, we've got Rolo now. Dogs are brilliant bodyguards. That may even be why Holmes had him. I'm sure he'll keep us safe even if things do turn nasty.'

Kitt pressed her lips together, clearly not thrilled with her own plan but seeing no other choice if they wanted to find out what really happened to Ralph Holmes. 'We'll have to strategize on the train there about how we're going to handle things. It's an hour or so to Edinburgh from Carlisle, which should be enough time to formulate a plan. I need some rest before I can even think soberly about it. Best-case scenario this man in the camel coat, whoever he is, will have something to say about Ralph Holmes, or at least give us a sense of who made his body disappear, and why.'

'And worst-case scenario?' said Grace.

Kitt looked over at Grace but didn't offer a verbal response. The grave expression cast across her face said it all.

CHAPTER NINETEEN

'I really don't like this,' Kitt said over comms.

'You can join the club on that one,' said Joe, holding a bounding Rolo tight on his lead. A quick online search the night before had confirmed what they had all hoped: that the Great Hall at the Institute of Art in Edinburgh was dog-friendly. Though dogs, understandably, weren't allowed anywhere near the exhibits, the venue did allow people to bring them into the entry area, where there were gift shops and a few pop-up food vendors. Joe theorized that the only reason the Institute of Art had made this exception was to maximize their chances of making money out of tourists. But right then, Joe wasn't too concerned about the rationale behind it all. He was just grateful to have Rolo by his side. There was no real reason things should turn ugly with the man in the camel coat but it would be a small mercy to have Rolo defending him if they did.

Had they been visiting Edinburgh for pleasure, Joe would

have rather enjoyed a trip to this particular attraction. He couldn't speak about the art housed in the exhibition rooms but the Great Hall was a marvellous space in the true sense of the word. The first thing that hit you when you walked in was the smell. If it were possible, the whole place smelled of culture. Which, as far as Joe could tell, was a blend of coffee and freshly printed paper. The hall also boasted several large skylights, through which beams of autumn sunlight flooded in, bouncing off the marble floors and pillars that were no doubt designed to give the whole building a prestigious air. Grace had been right about the noise levels. Visitors of all kinds, families, couples, friendship groups, were engaged in lively conversation that echoed off the hard flooring.

It wouldn't be impossible to overhear or record a conversation in this place, but it would be difficult, there was no doubt about it.

It was now three minutes to midday and Joe was lingering by a coffee stand not far from where the Venus statue was being displayed. He glanced down the hall to see that Kitt was pretending to browse postcards outside the gift shop area and Grace was by the reception desk, looking harder than anyone would ever need to at a map of the building.

'I want it stating for the record, for the next time Kitt asserts that I'm far too giddy for my own good, that I was the founder of the "Not Liking This Situation One Bit Club",' Grace said over comms. 'This is not my idea of a fun outing to Edinburgh. Any sign of our mystery man yet?'

'Nothing yet,' said Kitt.

'Wait,' Joe said. 'I see him. He's just walked in through the revolving doors.'

'I see him too,' Grace said. 'He's bigger than he looked in the picture, isn't he?'

'Thanks for that reassuring observation,' Joe said drily. During their brainstorming session on the train, Kitt had quickly dismissed the idea of Joe going to the meeting to pose as Holmes. 'Too many risks, and likely to escalate the situation,' that's what she'd said. But since they had no idea whether the man in the camel coat had ever met Holmes before, Joe had seemed the best candidate to send in, albeit while on comms to Kitt and Grace to ensure his safety. If they were lucky, the man in the camel coat might not know what Holmes looked like and mistake Joe for Holmes. If that happened, it was likely the man would give away some crucial information without Joe committing an out and out subterfuge that would only anger him.

There was also a chance that the man in the camel coat might mistake him for someone sent by Holmes in case of his death. Although Kitt had cited an article she'd read about how women make the best spies, they'd all agreed that it was still likely to be a male-dominated profession. Thus they had pinned their hopes on Joe passing himself off as someone involved in intelligence.

At the time they'd all agreed this, Joe was glad he was

the one taking the biggest risk. He'd even been a little bit excited by the prospect of such an operation.

All that excitement had dissipated the moment he set eyes on the man in the camel coat. After all that had transpired over the last forty-eight hours, Joe wouldn't have been surprised if he was hiding a pistol with a silencer under that camel coat. In his panic, Joe imagined that after shooting him the man would just wrap a scarf around his neck to cover the gunshot wound and lay his head back gently on the seat as if he was sleeping. And Kitt and Grace would be too late to save him and nobody else would realize what had happened until the man in the camel coat had escaped . . .

Or maybe that was too far-fetched even after what they had uncovered in the short time they'd been in Cumbria.

He was just going to have to take the meet one step at a time.

Joe watched the man in the camel coat walk in a straight line towards a bank of seating in the middle of the hall. He knew Kitt and Grace would be watching the man just the same. And by the man's manner, just for a moment or two, Joe wondered if they'd jumped to completely the wrong assumptions about this person. It was clear the man knew where he was going by his confident strides but he was in no rush. He took his time and didn't look in the least bit on edge. They had assumed the man had visited the Institute of Art to conduct some kind of clandestine meeting. But he didn't once look over his shoulder. His eyes didn't dart around, checking for anyone watching, waiting or listening. He looked as casual as he might if he had been popping into one of the exhibits. He even smiled at a little girl who had knocked into him while charging around the open-plan space with the carefree glee only little children can.

The girl's mother looked to be making some apology but he gave a dismissive wave and a broad smile to show there were no hard feelings and then continued to make his way towards the small row of wooden benches he had clearly been aiming for all along.

The moment he was sitting down, Kitt's voice came over comms.

'I suspect whoever he's expecting to meet would be on time. Espionage may be a strange profession but it's a profession nonetheless and I doubt such people are late for things. It's time to go in but for heaven's sake be careful. Don't do anything rash and listen to my instructions.'

'Received,' Joe said, acknowledging all Kitt had said.

Slowly, as previously agreed, he made his way over to where the man in the camel coat sat. As he did so, he looked at the man's features and tried to figure out if he looked like a good guy or a bad guy. How did one tell such things about another person? He didn't have any obvious scars on his face that might suggest he'd been in numerous fights. His nose protruded slightly further than most but it hardly seemed fair to judge a man on those terms. His short grey hair was carefully combed. Perhaps too carefully combed? The kind of perfectionism only a warped mind might dabble in?

Nope. As much as Joe tried to assess this man, he couldn't find anything concrete that betrayed the man's disposition one way or another. Even his expression was neutral.

Joe sat next to him. The man, at once, looked the other way. Not at anything in particular, he just allowed his eyes to roam around the room. Anywhere but at Joe and Rolo.

'So H has got you looking after his dog, has he?' the man said.

H? Holmes?

'I don't mind,' Joe said. 'I quite like having him around.'

This was a good way in. Joe hadn't had to stretch the truth, not yet.

'I didn't know if Uncle would send anyone today. I've been off-comms since H missed the agreed dead drop last Thursday.'

'Uncle is a term espionage agents sometimes use for head-quarters,' Kitt whispered over comms. 'It looks as though Holmes was supposed to leave something at a particular place last Thursday – the day we can't account for. Tell him he was sensible to follow protocol.'

'You did right to follow protocol,' said Joe in as confident a tone as possible. Was Kitt getting these lines from genuine knowledge of the world of espionage or was she repeating things she'd read in her books? If it was the latter, their luck might run out sooner than later.

The man glanced at him then. 'Why did H miss the dead drop at St Michael's? Was he worried it might fall into the wrong hands? I know he was convinced someone else was after the package. Someone outside the British network. Maybe he found out who?'

So, the man in the camel coat did work for British intelligence . . . or so it seemed.

But what about this package?

'Don't ask any questions about the package,' said Kitt. 'It could have been the briefcase but that was back at the hotel and we know Holmes didn't make it back to his boarding house after his visit to St Michael's. So it must be something else altogether. Tell him the truth. Tell him Holmes is dead. See how he responds to that.'

'Is everything . . . H did acquire the package to make the dead drop, didn't he?' the man in the camel coat pushed.

'I'm sorry to be the one to tell you,' said Joe. 'But Holmes is dead. That's why I am looking after his dog.'

The man in the camel coat narrowed his eyes at Joe then. Joe didn't know exactly what had given him away – something he had said or not said? Perhaps he shouldn't have called Holmes by his full name. Perhaps that was the giveaway? Regardless, the shadow falling over the man's face told him the game was up.

'Who are you?' the man in the camel coat hissed.

'Er . . . Joe,' Joe replied. He wasn't about to hand out his last name to this guy in a hurry and the moment he said it aloud he at once regretted even giving his real first name. How hard would it have been to say James or George or Adam?

'Joe,' the man in the camel coat almost sneered, 'you don't work for us.'

'I'm sorry,' said Joe. 'I've not come here to deceive you. I really am looking after Holmes's dog because he died. But I am a civilian. Me and my colleagues at a PI agency uncovered Holmes's body. But now the police are saying the body has disappeared and we just want some answers.'

The man's face paled, and a veil of confusion fell over him but he quickly corrected it. 'You'll just have to accept that you'll never have the answers. This meeting never happened.'

The man in the camel coat stood. Joe followed suit.

'It didn't really happen. You haven't told me anything,' said Joe.

'And I'm not going to. Whatever you know, just forget it,' the man said, and before Joe could say anything else he strode off towards the door at breakneck speed.

Joe started after him.

'No, Joe. Don't follow him. We don't know what he'll do if he's backed into a corner. He could be armed for all we know,' Kitt said over comms. But Joe paid her no heed.

Encouraging Rolo to run with him, he followed the flash of pale, camel fabric out onto the streets of Edinburgh's Old Town. At first, Joe had thought he'd lost him in the crowds. But then he caught sight of him again, running towards a medieval-style building. Without thinking at all, Joe started running in that direction. He must have been out of range of Kitt's comms as all he could hear now was static in his ears. Which meant, besides any assistance Rolo might be, he was going to have to deal with this situation alone. He really didn't want to lose the man in the camel coat the same way he'd lost the man – or woman – who had been spying at St Michael's churchyard.

'Come on, boy!' Joe said to Rolo and in just a few moments they were sprinting past what turned out to be the Writers' Museum. Joe took a sharp right onto a long, straight stretch of road bordered by various eateries and tourist shops. He kept his eyes firmly on the man in the camel coat. Even though once or twice he disappeared into the crowds of tourists, he always resurfaced a moment or so later. Joe had to hand it to him, the man's hair may have greyed but he hadn't let his fitness levels slip. He himself was struggling to keep up. Perhaps the man in the camel coat was used to finding himself in situations he had to run from.

Joe's chest burned as he gave chase. He wasn't used to running this fast and he would no doubt run out of puff in less than a minute if he didn't manage to catch up with the man. At least he wasn't alone in his struggle. Rolo panted heavily as he did his best to keep up with Joe's pace while avoiding the heavy feet of tourists and shoppers.

In spite of the pain he was in, Joe willed his legs to pump faster.

'Come on, boy, you can do it,' he gasped out to Rolo, but this time it felt as though he was, at least in part, talking to himself.

He gained a little on the man, which in turn gave him the enthusiasm to run that little bit harder. Within twenty seconds, Joe was almost in arm's reach of his subject. He tried to grab at the back of his coat but just as he did another man – another runner – barged into him and knocked him sideways. Joe landed on the pavement with a large thud while crowds of tourists merely walked around him. Rolo, seemingly glad of the rest, took the opportunity to pause and lick Joe's face.

'Sorry,' the man who'd knocked him over said, 'didn't see you there.'

The moment he saw Joe sit up, however, the man moved on. Seemingly not interested in hanging around long enough to see if Joe was going to make a full recovery.

Wincing from the jolt, Joe stood just in time to see the man in the camel coat turn into Greyfriars Kirkyard.

Limping along after his subject, and tugging the dog along with him, Joe did what he could to catch up, but deep down, he knew it was no use. By the time he turned into the kirkyard himself the man in the camel coat was nowhere to be seen. There was only a small crowd of visitors patting the statue of Greyfriars Bobby for luck.

'I've lost him,' Joe whispered over comms. But still all he received back in return was static. At this he bent double and placed his hands on his knees to try and recover from both the run and the fall. Rolo whined and looked longingly over at an ice-cream stand a few feet away. In his despair, however, Joe couldn't bring himself to respond to the dog's cries of longing.

He'd completely failed Kitt and Grace, again. Not to mention Carly. This meeting was supposed to give them something to go on. The man in the camel coat was the last clue, the last chance they had to really understand what was going on here. Now they had nothing.

CHAPTER TWENTY

'Shame there wasn't time to visit any of Edinburgh's book-shops,' Kitt said ruefully as she sipped tea from a paper cup at a cafe outside Waverley train station. 'There are some wonderful independents here.'

'Haven't we got rather bigger things to think about?' said Joe, trying not to make his tone sound too gruff as he did so. He was only frustrated with himself after all, nobody else should have to bear the brunt of that. Still, his experience with the man in the camel coat had undoubtedly left him shaken. He watched all of the people milling up and down the escalators at the entrance to the station, his eyes flitting from one to the next, as if the act of merely looking hard enough into the crowds was enough to provide him with a stroke of luck and the man he'd lost track of an hour ago now would appear. Running to catch his train out of the city. And then Joe would be able to do what he'd failed to do before: apprehend him and get some answers.

Kitt looked at Joe for a long moment before responding to his prior comment. 'Even if you'd caught up with the man in the camel coat, it was obvious he wasn't going to tell us anything.'

'We can't know that for sure,' Joe snapped. He hated the edge in his voice. But he couldn't help it. The case was in ruins now and it was his fault.

'Now listen here,' Kitt said, her tone quiet and stern. From little hints Grace had dropped here and there, Joe was well aware that Kitt was not a woman blessed with a lot of patience and Joe knew he'd been skating on thin ice with his attitude all the way back from the Old Town. 'You might not feel it, but you were lucky today. It's looking increasingly likely from what he said that he works for British intelligence and that, by proxy, Holmes did too. But I'm sure he still has his orders about how to deal with difficult circumstances. If you had caught up with that man, there's no telling what he might have done with you and then I'd have had that on my conscience. You shouldn't have gone after him. I made that clear.'

'What else was I supposed to do?' Joe heard himself say, though he had no idea why he felt so keen to push his luck.

'What you were told,' Kitt said. Her voice may have been perfectly calm but there was no missing the hard quality to it. 'I told you not to follow him.'

'I know . . . you're right, I'm sorry,' Joe said, frowning into his coffee. 'I just . . . he probably knows why Holmes was killed. He probably has all the answers.'

'He probably does,' said Grace, 'but as Kitt said, on these cases, we have to work as a team otherwise sooner or later it's going to be game over for one or all of us.'

Rolo let out a long whine at this comment. He was lying at Joe's feet under the table. Whether or not the dog understood the nuance of the conversation or was simply responding to the tone in their voices, he couldn't say. But Grace was right. Splitting from the group had been a rash thing to do under the circumstances.

'I understand,' Joe said. 'I thought it was worth the risk but I know I'm not experienced enough to make a judgement like that. I should have listened to you.'

'Nothing's worth your life,' Grace said, putting a reassuring hand on Joe's arm. 'And Kitt's right. He probably wouldn't have told you anything.'

'I didn't mean to put any of us at risk, of course,' said Joe. 'But how can you be so calm about that? About the man in the camel coat not cooperating.' He couldn't understand it. They'd had a man in their grasp who could have been the key to understanding everything but Kitt and Grace were behaving as though it was no big deal that he'd got away.

Kitt shrugged. 'In this game, you can only work with the people who are willing to give you something. In a lot of respects, the man with the camel coat gave more away by being secretive than he might if he'd spilled his guts.'

'Well, not quite that much,' said Grace.

'No, not quite,' said Kitt. 'But it's obvious we've stumbled onto some kind of conspiracy here. The more I think about it, the more I'm convinced that Garner, Drummond and Stark don't work for the police at all. I think our call was intercepted by whatever government agency Holmes was involved with. I think they dispatched Garner, Drummond and Stark and then gave orders to Cumberland police station to keep a lid on whatever's going on here. Oh, and don't worry,' Kitt added. 'I do understand how incredibly outlandish that sounds but it's the only reasonable explanation I can come up with for why Cumberland police station claimed that Garner, Drummond and Stark didn't exist.'

'So many questions,' said Grace. 'I'm trying to think of reasons why a government agency would want to cover up the death of one of their agents. There has to be a reason that they're doing this. Maybe understanding that will give us some way forward with this debacle.'

'What if they discovered Holmes was a double agent?' said Kitt. 'Pretending to work for British intelligence services while remaining loyal to a foreign power. What if his initial disappearance somehow tipped them off to his betrayal, and then he turned up dead and they needed time to work out how and why he'd been killed without any involvement from civilians?'

'Is that . . . likely?' said Joe.

'No . . . none of this is likely,' said Kitt. 'And if that was the case, frankly I think they would have just come up with some cover story for Carly. So it probably doesn't quite add up.'

Joe ran a hand through his brown hair, trying to think. This all seemed so unthinkable. He was used to life feeling somewhat surreal. That's how it had felt when the doctors told him there was nothing they could do for Sarah, and then again later when she died. Experiences of this magnitude left him feeling very much an outsider in a strange world and he imagined almost anyone else who had experienced similar felt the same. Until something like this happens, you go along living your life oblivious to the chaos and uncertainty other people are grappling with. Then it strikes you and you realize just how fragile your illusions about the world really were.

'I know losing the man in the camel coat was a blow,' said Kitt. 'But let's at least try to fit the things he said into a timeline, based on what we know already. If we do that, perhaps we'll strike on something to work on when we get back to Carlisle.'

'It sounded to me as though Holmes was expected to leave something at St Michael's Church. The package, whatever that is,' said Grace.

'And Holmes was meant to drop the package on Thursday,' Kitt said.

'He must have left the church alive, though,' said Grace. 'Because he left that voicemail for Carly on the Friday.'

'What if he did make the dead drop and left the package, whatever it was, at St Michael's Church? In the agreed place? But then someone else, an enemy, caught up with Holmes?' said Joe.

'The man in the camel coat did say, or at least suggest, that someone else was after the package,' said Grace.

'Would that work?' Kitt said, narrowing her eyes as she muddled it all through. 'We don't have any evidence that he did make that dead drop. We know he was buried at the church but we don't know exactly where he was killed or the circumstances under which he was brought to the cemetery. The graveyard may have just seemed like the nearest convenient place for the killer to hide a body. And though I hate to admit it, it was a pretty clever place to hide a corpse. In a gravesite from over a hundred years ago. It's unlikely anyone would go looking there.'

'But what put the idea in the killer's head to go to that church specifically?' said Joe. 'And wherever he went on the Wednesday evening, why didn't he just go back to the boarding house for his dog and his briefcase after? It seems to me that Holmes might have realized somebody was following him or was on to him and didn't dare go back to the boarding house in case they were waiting for him there.'

'But even if somebody was on to him, they wouldn't know the exact protocol for the dead drop,' said Kitt.

'Exactly,' said Joe. 'You heard what the man in the camel coat said – he'd been off-comms for a week. If something doesn't go to plan, the agents are clearly taught to lie low. If I work it through, I think I can just about see a scenario where Holmes didn't return to the boarding house for fear of someone waiting for him there. Then maybe he lay low for twenty-four hours, somewhere else so he could make his dead drop.'

'But then the next day,' Grace said, 'the people who were following him, the other people who were after the package, they caught up with him.'

'Forced him, possibly tortured him, to show them where the package was buried,' said Kitt.

'Then once they had what they'd come for, they shot him and buried him in the cemetery,' said Joe.

'But not before they forced him to call the one person who might come looking for him,' said Kitt.

'Carly,' Joe said. 'But . . . if Holmes is an agent, trained to manage situations just like these, he must have known they weren't going to let him go, even if he cooperated and convinced Carly he was going away to start a new life. Why would he do what they said?'

'Because they'll have threatened to kill Carly if he didn't,' said Kitt.

Joe felt tears rise in his eyes at this. Of course that's why Holmes had left the voicemail on Carly's phone. Before they'd known he had anything to do with espionage, they'd thought of him as a frightened civilian who had got himself into some trouble he couldn't get out of. Someone who was making decisions based on self-preservation. But Holmes will have known when he made that call to Carly's phone that he had little time left to live. And that if he didn't convince her he was going away, if he didn't ensure she didn't come looking for him, she would suffer the same fate.

'If any of this is even close to the mark, it's just tragic,' said Grace.

'I do hope I'm wrong about why Holmes left that message,' said Kitt. 'After everything that's already happened to her, I've no idea how Carly will react if she discovers Holmes gave his life for hers.'

'And if these people, whoever they were, have already got the package,' said Joe, 'if they managed to break Holmes, which given where we found his body they probably did, then whoever shot him will probably be long gone.'

'I did keep an eye and an ear on the forensics team while I was being questioned,' said Kitt. 'I overheard them say that Holmes didn't have any personal effects on him other than a wrist watch he was wearing.'

'It's all so convoluted,' Grace said.

'I'm not sure it's any more convoluted than some of the other cases we've worked in the past,' said Kitt. 'A person, Holmes, is in possession of something somebody else wants, and is killed for it. The only complicated aspect is the cover-up that's clearly going on. I'm still in shock that the police would play along with this. Halloran was adamant that he's just never heard of anything like this happening.'

'If this situation involves government agencies, the odds are whatever the package is, it's a high-value item,' said

Grace. 'Maybe the police had no choice but to go along with the story they were being told to sell.'

'Perhaps the package is very, very important information. Something that might even leave the UK vulnerable to attacks from foreign powers,' said Kitt. 'I can see those in power taking extreme action under those specific circumstances, even if I don't agree with the way they've gone about it.'

'So, where do we go from here?' said Joe. 'We've exhausted all leads from the briefcase and although we did get one or two pieces of information from the man in the camel coat, we still don't have a name. Someone to pin down and get some answers from.'

Kitt took her last sip of tea and set the cup down on the table before answering. 'I'm not sure we've got much rope left on this investigation considering what we're up against,' she said. 'But for Carly's sake, I think we should give getting to the truth one last shot. We're going to head back to Port Carlisle. Specifically, to the pub. The local news might not have reported anything about the body being found in the churchyard but I very much doubt that anyone, not even a government agency, could stop the village rumour mill from churning.'

'How will that help us?' said Joe.

'People will likely be talking about what they saw or heard around the time Holmes was killed,' said Kitt. 'You never know when someone is going to accidentally let slip something of profound importance. Often without them even realizing the significance of what they know. It's one of the perks of conducting an investigation in such a small place. Chins will definitely be wagging and we want to be there when they do.'

CHAPTER TWENTY-ONE

If Joe was honest, the last thing he wanted to do after their catastrophic jaunt to Edinburgh was return to the pub at Port Carlisle. The pub was nice enough and the warmth and light from the open fire certainly went some way to lifting his spirits. But this case was becoming more of a tangle by the hour, and it was getting to the point where Joe couldn't fathom which way was up. Two crucial but shadowy figures lingered on the periphery of any theory they came up with. The figure dressed in black who had been watching the police at the cemetery and the man in the camel coat. They were no closer to knowing who those people really were, except that the man in the camel coat seemed to work for some kind of British intelligence agency. Joe didn't know how, precisely. But he suspected both of these figures were integral to unravelling all that had happened to Carly's uncle.

One thing he did notice was that Donna was much

quieter than she had been the last time she'd served them. Joe couldn't quite say it was unusual because he'd only met the woman once, but she certainly seemed different in her demeanour. She hadn't appeared particularly pleased to see them. The welcoming smile she'd issued earlier in the week was now nowhere to be seen. Last time they had visited she'd been full of questions and taken the time to chat. This time she barely said two words to them as she served their drinks. Had she been silenced by someone? Told not to talk to them? Or was the botched meeting with the man in the camel coat merely playing on his mind? Making him paranoid?

Joe took a deep breath and tried to calm himself. He took a moment to focus on the logs crackling on the open fire. A sound he could just make out over the low murmur of conversation. He tried to concentrate on Kitt and Grace's chatter as they sat around one of the small mahogany tables set away from the bar. They sipped their drinks and somehow managed to smile and chuckle together even after a day that could only be described as taxing. Joe should have felt at ease here. It was a cosy enough pub and the company was as good as it came. For some reason, however, there was a knot in his stomach that just wouldn't untangle.

'Holmes told Carly he was going to rehome the dog,' Kitt said out of nowhere. Joe's attentions were piqued by this and he wasn't the only one to take note. At the word 'dog' Rolo's ears pricked up. He was sitting by Joe's feet looking as morose as Joe felt but it seemed he understood when he was being talked about.

'Yes, but he didn't go through with it,' said Grace.

'Maybe it wasn't a matter of choice,' said Kitt. 'If we're to take what the man in the camel coat said at face value, it's likely that Holmes was working for a British agency and was sent here on some kind of task or operation.'

'So, where does the dog come in?' said Grace.

'He left a voicemail for Carly to essentially warn her off looking into his disappearance. He said he was going to rehome the dog. Perhaps he tried to but couldn't find anyone to take him. Perhaps he did all of this because he knew this operation was going to be particularly dangerous.'

'You mean, you think Holmes might have had some idea that he was going to die?' said Joe, gravely. He'd never known how Sarah had made her peace with dying. He'd certainly yet to accept how she'd been robbed of all the years they thought they would spend together. Nobody is a stranger to the idea that we're all mortal, of course. But Joe could not contemplate how anyone dealt with the knowledge that their death was likely to be imminent.

'I imagine most people in Holmes's line of work get used to the idea that any operation, no matter how straightforward it might seem, could be their last,' said Kitt. 'But his behaviour around this particular mission, it does seem different. Carly's never had any information on his profession before, for example. Not even a cover story like the one he gave her in the voicemail.'

'It has to be about the contents of that package he was going to dead drop,' said Grace. 'Whatever was in it, it was so important that somebody else was after it and likely killed him for it . . . Maybe that's as close to the truth as we're ever going to get.'

'I think you might be right,' said Kitt. 'When it's the police handling the investigation, I can usually find some way to make a connection with them. Even if I'm kept on the outside, they'll at least allow me to pursue less urgent leads in the hope that they provide something new to go on.'

'But unless you're going to ditch Halloran and start going out with a top-secret government agent, we might have taken this case as far as we can.'

'Yes, well,' said Kitt. 'I'm in Halloran's black books enough as it is without dumping him for a higher ranking government official.'

'He didn't approve of the Edinburgh mission, I take it,' said Grace.

'That's one way of putting it,' said Kitt. 'I've never heard him quite so angry as he was over the phone earlier. You'd think he'd be used to me swanning off into dangerous situations by now. I have been a part-time PI for, oooh, must be going on for five years. And I've only come close to death once or twice – which when you think about it is quite good odds.'

'This case is a little different, though,' said Grace.

'You can say that again,' said Kitt. 'Although Halloran did jump off the deep end . . . well, I don't want this to get back to him or anything but he might have a point. We have stumbled into a rather more dangerous situation than we're used to here. We don't have the local police on side. In fact, we don't have any allies in this situation at all.'

'So, you think we should just tell Carly the vague gist of things, the fact that her uncle was exchanging a package of great importance and that he was killed for it and then . . . give up?' said Joe. He couldn't help but sigh at the thought that his very first case of magnitude might yield no concrete answers for the client.

'We'll do what we agreed,' said Kitt. 'We'll hang out here for the evening and keep our eyes and ears open. But if nobody is talking about what happened yesterday at St Michael's, I think we will have to accept we've hit a brick wall, explain the information we have recovered to Carly and make our way home.'

'But . . . if we do that . . .' Grace said.

'I know,' said Kitt, putting a hand on Grace's. 'It'll be the first case we haven't cracked. That wounds me just as much as it does you but we can either continue to go round in circles or we can cut our losses, go home and give our time to someone else who needs our help.'

Joe nodded simply because Kitt was in charge and he had no choice but to bow to her judgement. But deep down, he ached at the thought of Carly going through all she had been through and not getting any answers. This world was hard enough without being denied the solace of closure.

'I thought Donna was a bit subdued tonight,' said Joe, grasping at any observation in the hope it might lead somewhere.

'She was definitely quieter than she was the other day, yes,' said Kitt. 'I'm not sure we can really read anything into that, though. She could just be tired from putting in the hours.'

'I notice the same vultures are perched at the bar,' Grace said, keeping her voice low so as not to be overheard. She nodded over and sure enough the same group of men who had been sitting around the bar were sitting there now.

Particularly, Joe noticed that the man in the grey tracksuit who had given Donna a fair bit of lip was sitting in just the same seat as last time. Joe wondered, in fact, if the man had actually moved since they were in on Tuesday. The man happened to turn his head in their direction and he at once clocked Joe looking over. He frowned hard enough for Joe to look away. Abrupt as the man had seemed, they didn't have any evidence that he knew anything about Ralph Holmes and Joe wasn't going to get into a bar fight for looking the wrong way at someone. 'They don't seem thrilled that we're back,' Joe said, following Grace's lead and keeping his voice low.

'Funnily enough, I don't feel inclined to go up to them directly and ask why,' said Kitt. 'Better to keep things civil.'

Just a few moments after these words had left Kitt's mouth, the door to the pub flew open and a biting gale blew in from outside. A man stood in the frame, someone Joe vaguely recognized. He'd been in the pub the first time Kitt, Joe and Grace had visited. His straggly brown hair had been twisted into a startling arrangement by the October winds.

'You'll never guess it. There's been a body found just out there on the marshes,' he announced, seemingly to the whole pub. 'A dead body,' he clarified to the sea of stunned faces.

The pub erupted as the locals began bombarding the man with questions about this discovery. It was so loud it was impossible to hear any individual query or answer given. In the wake of the hubbub, Kitt blinked and sat up straighter in her seat while Joe and Grace exchanged a wide-eyed look.

Another body.

Less than a mile from where Holmes's body had been found just yesterday. Something told Joe that couldn't be a coincidence.

CHAPTER TWENTY-TWO

'Bernie, isn't it?'

It had, quite understandably, taken a while for the clamour caused by the man's announcement to die down in the pub. The man in the grey tracksuit and several others sitting at the bar hadn't wasted a second in learning all they needed to know about what had happened down on the marshes. Having already decided to keep their distance from the crowd at the bar, Joe, Kitt and Grace had remained in their seats just out of earshot. Bided their time while keeping their eyes on the man Kitt had remembered as Bernie. At least, that's what Donna had called him when he had passed some comment the day before last. She had also said, in a rather long-suffering manner, that Bernie was prone to dreaming up conspiracy theories. After all Joe had seen on the case so far, he wondered if Bernie was a lot closer to the truth with his theories than many of the locals realized. As long as he didn't leave, they'd decided, it didn't matter if they had to wait a few moments more to talk to him. The main thing was to get a quiet word without an audience. Quite a difficult feat in a small village pub.

'Aye, that's right,' Bernie said, his eyes narrowing as he looked up at Kitt.

'May we sit with you?' Kitt asked.

Bernie didn't verbally respond but waved a hand at a couple of nearby stools. Kitt, Joe and Grace all grabbed one and pulled them up to Bernie's table. Once the ruckus had calmed down, he'd ambled over to the same table he'd been sitting at a couple of days ago. It was far enough away from the bar that Joe was pretty confident they couldn't be overheard by the men who never seemed to leave their posts. Still, he would keep an eye out in case anyone did try and listen in.

'Me and my associates were in the pub a few days back, that's how I remember your name,' said Kitt. Despite the clarification, Bernie's eyes remained grey-blue slits and he momentarily glanced in the direction of the men at the bar, as if he thought they might take exception to Kitt talking to him. They were huddled in their own conversation, how-ever, and didn't pay theirs any heed.

'I recognize you,' he said at last, wagging a finger at Kitt. 'I never forget a face.'

'Nice to meet someone as observant as I am,' said Kitt.

'Spend twenty years in the navy and nothing'll get past you either,' said Bernie, before taking a gulp of whisky.

'I don't doubt it,' said Kitt. 'Twenty years. That *is* impressive.

Perhaps if you were in the navy for twenty years, the discovery you made out on the marshes tonight wasn't quite the shock it would be to somebody else.'

Bernie gave an almost imperceptible nod. 'I've seen a few bodies over the years. Most of them people who've drowned. I don't think it's a good idea to ever get used to seeing them, mind. Seeing someone who's left this world, it should always be a bit unsettling, if you want to stay human.'

'I couldn't have put it better myself,' Kitt said, admiration gleaming in her steel-blue eyes. 'I hope you don't mind but I'd like to ask you a few questions about what you saw. We uncovered a body ourselves just yesterday, a little further up the coast, and we're concerned the two might be related.'

'If you found them within a mile or two of here, it seems almost unthinkable that they're not related,' said Bernie. He paused then, looking between the three of them in turn. 'There are some strange doings going on round here. Nobody believes old Bernie, of course. They think I'm mad as a bag of badgers.'

The man paused then and Joe was sure he saw the prior light that had been shining in Kitt's eyes dim somewhat. He couldn't blame her. All they'd been looking for on this case was a reputable source of information and they had been thwarted at every turn. Kitt likely didn't relish taking intel from a man who was known for being 'mad as a bag of badgers' but on reflection Joe had to ask himself, at this point in the proceedings, what choice did they have?

'I'll tell you what I know,' said Bernie. 'But I don't want to get into any trouble. I've had plenty of that in my life and I don't need it. So if anyone asks, I don't want you telling them you heard it from me.'

'I work with anonymous sources on a regular basis,' said Kitt. 'I assure you, I can keep your identity private if you share what you know.'

'What I have to say might sound . . . odd,' said Bernie. 'But like I said, some strange things happen in these parts.'

'Strange, how?' said Grace.

'Strange. Things,' Bernie repeated, the hardness in his eyes making it plain he wouldn't be drawn any further on that particular point.

Without wasting another moment, and likely to prevent any more avoidance from their interviewee, Kitt pulled a notebook out of her pocket. 'I won't write down your name, Bernie, but I might need to make one or two notes as you speak. Otherwise, I am prone to forgetting things.'

Bernie didn't look enthused by the presence of the notebook but he didn't get up and leave the table either, which was permission enough for Kitt to proceed.

'So, this body on the marshes tonight. Did you find it first?' said Kitt.

'No,' said Bernie. 'Somebody else found it. I heard them screaming for help. They'd clearly never seen owt like it before to carry on the way they were. I could tell by the tone in their call, you know, that they were in real distress.

They'd already called the police but must've been spooked to be standing out there on the marshes alone with a dead body.'

'Can't blame them for that,' said Grace.

'So, you went to the person's aid when they called?' said Kitt.

'Aye, a woman who lives in a house at the edge of the firth found the body. I don't know her to speak to but recognized her face, you know. When I saw the body for myself, I understood why she didn't want to be alone with it, mind.'

'What makes you say that?' said Kitt.

Bernie paused again, and looked down into his whisky glass before responding. 'The police were telling the woman, and tried to convince me, that the man had drowned.'

'What do you mean, convince you?' said Kitt.

'I mean, it was plain to me that's not how the man died. There was a bullet in him,' said Bernie, lowering his voice.

Just like Ralph Holmes, Joe thought to himself. Kitt must have been thinking along similar lines as she pulled her phone out of her pocket and turned it towards Bernie. 'I don't suppose you've seen this man around the village, have you?'

Bernie looked at the photograph and then up at Kitt. 'I've seen him. In here, in fact. It was a good few nights back now. Over a week ago. Last Tuesday maybe? Anyway, that fella, he was sitting over there by the fire, having a heated conversation with a woman.'

Last Tuesday? Joe thought to himself. Donna said she'd seen Holmes in here on that same Tuesday and she'd never mentioned a woman. Why? Joe tried to think back to the conversation they'd had with Donna. She'd had a hard time remembering which day it was; had she misremembered the day? No. That wasn't it. The answer came to Joe. She said she worked the day shift on the Tuesday and her son worked the evening. So she wouldn't have seen this mystery woman. Whoever she was.

'Can you describe this woman?' said Kitt.

Bernie shrugged. 'I'm pretty observant but there wasn't much to distinguish her. She had long brown hair. That much I remember about her. Quite tall. She was dressed in black trousers and a black roll-neck jumper. But I didn't think much of that because from what I hear from the women I know, black's considered slimming.'

Kitt nodded along and jotted down the description in her notebook. Joe wagered she was thinking the same thing he was. They still had no idea who the figure in black at the cemetery had been. It could have been a coincidence that this woman with the long brown hair was dressed in black, of course. But something deep down tingled in Joe. Some intuitive sense that the connection he'd made in his mind shouldn't be so quickly disregarded.

'Not that we encourage earwigging,' said Grace. 'But I don't suppose you heard what they were talking about?'

Bernie shook his head. 'I could just tell from the expressions and the hand gestures that whatever they were talking about, it was important to them. Maybe I was wrong to describe the conversation as heated. It was more ... the atmosphere between them was cold. Stone cold. They looked pretty angry with each other but to me it just looked like a domestic. Not uncommon. People go away on holiday to a picturesque place like this thinking they're going to escape all their troubles but they just bring their troubles with them.'

'I'm sure you're right,' said Kitt, making one last note in her notebook. 'This has been really helpful, thank you for taking the time to talk to us.'

'Not a bother,' said Bernie. 'But I would prefer you keep me out of whatever it is you're doing with this information.'

'I'm sure we'll not have to pester you again,' Kitt said with a warm smile as she stood from her bar stool and arranged her maroon trilby on her head. A signal to Joe and Grace that they would soon be leaving.

'Oh, actually,' said Kitt as she pulled her coat back on. 'One thing I did mean to ask. You said some police arrived at the scene?'

'Aye, that's right,' said Bernie.

'Did they give you their names?' said Kitt.

'DC Drummond and DC Stark,' said Bernie. With little more than a rushed goodbye to their source, Kitt, Joe and Grace exchanged wide-eyed looks and dashed out of the pub.

CHAPTER TWENTY-THREE

Back at the hotel, Joe curled up on Grace's bed with Rolo while Kitt made the tea. He pushed his fingers through Rolo's soft fur, trying to find some comfort.

After Bernie had told them that it was DC Drummond and DC Stark who had attended the scene of the second body – the same officers that the local police station had denied all knowledge of – Kitt, Joe and Grace had raced out to the marshland. They needn't have bothered rushing. The officers had already gone; there was no sign of any law enforcement vehicles along that whole stretch. Not one flash of yellow tape. Not one blue light. For one twisted moment the trio had wondered if Bernie had made it all up after all but then they remembered their own experience with these mystery officers in the cemetery. Bernie was almost certainly telling the truth. Otherwise, how would he have known the names Stark and Drummond?

After that, they'd had nothing better to do but trudge

back to the car in the cold and drizzle while pondering whether this second corpse, whoever they had been, was the second body Drummond and Stark would make disappear this week.

'My head hurts,' Grace said, pressing both hands to her temples. She was sitting cross-legged on the other side of Rolo and looked as frustrated as Joe felt. 'I am going around in circles about who this second body is and how it connects with Holmes.'

'I know, I'm right there with you,' said Kitt, handing Grace, and then Joe, a cup of tea. 'But without seeing the body for myself, it's difficult. I've gone round and round with it and there are now two prominent possibilities forming.'

'And what are they?' said Joe, who had been as lost in his own thoughts about this new development as Grace had been in hers.

'Either Holmes and his killer came face to face and both of them got a shot out of a gun at each other at pretty much the same time.'

'You mean, Holmes was killed instantly and the other man wasn't?' said Grace.

'It's a possibility,' said Kitt. 'We don't know exactly what organs the bullet hit or missed in that second body. Maybe it took some time for them to die.'

'But whoever killed Holmes buried him,' said Joe. 'Would you really be able to bury a man while slowly bleeding to death from a gunshot wound?'

'It's not impossible,' said Kitt. 'But I agree it's not likely. Which leads to my other theory – that there's a third assailant in the mix.'

'The woman in black,' said Grace.

'Good book that,' said Kitt. 'And set in a watery locale not dissimilar to the firth. But yes, if I had to bet on it, I'd say this woman who was having some kind of difficult conversation with Holmes was the likely culprit of the two killings. Possibly the same person who was after the package – whatever that is!'

'But how can we be sure?' said Joe.

'We can't be sure of anything,' said Kitt. 'And we're going to have to make our peace with the fact that there's no point going to the police. You heard what Bernie said, Drummond and Stark were already telling local people it was a drowning when Bernie saw a clear gunshot wound.'

'But we do only have Bernie's word for that,' said Grace. 'I mean, he seemed a nice enough chap but we don't know him any better than we know Stark or Drummond really. And he even said himself his word wasn't worth much. Donna said he was always coming out with conspiracies. He's not the sturdiest of witnesses.'

'True,' Kitt said, pouring some tea for herself into some travel china she'd brought with her.

'I'm beginning to wonder how we're supposed to trust anyone's account of anything in this case,' said Joe. The sheer amount of second-guessing was leaving him dizzy.

'Well, look, Bernie seemed harmless enough. Just because he's paranoid or prone to believing conspiracies doesn't mean he's not right in this instance,' said Kitt. 'But we didn't see the body for ourselves, so it is second-hand information. I know what you mean about the trust issue. Garner, Drummond and Stark all seemed very plausible police officers to me – and I live with one. But they turned out to be not who they said they were. When events seem to be being manipulated left, right and centre, it makes you think twice about everything – and everyone.'

Joe sighed. 'Is it even possible to solve this case if there's not just one bigger agency or force involved, but potentially more than one?'

'The truth is, I don't know,' said Kitt. 'I've never quite worked a case like this one. There are potentially too many players in the game that we can't identify in any meaningful way. The man in the camel coat. The woman in black. These are hardly in-depth profiles.'

'If I had to guess based on what the man in the camel coat said, though,' said Joe, 'I'd say you were right about the woman in black potentially being the other person who was after the package.'

'I'm not sure we've anyone else to suspect,' said Kitt. 'She is the only additional party we've heard of. The only real candidate. Though it is pretty bold for her to go and argue about something like that in a pub so small where anyone could overhear you. I . . . What? What's the matter, Grace?'

Joe looked over to see that Grace was frowning. She was staring intently at her mobile phone which she had picked up, presumably to look something up on. She moved to the left and it emitted a sort of crackling noise. When she moved to the right it went silent again.

So again she moved to the left, and kept shuffling left along the bed until she was very close to a lamp sitting on a small table. By this point, her mobile phone was almost screeching with feedback.

'That's right weird that is,' said Grace. 'What do you think—'

But Grace stopped talking then. Because Kitt's whole body had tensed and she had brought a finger to her lips to suggest that Grace should stop talking right away.

Slowly, Kitt walked towards the lamp and, doing what she could to keep each movement silent, she picked it up and examined the base. Switching off the bulb and reaching across to turn the wire off at the plug, she then began to fiddle with the base, turning it this way and that until it was clear she was able to unscrew a section.

Grace and Joe looked at each other and then back at Kitt. Neither of them daring to speak. For her part, Kitt drew a sharp breath as she reached into the wiring and pulled out something small, flat and circular.

Kitt gestured for Grace to hand over her mobile and when she did so, Kitt waved it over the small piece of metal. A similar feedback sound was heard as before. Without a word,

Kitt took off the silk turquoise scarf she was wearing, folded it and began wrapping the small circular object in the scarf. She then placed the scarf in a drawer of the dressing table and closed it tight.

She turned back to face them, her eyes still wide. Kitt looked to Joe and Grace in turn before providing any explanation.

'Somebody's listening,' Kitt whispered the words. They were barely audible but each horrifying syllable sent a shiver straight through Joe's body.

CHAPTER TWENTY-FOUR

Moments after Kitt's discovery, she had ushered them into the bathroom, leaving the device – whatever it was – wrapped up in a scarf in the drawer. Once the bathroom door was closed, she turned on all the taps and the shower to boot before speaking.

'On my private investigator's training, we did a whole module on surveillance technology,' said Kitt, still keeping her voice low despite all the precautions she had taken. 'We were taught that sometimes, taps or bugs could create feedback on cellular or radio devices, depending on the model of the phone and the model of the bug. It was taught as a warning that one should never plant listening devices in a subject's house or private quarters. That such behaviour was illegal and if it were discovered, you'd lose your business and accreditation, everything really.'

'So, somebody has been listening to everything we've

been up to in the room all this time?' said Grace, looking a little flustered.

'I don't know how long they've been listening to us . . . Why?' Kitt said, seemingly sensing her assistant may have something to confess.

'Nothing . . . it's just, well, while you were taking a shower I took the liberty of performing the "Thong Song" at full volume in front of the mirror.'

'What is it with you and that song?' said Kitt, shaking her head, while Joe tried to keep a straight face at the image that had formed in his mind. How was it that in the grip of such a mind-bending discovery, Kitt and Grace could completely distract him from the issue at hand?

'I don't know,' Grace said. 'It's one of life's unsolved mysteries. But in my defence, I didn't think anyone could hear me, did I?'

'Whoever is at the other end of the line, I suspect they've heard worse,' Kitt said, though she couldn't resist adding, 'probably.'

'Who is listening to us?' Joe said, his smile fading at the sobering thought that they'd been monitored without their knowledge. Kitt had just said that the people who had taught her about surveillance considered it an illegal practice to place recording equipment in a civilian's personal space. Did that mean whoever had done it considered themselves above the law?

'I'm afraid that's quite difficult to narrow down,' said Kitt.

'There are likely to be a couple of parties at play here. And we don't know who is working with whom. The man in the camel coat seems to have been working with Holmes. So their employers could have planted something. Then there's Garner, Stark and Drummond. Garner took the name of our hotel and our room numbers. We don't know if she works for the same people as Holmes did.'

'Or do you think Cobb or Jessops could have planted the bug while they were here?' said Grace. 'I wasn't really paying attention to their movements the whole time. I was too taken aback by the discovery we'd made. Maybe they did have an opportunity to do something like that and we just didn't notice.'

Joe was left open-mouthed even at the idea of this. It was one thing to think about some kind of clandestine operation happening behind your back. It was quite another to think about someone planting a bug in your hotel room right in front of you.

'I think it's unlikely,' said Kitt. 'Not only would they have had to unscrew the base of the lamp without us noticing but there was a detective inspector in the room with us at the time. By anyone's standards that's a pretty brassy move. Besides anything else, even if he is cooperating in the cover-up, I doubt he's involved in any high-level tactics given he's a police officer. I imagine most agencies do their own dirty work to keep operations classified.'

Kitt paused then, thinking.

'On reflection, whoever planted this device, I doubt they planted it straight after we found Holmes's body,' she said. 'For one good reason. We discussed our trip to Edinburgh in this room. To meet the man in the camel coat. If they, whoever they are, had overheard that conversation, they might have followed us or tried to stop us from going to the meeting. Surely they would have intervened in some way in that meeting if they're part of all this?'

'So, our best guess is that the bug was planted while we were in Edinburgh?' said Joe. 'In which case, they can't have been listening for that long . . . I feel like I should be more relieved than I am.'

'I know, being snooped on in any capacity is enough to make your skin crawl. But while we were in Edinburgh, yes, I would say that's the most likely scenario,' said Kitt. 'We were out of the room for an extended period of time. We took the dog with us so there was nobody – human or animal – to monitor what was happening in here. It would have been the perfect opportunity.'

'Doesn't say much for security at this hotel if someone was able to break in and plant a bug,' Joe observed.

'It's not likely that they broke in,' said Kitt. 'There's certainly no damage to the door that would suggest so. I opened the window earlier and there was no damage to that either. If they are an agency that works in the field of espionage, they will have found another way, like copying a key card or feeding some story to the staff. Something more surreptitious.'

'This is bad,' said Grace. 'Really bad.'

'And the Understatement of the Year Award goes to . . .' said Kitt.

'What the hell do we do now?' said Grace, for once ignoring Kitt's invitation to a banter session. 'If we go quiet and throw the device out of the window or something, they'll soon figure out that we've discovered it and then goodness knows what will happen. With each hour that passes this situation just gets worse and worse.'

'I know. We need to bide our time,' said Kitt. 'I need to talk to Halloran for one thing. I know he's busy with that fraud case but we're decidedly out of our depths here.'

'On the biding time front, we could go back out there and put on a show for the microphone,' said Grace.

'They've already heard you do the "Thong Song",' said Kitt. 'I doubt they want an encore.'

'Not that kind of show,' Grace said flatly. 'We'll say we're all going to bed now, et cetera, and then arrange to either call or meet Halloran somewhere else tomorrow via text message, depending on if he can get away from York for the afternoon.'

'I doubt I'm going to sleep a wink knowing that device is in the room,' said Kitt. 'But yes, it's probably wise to at least act normally for now and give ourselves some time to think. But . . .'

'What?' said Joe.

Kitt ran her hands through her long red hair before responding. 'The trouble with this situation is, we've no idea how far they've taken their surveillance of us. We don't know if Joe's room has been bugged too. If they're listening to our phone conversations, or what.'

'I get that,' said Grace. 'But if Halloran can only talk over the phone tomorrow, you can call him from a payphone . . . assuming they still exist. If we can't find one of them, well, you could ask to borrow someone else's phone. Say your battery's flat and you need to make a call.'

'Oh, that's good thinking, Grace,' said Kitt. 'And it solves one problem, at least. I'm just concerned that if they're willing to go this far to hear what we've been talking about, then there could be protocols in place that we're not aware of.'

'Like what?' said Joe, though he genuinely didn't want the answer. In his wildest dreams he never thought it would come to this. Being afraid every word he said might be overheard, scrutinized. He could easily see how working in the navy, like Bernie had, might make a person paranoid. Officers in that line of work were probably privy to the kind of information that would leave most civilians in shock.

'I don't like to think about it,' said Kitt, 'but one possibility, assuming they have the resources, could be physical monitoring.'

'You mean . . .' Joe started the sentence but was almost afraid to finish it.

'I mean, they could be having us physically watched and followed whenever we leave the hotel,' said Kitt. 'Why, I don't know. Possibly because we've seen more than we should have in uncovering Holmes's body and briefcase. But if they're willing to plant a bug, I don't think we can rule much else out.'

'I did say I felt as though we were being watched,' said Grace.

'And maybe there was something to that,' said Kitt. 'We can't know for sure and, though I hate to say it, we can't be sure we have a sense of who's listening either.'

'How do you mean?' said Joe.

'For all we know the people listening are the same organization the man in the camel coat works for. And from the way he conducted himself in the meeting today, I'd say he was British intelligence. But we can't discount the idea that it could be someone else, a person or agency who has yet to identify themselves in this mess. Remember that there could still be a killer out there, someone who shot Ralph Holmes, or that other unidentified man found in the Solway, or both in cold blood, assuming they didn't shoot each other.'

'So, you think the person, or people, watching us could be responsible for one or both of those deaths?' said Joe.

'It's one of several possibilities,' said Kitt. 'All I know now for sure is, after everything that's happened, we can't assume anything. And we certainly can't take any chances.'

CHAPTER TWENTY-FIVE

'Why am I not surprised you chose this cafe as a meeting place?' said Halloran as he approached their table, which was small, square and surrounded by a range of different sofas.

The sofas were just one of the many features that made this cafe particularly cosy. The smell of brewing coffee hung thick in the air and the servers behind the counter chatted merrily over the clatter of plates and clinking of teacups.

'I'm sure I don't know what you mean,' said Kitt.

Joe frowned, waiting for Halloran to clarify. He really didn't know what Halloran meant.

On noticing Joe's expression, Halloran added, 'It's called Bookcase, and it's attached to a bookshop. I had to walk through several rooms of books just to reach the cafe.'

Without waiting to gauge Joe's reaction to this information, Halloran leaned down towards Kitt and delivered the kind of kiss most people would probably reserve for behind closed doors. Halloran had done this every time he'd called on Kitt and, so far as Joe could tell, it was a sure sign that he didn't care who was watching when it came to showing affection to his partner. Joe had always been much more reserved in his relationships. He had never mastered public displays of affection. By the look on her face, neither had Grace. She was poking two fingers into her mouth in a pretence of being sick. She decided to cross her eyes at the same time for the maximum funny face effect.

Joe did what he could to keep from chuckling at her antics but it was no easy task. Especially when Halloran opened his eyes after the kiss and Grace was still pulling her odd, tortured expression.

Halloran cleared his throat and sat next to Kitt on a dark green settee. The sight of Grace openly mocking him, however, only temporarily interrupted his goading of Kitt.

'And here I was,' Halloran continued, 'under the impression that this meeting was urgent? If you've got time to browse the latest hardback releases, I'm not sure this counts as an emergency. Do you know how many miles I've done in that bloody car this week?'

'Yes, well,' Kitt said. 'Given the level of inconvenience, it's a good job you love me, isn't it?'

'It certainly is,' Halloran said, a warm smile surfacing behind his beard.

'I am sorry to drag you across the Pennines a second time, though, love,' said Kitt. 'You know I wouldn't have had you drive all the way back over here unless it was a serious matter. Mind you, since you bring it up, is there anything so wrong with hedging your bets that you might get a little bit of book shopping in?'

'Because that's just what we need at the cottage, more books,' said Halloran, his smile becoming just a touch cheekier. 'And should we be discussing whatever the matter is in public if it's that serious?' He looked over his shoulder to see if there was anyone sitting near enough to overhear them. As it was, there was only one other table in and they were sat at the other end of the narrow rectangular room.

It was clear from this comment, however, that Kitt had been super cautious about what she'd relayed in her text messages about their situation. Perhaps she suspected even they were being monitored.

'The hotel is no longer a safe place to talk,' said Kitt. 'And no, before you ask, I'm not even sure this is but we took all the precautions we could to make sure we weren't followed here and, frankly, we need your advice so we're going to have to talk about it sooner or later.'

'Hotel . . . not safe? Followed? What exactly has been going on while my back's been turned?' said Halloran. He had the same expression Joe might have had if he'd walked into such a conversation cold. When one said these things out loud, that they were being monitored, possibly followed, it sounded as ludicrous as Halloran's face might suggest. But Joe had been there and seen it for himself. That tiny little device Kitt pulled out of the lamp. This was really happening to them, and there was no denying it.

Following Halloran's question, Kitt went on to describe, in as quiet a voice as possible, the bug they'd found in their room. The precise details of all that had happened with the man in the camel coat and their concern that they'd roused the attentions of an agency or individual who might be a threat to them. When she had finished, Halloran was silent for what seemed like for ever, but couldn't have been more than a minute.

'From everything you've told me, it sounds like the work of a government agency.'

'Like MI6 or something,' said Grace.

'I don't know,' Halloran said. 'There are many different sections of intelligence in the UK. More than most people know about. We can't even be sure if it is a British agency or if it's a foreign agency involved in espionage in this country. But if I had to reason it through, I'd say the odds are the device was planted by a British agency.'

'What makes you say that?' said Kitt.

'Because of where you found the bug,' said Halloran. 'According to what I've read, and learned through working with the odd officer over the years, lamps are one of the favoured places to plant listening devices.'

'And a foreign agency couldn't be adopting the same strategy?' said Kitt.

'It's always possible,' said Halloran. 'But again, based on what I've been told, not very likely. Foreign agents tend to plant devices on a person by brushing past them, or bumping into them and such. It's easier than trying to track a person's place of residence, especially when a lot of foreign agents are operating with far fewer resources at their disposal because often they can't keep large stores of equipment in case they are caught and, besides, lots of high-tech equipment isn't very portable. These people tend to move around a lot.'

'So, the odds are this device was planted by the British,' said Kitt. 'I feel like I should be more relieved ... Look, I know you'll want us to leave well enough alone but I really think it's too late for that. We can't spend our lives looking over our shoulders, wondering if we're being listened to or tracked. We need to get to the bottom of what's happened here, and not just because Carly is paying us double to do so, but for our own peace of mind.'

Halloran nodded. 'I do live with you, you know. I don't relish the idea of being monitored by some unspecified agency by proxy because you stumbled across something you shouldn't have on one of the many investigations I think it would have been wiser to say no to.'

'When you're quite finished,' Kitt said, her nose crinkling at Halloran's little lecture.

'All right, I know, I know, it's your business now,' Halloran said, running a hand over his beard. 'But I have to advise you, even if you do try and get to the bottom of this, you might never know the full truth of the matter. It sounds to me like you're dealing with people trained in covert operations. No matter what you do, you're likely to be left with unanswered questions.'

'I know,' Kitt said. 'But we have to try. Someone is monitoring us and even if we never learn the whole truth, I need to do everything I can to find out who it is. I fear if I don't, I'll never feel quite safe again.'

'Seconded,' said Grace. 'Difficult to relax at home when you don't know if someone's listening to everything you're saying.'

'OK,' said Halloran. 'I think I have an idea. But we'll need to go back to the hotel to execute it.'

'Oh,' Kitt said, not nearly as excited as Joe would have expected her to be now that Halloran had come up with a way of finding out who was monitoring them. 'Do we have to go right now? This instant?'

Halloran shook his head. 'Only you would prioritize book shopping over the possibility of uncovering some grand scheme of international espionage.'

'I must admit, it's a bit of a toss-up about which I want to do more,' Kitt said, smiling.

*

Once they were back in Kitt's hotel room, just as Halloran had instructed her on the walk back to their accommodation,

Kitt unravelled the bug from the silk scarf it had remained wrapped in since that morning when they'd all had a very loud and cheerful conversation about how they needed some time away from the case and were going to go into town for a cuppa. They had hoped that this would be enough to throw whoever was listening off their scent and that even if they'd followed them to the cafe, they wouldn't bother following them inside.

Once the bug had been unravelled, Kitt looked at Halloran to check the plan was still in place. When he gave her the nod, she started speaking.

'We know you're listening,' she said. 'And we know what you want. We've uncovered the package and have hidden it at a secret location. We want you to leave us alone. So we're proposing a trade. We'll hand over the package if you never covertly monitor us or otherwise interfere with us again. If you agree to these terms, meet us at the travelling fairground at Silloth, next to the carousel, at five p.m.'

After these words, Kitt took pains to wrap the silk scarf back around the bug and place it in a drawer in the dressing table.

Joe looked at his watch. It was only two o'clock. It was going to be a long wait between now and five. And who knew if the agency in question would wait that long, or stick to the terms of the deal? If they had the power to plant fake police officers at a crime scene and intercept more than one call to the local police station, then they had the power to abduct a small group of amateur sleuths, even if there was a police officer among their number. With all this in mind, Joe was going to have to work hard to keep it together.

CHAPTER TWENTY-SIX

Several hours later, Joe, Kitt, Halloran and Grace stood next to the carousel near Silloth beach. The sun was lowering in the sky, creating orange and pink shockwaves across the clouds that had gathered around the rugged terrain of Scotland on the other side of the water. Like most fairgrounds, this one smelled of hotdogs, tobacco and damp banknotes that had been through too many hands. Ordinarily, the jaunty music of the carousel and the predictable rise and fall of the horses would have brought a smile to Joe's face. As would the laughter of those who had decided to take their kids for a treat at the fairground that night, before the unforgiving chill of winter set in. But under the context of this meeting, both the music and the laughter sounded eerie, almost tragic.

It was now five minutes past five. After all the silent anxiety Joe had pushed through that afternoon, he began to question if any representative from the agency that had been monitoring them would show up.

Kitt looked at her watch, and when she spoke, echoed Joe's thoughts. 'Maybe we didn't give them enough notice for the meeting. We sort of assumed they were listening to us live. That might not have been the case. They may have recorded us and reviewed the tapes at a later hour. If that's the case, they won't even know we're waiting here for them.'

'Maybe,' Halloran said with a nod. 'But if you'd given them too much notice, they might have prepared some kind of counter-operation.'

'I'm not really sure what that would entail,' Joe said. 'But I have to admit, it doesn't sound good.'

'It might be even simpler than that. Maybe they're not interested in the package,' said Grace. 'Or worse, maybe they already have the package and know we're bluffing. I can't think we've ingratiated ourselves with them if that's the case . . . and for the record, when I said I wanted to visit the fairground at Silloth, this wasn't really what I had in mind.'

'Nothing untoward is going to happen while I'm here,' said Halloran. He was so confident in his tone that Joe found himself believing him. Or perhaps it was simply because he really wanted to believe him. 'We'll give it one more minute,' said Halloran. 'But I admit this is starting to look like a no-show. I really wouldn't expect someone from a government agency to be anything other than on time for a meeting like this.'

A silence fell over the group and Joe watched the families, happily selecting their horse and climbing up on the stallions, waiting for the ride to begin. It was strange to watch people having such blissful fun when you found yourself suffering through what could only be described as turmoil.

This wasn't the first time this thought had occurred to Joe. He remembered the days and immediate months after Sarah's death. How the world had seemed so utterly grey to him. And yet he could see other people taking pleasure in dining out and taking leisurely strolls and having conversations about *Strictly Come Dancing*, as though such merry experiences were the only kind that existed. Joe had been like that once. Not a *Strictly* fan – he had trouble doing the 'Time Warp' and that came with instructions. But he had been someone for whom positive experiences could be enjoyed without any bittersweet edge. He had hoped the world of private investigation would take him away from those somewhat jaded feelings but as it turned out, he had only been confronted with them more fiercely.

'Nope, I'm calling it,' said Halloran. 'They're either not coming or they're planning something we don't want to hang around for.' Joe's heart sank as he heard those words. This was their big shot at finding out who had been listening to them, and it was a no-show. Now they may never know who had killed Ralph Holmes, why Garner and those other officers had been planted in the churchyard that day and why their conversations were being listened to by some unknown entity.

'Come on,' said Halloran, when not one of them made a move to leave. 'I know it's not the outcome we wanted. I wanted to know who was behind all this as much as you did. But there's no point dragging it out any longer. We'll regroup back at the hotel.'

Grudgingly, they made their way back to the car park. The sounds of the screams and the jolly music of the rides fading as they did so.

They had no sooner got back to Joe's car when Rolo, who had been left in the back seat with the window ajar, began barking and running up and down the back seat as though some kind of unearthly devil was chasing after him.

'What the bloody hell's got into him?' Halloran said. 'He's usually quite placid. Well, from what I've seen of him.'

'I have no idea,' said Joe. 'I've only had him a few days but I've never seen him react like this.'

'Kitt Hartley, isn't it?' said a cold, clipped voice from just behind them.

All four turned in unison to see who the voice belonged to. A tall man in a long, grey coat stood a few paces behind them. His hair was mousey in colour and combed neatly at the sides. His dark brown eyes surveyed each one of them in turn. All the lines on his face, his mouth, the wrinkles near his eyes and across his forehead were level, betraying no emotion whatsoever as he looked at them.

Kitt cleared her throat. 'I am Kitt Hartley. And who are you, may I ask?'

The man broke into a smile then. Not a welcoming smile. Nor a kind smile. The sort of smile that signals the person you're talking to knows much that you don't.

CHAPTER TWENTY-SEVEN

'Names are of little relevance,' the man said after a moment's silence.

'That's easy for you to say,' said Kitt. 'You know mine, and if what we've been through over the last few days is anything to go by, you probably know a lot more than that.'

'I'm not here to unnerve you, Ms Hartley.'

'Well, for someone who's not even trying you're doing a good job,' said Grace. 'Creeping up on us in the dark, refusing to give your name. What part of that isn't unnerving?'

Joe couldn't help but notice that Grace was talking at a higher octave than usual and he couldn't much blame her. This man, whoever he was, had gone against the agreement of meeting in the more public space of the fairground. The car park wasn't completely empty but there were only one or two others in there and they were some way off. The man must have had his reasons for wanting a more isolated meeting place. Joe could only hope that those reasons weren't nefarious.

'I believe DI Halloran will understand that when it comes to matters of national security, the less information that is shared with the public, the better,' said the man.

'So, you do work for a government agency, then?' said Halloran. 'A UK government agency?'

'That's correct. And if names are so important to you, you can call me Alfred Smith.'

'A. Smith?' Kitt said, her tone incredulous.

'It is not my fault my parents gave me such a common name,' said Smith, with a wave of a gloved hand. 'It's made any kind of family tree search impossible, I can tell you. Quite useful in my line of work, though.'

'Which agency are you working with? If you're above board, there should be no issue in telling us that much,' said Halloran, his tone still dubious. Joe was just as suspicious. Garner, Drummond and Stark had all presented their identification and all turned out to be deceivers.

'There are many subsections of our government network so the name Section Forty-Seven won't mean much to you,' said Smith. 'But I am working for crown and country. And the package you've acquired is of great value to us. Recovering it could see you on the honours list, it's that important.'

'Oh . . . er,' Kitt said. It was getting dark but Joe could still make out a blush rising in Kitt's cheeks. Seemingly she was willing to believe this man was who he said he was. Either that or she didn't want to face the consequences of wasting an agent's time if he was who he said he was. 'The thing is, we don't actually have the package.'

Smith blinked in quiet surprise and Joe held his breath, waiting to see how he might react to this news. As it was, Kitt didn't give him much of a chance to respond. Quite uncharacteristically for her, she started babbling.

'You see, we found the bug you planted and from what Halloran knew about British espionage we had a fair idea it was a UK agency listening in and we really just needed to know why we were being watched, so I'm afraid we only used the package as a way of drawing you out. And actually using the package as bait was all Halloran's idea.'

'Good to know you're always willing to throw me under the bus when it comes down to it,' said Halloran, shaking his head at Kitt.

There was a quiet moment in which Kitt digested all she'd just blurted out.

'Sorry, love,' she said, squeezing Halloran's arm. 'I panicked.'

'That is not good news,' Smith said, his shoulders slumping as he understood that the package, whatever it was, was not going to be presented any time soon.

'I'm ... I'm sorry,' said Kitt. 'We didn't know what else to do. We were really worried about the fact that you were keeping tabs on us. Perhaps we can make amends somehow.

I am a private investigator by trade, after all. If I knew what the package was, what it was you were looking for, maybe we could help you uncover it.'

Smith was quiet.

'We know that Holmes was in possession of the package and that, while investigating another party who was after it, he was shot and murdered in cold blood.'

'I don't mean this to sound rude,' said Smith, 'but it's clear from what we've heard over the device we planted that – with the exception of the lyrics to the "Thong Song" – you know nothing.'

'Holmes wasn't in possession of the package?' said Kitt.

'Oh no, that much is correct,' said Smith. 'But we've never heard so many wild theories floated as the ones you discussed last night in your hotel room. Gave the team quite a chuckle.'

'Well, I'm glad you're entertained,' said Kitt, the edge to her voice returning. It seemed, after her initial wariness around Smith, that she'd recovered herself. 'Two people are dead and you are sitting around the office making jokes at our expense.'

'Forgive me,' said Smith. 'I didn't mean to imply we found sport or humour in the death of our colleagues, it's just when you're working a case this serious, well, any light-heartedness is welcome.'

'I wholeheartedly agree,' said Grace. 'I've been trying to tell Kitt this for years.'

'Grace . . .' Kitt said. Her voice had a quiet warning to it.

'At any rate,' Smith continued, 'I was surprised to hear you'd recovered the package given what we'd heard. Now that you've come clean about fabricating that, well, that makes more sense. But it's the very fact that you know nothing about all this mess that prompted me to meet with you.'

'Why?' said Halloran.

'Because it means we can trust you, something we haven't been sure about since you handed in that briefcase,' said Smith.

'Why wouldn't you think you could trust us?' said Kitt. 'We cooperated with the police, we handed the briefcase over to the authorities and we're not the ones who dispatched fake police officers to more than one murder scene with the agenda of making the bodies disappear.'

'The bodies have not disappeared,' said Smith, 'they are simply being held in a secret location until we've run the necessary tests on them. And agents Garner, Drummond and Stark were merely doing what I tasked them to do at the crime scenes.'

'Why send them instead of police?' said Halloran. 'I've never heard of anything like this being done before.'

'It's not something we do often,' said Smith. 'But in this instance it was necessary to compartmentalize all information and interactions. In short, I'm afraid we needed to play you.'

'But why do that to us when we were only trying to find out what happened to Holmes?' said Kitt.

'We didn't know that was your agenda,' said Smith. 'When we found out that the police had had a briefcase handed in containing all the things our agents carry, we visited your hotel the morning after you spoke to Cobb and monitored your movements. After that, we felt we needed control over what information was given to you, and the person we believed to be your associate.'

'Our associate?' Kitt said, shaking her head, unable to fathom who Smith was talking about.

Smith paused again. There was clearly something vital he had yet to tell them and he seemed to be weighing up exactly what to say next.

'How did you find out about Holmes being missing in the first place?' Though Smith had asked a clear question, he did so in a tone that left Joe suspecting he already knew the answer.

'His niece came to us because she'd received a voicemail from him, saying that he was going away to start a new life and was cutting off all contact from her. She thought the voicemail sounded strange, unlike him, and was worried he'd been coerced into disappearing . . . or worse.'

'His niece,' Smith said. His voice had a peculiar tone to it. Joe couldn't quite make out what Smith was feeling from it.

'Yes,' Kitt replied.

'That's what Cobb told Garner you'd said when you

handed in the briefcase. So, I suppose that's really the story she fed you.'

'Story?' said Kitt.

Joe's stomach turned over and goosebumps ran up his arms as he started to suspect something, something that was the last thing he wanted to be true.

Smith took a deep breath and looked at each of them in turn. He pulled his phone from his pocket and swiped the screen a few times. When he turned it towards them, they all took a step closer to properly examine the photograph.

'Was this the woman who came to your agency?' Smith asked.

On Smith's phone there was a photograph of a woman. Not just any woman. She had piercing green eyes and thin, petite lips. It was a picture of Carly. And in the photograph, she had long brown hair.

Slowly, Kitt nodded to confirm that yes, that was the woman who had sought help in finding her uncle.

'I'm sorry to tell you Ralph Holmes doesn't have a niece,' said Smith.

CHAPTER TWENTY-EIGHT

Kitt's jaw dropped open at these words and Joe's jaw wasn't far behind hers.

'But . . . but . . . the voicemail, she played it to us,' said Kitt. 'We heard Ralph Holmes address her by name. We heard him explain that he couldn't be in contact with her any more because he was starting a new life.'

'Had you ever heard Holmes's voice before that moment?' said Smith. 'Or have you heard it from some other source since?'

Slowly, Kitt shook her head. 'No . . . we hadn't and haven't. You're right. We took it on faith that the voice we heard was that of Ralph Holmes. For goodness' sake, it could have been anyone. Why didn't I think about that?'

'But we did checks on Carly. Everything about her checked out,' said Grace. 'It's the same checks we do for all our clients. They give you a pretty good picture.'

Smith took a deep breath and nodded. 'Where the

voicemail is concerned, I see two likely possibilities. Either this woman, who we know by the codename Snow Queen, had an actor record it, knowing you'd never heard Holmes's voice and therefore couldn't verify either way whether or not the voice was his. Or secondly, she may have somehow come into possession of a digital recording of this voice and used AI technology to recreate the message she wanted you to hear. Just in case you stumbled across anything that contradicted the message she'd created.'

'Can AI really do that?' said Grace. 'The voice didn't sound like a robot.'

'The latest AI renderings of a human voice are extremely convincing,' said Smith. 'Like anything, of course, it can be used for good or evil. It could allow a widow to hear the voice of her lost husband many years after they're gone. But the people we deal with, they're not using it to make the world a better place. Most of the strange intonation which has historically been a dead giveaway has been eradicated. In my line of work it's got to the point that unless you're talking to a person face to face, it's very difficult to know if you're actually listening to their voice.'

'That's beyond scary,' said Grace.

'I know,' said Smith, 'it's one of many technologies that are making our job harder. But when it comes to the checks you carried out, though I'm sure they were as rigorous as possible, they would never have been enough.'

'Dare I ask why not?' said Halloran.

'The Snow Queen isn't just anyone. She's a sleeper agent who has been living in the UK for many years. She's been trained to very slowly infiltrate the UK intelligence network,' said Smith. 'She is the kind of agent who is playing the long game and essentially hiding out in society until she is tasked to an operation. Such individuals build extremely credible covers. It would be almost impossible to spot unless you knew what you were looking for.'

'Which would be what, exactly?' said Kitt.

'Certain companies are known for giving covers to foreign intelligence agents. It's not something that is easily proven, otherwise such enterprises would be shut down. But if you suspect someone is a foreign agent, finding out that they work for a particular company can be a giveaway, but you have to be in the intelligence network to know which companies those are. To a civilian, it would appear a perfectly credible cover.'

'And when you saw us with Carly at the breakfast table in the hotel, the morning after we'd contacted the police about the suitcase,' said Kitt, 'all of us, including Halloran, you weren't sure where our loyalties lay?'

'That's the issue exactly,' said Smith. 'We had picked up her trail a few days after Holmes had gone radio silent. At that point we didn't know if she had the package or where Holmes was, so rather than bring her in we decided to follow her in the hope of learning more. But she's very good at slipping surveillance, so we lost track of her, until she turned up at your hotel that morning.'

'So, what we're saying here,' said Joe, barely able to process the information, 'is that Carly Lewis isn't really Carly Lewis at all? That she isn't Holmes's niece? That she wasn't concerned at all for his safety? That every sob was faked? That she was just using us to try and find information on him?'

'I'm afraid so,' said Smith. 'We thought you might have been an ally of hers, either working to help her uncover the package that Holmes was killed for or carrying out some other related task. So we arranged to feed you false information. Information that we hoped would frustrate you and ultimately the Snow Queen into doing something rash. Such as going to an even bigger fish in the pond.'

'I can only reassure you of our allegiance to this country,' said Kitt. 'You can probably tell from the look on our faces, we had no idea who Carly really was and the fact that you were deliberately giving us false information certainly makes a lot more sense than any of the other theories we've come up with while we've been caught up in this mess. And of course, the case we worked was a complete farce. We were working to the wrong timeline because of the voicemail. Making assumptions about Holmes's disposition based on the fact he'd allegedly told Carly he was going to rehome his dog. Which was just a cover for the fact that she didn't know he travelled with his dog. Oh, what a terrible waste of time. But what I don't understand is why? Why would Carly go through us to get information on Holmes? If she is part of the intelligence network, she must have access to all kinds of resources.'

'Not necessarily,' said Smith. He took a deep breath and paused. 'You've already heard what must seem like quite a lot of startling information. But I'm afraid we've only scratched the surface of how deep this goes. What I'm about to tell you cannot leave this circle, agreed?'

Joe, Kitt, Grace and Halloran all agreed in turn.

'There is a logistical reason that the Snow Queen, or Carly as you knew her, will have used your organization and I'll get to that in a moment. But what you need to know first is that before he went missing, Holmes had just uncovered information on a North Korean spy network trying to infiltrate the British naval base not far from here.'

'What were they after?' said Halloran.

'We don't know what their end game was. Only that they wanted to infiltrate the base. The package consisted of files Holmes uncovered from an office building on the outskirts of Carlisle. He'd found out that the North Korean network were using the office space as a base. The last we heard from him, Holmes had been able to access the building and copy the files. The files in question were going to be of immeasurable help in maintaining national security. They were going to show us inside this enemy spy network. Their end goal. How far it reached.'

'And that was what Holmes was supposed to leave at St Michael's Church,' said Kitt. 'Presumably so another one of your agents could collect them.'

'That's right,' said Smith. 'We arranged a dead drop so he could quickly pass the files on. That was scheduled for Thursday evening at St Michael's Church. He was to leave the package in a litter bin that evening and it would be collected within the hour by another agent.'

'But he never made his dead drop,' said Kitt.

'No,' said Smith. 'We lost contact with Holmes on Wednesday lunchtime. Time of death has been narrowed down to that evening. When our agent went to collect the package, he did a quick search of the churchyard but saw no sign of Holmes. He didn't notice the disturbed gravesite as you did, Ms Hartley, but in the agent's defence he had no idea that Holmes was missing.'

'If Holmes was murdered on the Wednesday evening,' Kitt said, 'that's why we've never been able to understand what he had been doing on that elusive Thursday. He was already dead by that point.'

Joe digested Kitt's words and of course she was right. Between the false information from Section Forty-Seven and the false information from Carly, they never had a chance of solving this case. No wonder they had been going around in circles.

'So, that's why Holmes didn't go back to the boarding house for his dog and briefcase that night,' said Kitt. 'He was already dead. But why didn't you? Why didn't you go and retrieve the briefcase?'

'There are such tight protocols for our agents in order to protect both them and the public,' said Smith. 'We work in extremely sensitive areas and as such we discourage agents from communicating their precise quarters when they're on an operation. If any messages get picked up by an enemy, they may seek out the agent but they may also endanger members of the public staying in the same place. Agents are also given intensive training on how to ensure nobody follows them back to their living quarters. More of our agents have been murdered while sleeping quietly in their beds than you would believe. We have no choice but to be extremely cautious.'

'So you couldn't retrieve Holmes's briefcase or his dog because you didn't know where he was staying?' said Grace.

'No, not precisely,' said Smith. 'And to be straight with you, we didn't know for sure that Holmes was dead until you discovered the body. We were on full alert to intercept calls to the police in that area but for all we knew, Holmes was lying low somewhere or had been captured.'

'So you don't know exactly how or why Holmes died, either?' said Halloran.

'Not exactly,' said Smith. 'In one of his last communiqués, Holmes said the Snow Queen had been so bold as to corner him in a pub he'd been sitting in very close to where he was staying. She had threatened to end him unless he handed over the package. Told him he was being watched.'

'A man we saw in the pub at Port Carlisle last night, ex-navy actually, told us he'd seen Holmes having a heated conversation with a woman,' said Grace. 'I'm guessing that was the Snow Queen, or Carly as we know her, making her threat to Holmes.'

'She will have approached him there because she knew he wouldn't have wanted a fight to break out in public. She was armed, according to Holmes's message. He was too, but he wouldn't have pushed a conflict in public. She could have taken hostages or done anything she wanted, in fact. And she knew he'd be far more concerned about loss of life than she was.'

'So, she'd tracked him to the pub, but not to where he was staying?' said Kitt. 'But the two places are only a mile apart.'

'I know,' said Smith. 'Holmes conveyed shock in his communications about being approached by her so close to where he was staying. He knew after that he had to take extra care to misdirect anyone who might be following him. If she'd known where he was staying, she could just have crept into his bedroom at night, killed him and taken the package and, believe me, she would have. The fact that she didn't means despite her insistence that they were watching Holmes, they weren't able to watch him all the time.'

'So did she follow him to St Michael's and kill him?' said Grace.

'We suspected that ourselves at first,' said Smith. 'But

then why would she need you to root him out for her? The way she approached you also tells us she doesn't have the package. That's really what she's looking for after all. She only wanted to get to Holmes – or his corpse – so that she could ascertain if he had the package. Which means on the night Holmes was actually murdered, she must have had someone else following him.'

'The man who washed up in the Solway,' Kitt said, piecing it all together just as the rest of them were.

Smith nodded. 'We think so. The best theory that we have is that Holmes went to the dead drop without the package to see if it was safe to leave the package there. Essentially to ascertain whether the Snow Queen really was having him followed. If he had dropped something in the litter bin and somebody had been watching him, they could have just picked it out before the agent arrived.'

'And they must have picked up his trail and followed him to St Michael's because he was killed there?' said Grace.

'I imagine so,' said Smith. 'You see, despite there only being a few miles between the two sites, Holmes won't have driven straight there. He'll have taken some convoluted route that perhaps took three times as long. This gives an agent time to see if anyone is following but, of course, it also means that someone might pick up your trail because you are on the road longer. As for what played out at St Michael's, when Holmes refused to hand over the package, we believe the agent who washed up in the Solway, who we have no record of, shot Holmes and buried him in a shallow grave,' said Smith.

'Wouldn't the agent have had more chance of recovering the package with Holmes alive?' said Grace. 'Why kill him?'

'That we don't know,' said Smith. 'But something played out between the two of them and Holmes didn't come out of it alive.'

'Then how did he get shot – the second man, I mean? Could Holmes have shot him before he died?' said Joe.

'No, I don't think that's what happened. We believe Holmes's murderer walked into the water and shot himself,' said Smith.

'Why?' said Halloran.

'Because he'd failed the Snow Queen,' said Smith. 'The first time she popped up on our radar was a few years ago. We've had limited contact with her personally because she's always got an extraction plan. But one thing we've learned about her is that she's notoriously ruthless and we've had other agents working with her who have wound up inexplicably dead. We've come to the conclusion that those who don't succeed on operations would rather die than face her.'

'But again, if she's that ruthless, why would she need us? You said there was a logistical reason,' said Kitt, 'but I just can't think of one.'

'Because she knew we were closing in on her and her network,' said Smith. 'She has a small network of spies working for her and we've managed to identify quite a few of them and put case files together on them. She's more than aware that we know what she looks like. What she doesn't know is which of her spies we have identified, and which we haven't.'

'So, if she sent one of her spies into the area to find out what happened to Holmes and the package, she couldn't know whether they'd be recognized or not by your operatives ... and if they were recognized, it would lead your agency straight to her,' said Kitt.

'That's right,' said Smith. 'She's been trying to keep both herself and her own agents at a distance, using you as a buffer of sorts. You see, we have a photograph of her but she is likely to have several aliases and unless we find out what those are, it's almost impossible to hunt her down. She'd have to come out in public, and she knows that. So she's stayed away from places associated with Holmes and his work. What she didn't know is, we were already keeping an eye on you. The moment we saw her arrive at your hotel, we knew who she was.'

'So, if you wanted to track her down so badly, why didn't you arrest her when she came to Cumberland police station?' said Kitt.

'Oh, I wanted to, believe me,' said Smith. 'Holmes was not the first agent we've lost to her network. But someone higher up the pecking order felt we'd learn more about her operations if she was followed rather than apprehended.'

'So, when she came to the station masquerading as a forlorn niece, you instructed the police to tell her Holmes didn't exist, closed ranks,' said Halloran.

'And then you hoped she'd do something rash that would give away more than she'd like about her operations,' said Grace.

'That was the hope,' said Smith.

'So, you knew we were going to meet the man in the camel coat, who I assume is one of your agents, in Edinburgh?' said Kitt.

Smith nodded. 'We hadn't planted the bug at that point, so we didn't know where you were going. Which is why we couldn't warn that particular operative that you were going to meet him there. Because we had followed you there, we were able to intervene when Joe gave chase to our agent, though.'

'Intervene?' Joe said, and then it hit him. 'The jogger who knocked me down. That was one of yours?'

'Sorry,' said Smith. 'We do have to protect our operatives as best we can and we still didn't know which side you were playing for.'

'So, are you going to continue following Carly?' said Kitt.

'We would but, unfortunately, we have hit a bit of a snag.'

'What kind of a snag?' said Kitt, a wariness in her voice.

'We had three agents tailing the Snow Queen but unfortunately as of three p.m. this afternoon, she's nowhere to be found. Somehow, she's slipped through the net again and with all that's happened with Holmes and the files that he found on her operation, I'm quite concerned that if we don't catch up with her soon, we may well lose her for good.'

CHAPTER TWENTY-NINE

Smith spent the next fifteen minutes standing several paces away from the group, making a number of important and somewhat heated phone calls. Joe, and the others, were standing too far away to glean exactly what Smith was saying, but before creating some distance between them he'd explained that he needed to formulate some kind of plan for apprehending the woman Kitt, Joe and Grace had only ever known as Carly Lewis. After Kitt's generous offer to do something to make up for the fact they had lured Smith to Silloth on false pretences, it seemed inevitable that whatever plan was hatched would somehow involve them. Perhaps by the time they'd formulated their approach, Joe would have come to terms with all that Smith had told them. For the time being, however, being left reeling seemed an acceptable way to pass the time.

'Can this be real?' Joe asked, while Smith was finishing up his phone call. 'It doesn't feel like it, but it must be, mustn't it? I mean, Smith seems to be who he says he is. He knows things only someone in his position could know.'

'I'm afraid it's all too real,' said Kitt, giving Joe's arm a gentle rub. 'All that's happened to us since Monday, well, this is the first time any of it has made sense. It's not a lesson I would have preferred you learn on your first big case, but so often when we're doing this kind of work, we cannot trust the people we want to. Even those who seem to be asking for help.'

'It's the depth of the deception, though,' said Joe. 'I mean, we had this whole conversation about being alone in the world. I told her about my wife dying and she sat there and empathized with me. And all along it was just a – a scam. A scheme. I mean, who does things like this?'

'When people believe themselves to be working for the good of their country, they can justify a lot,' said Kitt. 'Though I must admit, very few have gone to the lengths Carly has to deceive us. I would call her the Snow Queen, but it's a bit too preposterous a name to say with a straight face. Who comes up with these things, I ask you?'

'I'm sure there was a big important meeting about it,' Halloran said, drily. 'They'll have thrown around some alternatives. Ice Maiden, for example.'

'Or Sleet Princess!' said Grace.

'Er, yes. Maybe,' Halloran said. 'And for reasons best known only to themselves, they'll have settled on Snow Queen.'

'And I thought meetings with Michelle about how to rejig the third-floor library displays were tedious,' said Kitt, with a wry smile.

Joe couldn't help but feel like the others were taking this whole situation more lightly than he was and he was at a loss as to how.

'You were sceptical, in the beginning. And I was all for trusting Carly, too blindly,' he said, trying to drum home how hard this was hitting him so that someone – anyone – might give him some steer on how to deal with it. 'I should have listened to you. If I had, maybe none of this would have happened. Or if it had, we would have been happily oblivious to it like everyone else. I'd still think that there was little more to PI work than administrative tasks and humouring Ruby when she insisted she could solve any cold case if you just gave her a candle and a circle of salt.'

Kitt shook her head and even managed a chuckle over Joe's words about Ruby. 'Joe, you're not the only one who has been taken in here. Without any obvious red flags, we would have taken this case even without your optimistic input. None of the checks we did raised any concerns. We did our due diligence. We didn't know at the time that we were dealing with a government-level cover. To us, everything seemed normal. And she's been nothing but the picture of innocence the whole time we've been working with her. Her true motives and identity are just as much a shock to me as they are to you, I assure you. It's just, well,

I've rather got used to this kind of situation rearing its head. For you, it's much more alien an experience.'

'Anyone can be duped by someone with the right amount of charisma, at any point in their career,' Halloran chimed in. 'I've got a fairly good radar for when people aren't telling me the truth. If I didn't, I'd probably have been put on desk duty a long time ago. But even I've been fooled a time or two. You have to remember that when that happens, when someone lies to you or betrays you, it's not a reflection of you. It does, however, say everything about them.'

'Thanks,' Joe said, with a grateful nod. Though he didn't really feel any better about the whole situation, he didn't want Kitt and Halloran to think their attempts to perk him up had gone unnoticed.

'Right,' Smith said, returning to the fold. 'I've cleared a Plan A and a Plan B with HQ. Both require your cooperation, but you can decide how deeply you want to be involved. I'll struggle to bring Carly – as you know her – in without your help but I don't want to force you into a situation where you might be put in danger. And Plan B definitely involves a bit of that.'

'Let's discuss Plan A first then, shall we?' said Grace. 'I've been in danger once or twice over the years and it's not a place I'm keen to revisit unless absolutely necessary.'

Smith almost cracked a smile at Grace's comment, but not quite.

'Plan A merely involves you calling Carly and feeding

her the same bait you offered us. You tell her that you've found the reason her uncle was killed – a USB containing what look like encrypted files. You then arrange to meet her somewhere isolated, with plenty of space so we can essentially close a net around her and capture her. As you know, we had hoped to follow her but we don't know how she slipped our team this time. We can't risk losing her twice, so HQ have agreed with me that rather than take a chance and lose her for good, now's the time to bring her in.'

'Where do you suggest we meet her?' said Kitt.

'We were thinking Anthorn might do the job. There's a naval facility nearby, no less than the one the Snow Queen was trying to infiltrate, and we'll be able to commandeer the use of some of their resources to apprehend her. There's a public footpath through some fields not far from the base that will likely make a good spot in which to arrange the meeting. But to be clear, in Plan A you wouldn't be expected to show up for the meeting.'

'So instead of meeting us there, you'd just be waiting for her and would ambush her?' said Halloran.

'That's the plan,' said Smith. 'But it has some strategic weaknesses. Without a distraction there, she'll be on full alert and will thus be more able to coordinate an extraction from any other agents who are backing her up. Given that she's slipped our surveillance team this afternoon, she's aware someone is following her and is likely to be on edge, which does make bringing her in more difficult.'

'By your wording,' said Kitt. 'I'm assuming Plan B is that we actually attend the meeting with Carly and provide the necessary distraction so that you can easily apprehend her.'

'If we do it that way, we can easily take out any back-up she may have without her noticing. Then we'll be able to apprehend her before she's able to signal for an extraction. It's your basic misdirection. We've completed many ops like this in the past and it's a proven method of ensuring the capture of an enemy agent.'

Kitt sighed and looked around the group.

'Before you decide either way,' said Smith, 'you need to know that we'll do everything we can to protect you if you choose Plan B. But it comes with an element of risk. Individuals in the espionage business are trained to fight for their lives, even when the odds are stacked heavily against them. They will do anything to avoid capture. To avoid truth serum and the possible relaying of national secrets. I can't say exactly what this woman will do when backed into a corner, but if agents are killing themselves to avoid her wrath, I'd say that speaks for itself.'

A grave expression fell over each and every face in the circle, and Joe felt his own expression follow suit. Naturally, he wanted nothing more than the opportunity to confront Carly for her betrayal but, reading between the lines, Smith was suggesting that such gratification may actually lead to extreme injury or death. Was it worth that? He thought back to the scars on Evie's face. How she'd described being kidnapped. Kitt too had, by the sound of things, narrowly escaped being incinerated. Though they both had their scars from these ordeals, physical and emotional, they had come out of those situations alive. But was there really any guarantee Joe would be so lucky? He'd heard first-hand some of the dark places these kinds of situations could lead. That said, how could he shy away from helping Kitt when she needed him most?

'I don't expect the rest of you to come along for the ride,' said Kitt, almost as if she had some idea what he might be thinking. 'Really, they only need me to execute Plan B. I'm the head of the agency. I don't think Carly would think twice about it if I showed up alone. Given the magnitude of the threat we're talking about here, that this is a matter of national security, I don't feel I can shy away from the call. If they tried Plan A and it failed, I'd always wonder what we could have prevented if things escalated in the future. It will be easy to spin some story about why the rest of you aren't there. I can tell Carly that I'm coming alone because I don't know if exposing you all to knowledge of the files might be dangerous to you. None of the rest of you need to follow on. It's an unnecessary risk.'

'That was quite a convincing speech,' said Halloran, 'but if you think I'm going to stand by while you go face to face with a North Korean spy, you've got another thing coming. You're not having all the fun.'

Grudgingly, Kitt smiled at him.

'It won't feel so terrifying if we go as a trio,' said Grace, 'and Halloran is pretty competent in situations of high jeopardy.'

'Thanks,' Halloran said, flatly. From stories Joe had heard over the time he'd been working with Kitt and Grace, he knew Halloran had saved both their lives on more than one occasion. Joe thought it was rather good of him not to point that out in the face of Grace's reserved comment.

'I'm coming too,' said Joe. 'I know what you're going to say, I only signed up for work experience. I'm not obligated, et cetera. But if anything happened to any of you, and I could have been there to help, I'd never forgive myself. I've stood by and watched one person I care about in this world die, I'm not about to do the same a second time. Not when there is something I can actually do about it.'

Nodding, Kitt turned back to Smith. 'Looks like we're all go for Plan B. What time should I set the meeting with Carly for?'

'Nine p.m. should give us enough time to assemble and dispatch a small team,' Smith said.

Without another word, Kitt dialled Carly's number on her phone.

'Carly?' Kitt said when she answered. 'How are you feeling? We've all been quite concerned about you after your uncle's body went missing.'

There was a pause while Carly fed Kitt some line or other. Joe felt his teeth clench even though he couldn't hear the exact words Carly was saying from this distance. Why would he need to? Whatever she told Kitt, however she answered that particular question, it was all a fallacy.

'Of course,' Kitt continued. 'It's totally natural to feel that way after everything you've been through. I . . . Look, I'm not sure if this is going to make matters better or worse but we've found something. Something that's obviously important and may even be the reason your uncle was murdered in the first place.'

There was another pause while Carly asked what it was Kitt had found.

'We went back to the boarding house your uncle had been staying at. Something was nagging at me about the room, I don't know what it was. Anyway, Yeats charged me another fifty pounds to view the room again but this time I checked all the floorboards and one of them was loose. Underneath . . . well, I'm not entirely sure what's on it but we found a USB stick. When we tried to open the files on Grace's laptop, they were encrypted.'

Another pause while Carly responded.

'Yes,' Kitt said. 'I don't know about you but I wouldn't go to the effort of encrypting files unless they contained something very important indeed. I can't say for sure, but the way it was hidden, and given where we found the USB drive, whatever's on it probably has something to do with your uncle's death.'

Again, Kitt paused while Carly responded.

'Oh, you do. Well, that is very fortunate indeed. I can certainly pass the USB stick on to you – after all, it was in the possession of your late uncle and you're his only next of kin. But I must insist we're careful about where we meet. It can't be anywhere too public. I am still worried that someone may be after this drive and I'd never forgive myself if something happened to you. If it's OK, I'll text you the location to meet and if you can make it, I'll see you there at nine p.m.'

There was one last pause while Carly confirmed she'd be at the meet and then Kitt dispensed some closing pleasant-ries and hung up.

'Wouldn't you know it,' said Kitt. 'Carly has a good friend who is a computer whizz and she's just sure he can decrypt the files we've found.'

'A friend, or a member of her network,' Joe said.

'There may be no friend at all,' said Halloran. 'She may be equipped with those kinds of skills. Or maybe she doesn't need to be. Maybe she already knows what the files say and just wants to make sure they never get into the hands of a British agency.'

'I'd say your last guess was the most likely,' said Smith. 'I'll need that phone number you just dialled, Kitt. We'll want to put a tap and a tracker on it in case anything goes awry, and she manages to escape.'

'Of course, here you go.' Kitt handed her phone to Smith so he could extract the number.

'Is there anything we can do to protect ourselves?' Halloran said.

'Have you trained in firearms as part of your work with the police?' said Smith.

'I've basic working knowledge but . . . No, not officially,' said Halloran. 'And up until this moment I'd had no regrets about that.'

Smith nodded. 'We can provide you with a taser.'

'I'm familiar with using those,' Halloran said. 'It's better than nothing given what you've said about how these people are trained.'

'Try not to worry too much,' Smith said. 'With a bit of luck we'll apprehend her before she even knows what's happening.'

Halloran offered a very thin smile that was barely visible behind his beard. Joe could tell from Halloran's expression that much as he might want to, he didn't fully trust Smith's words. And try as he might, Joe couldn't quite bring himself to either.

CHAPTER THIRTY

Joe was glad of the extra layers he'd put on by the time they got to the field Smith had picked out on the outskirts of the village of Anthorn. It had turned into a chilly evening with quite a strong breeze. Joe wondered, however, even if he had attended the meeting with Carly in a T-shirt if he would have felt the cold, so fast was the adrenalin pumping through him. Without any street lights the dark seemed to close in all around them. The only immediate light to see by was the beams from the torches they'd brought. Kitt had brought one of her own, of course – ever prepared. The rest had to be bought from a supermarket they'd passed on the drive here from Silloth.

None of them had said much of anything on the journey here. Even Grace was unusually subdued. They were all no doubt mulling over similar thoughts.

What would they do if Carly went on the attack? If the agent who had shot Holmes had killed himself just so he didn't have to face her, what did that say about her level of mercy? And then there was the revelation that she'd had the audacity to meet Holmes in the pub and threaten him to his face. Smith had said she was armed. That meant she would likely be armed tonight too. Which very much put her at an advantage. Besides the taser Halloran was carrying, they had no such force on their side.

Between arriving at the location and walking to the meeting point, a thousand terrible scenarios had whirled through Joe's mind. All of them depicting in graphic detail how this situation could quickly turn south. Perhaps his biggest fear was that Smith's team didn't take Carly out quick enough if she did turn on them. Smith himself was overseeing the operation from the nearby base. He'd dispatched a small team of field agents. Plenty to apprehend someone even as ruthless as the Snow Queen was meant to be. But what if the team failed in some way? They were having to place an incredible amount of trust in Smith and the people he worked with to ensure their safety.

Unfortunately, one terrible thought only led on to another, and he cursed himself for not being able to pull himself together better than this. To prevent his mind from pondering the fact that he may be joining his beloved Sarah sooner than he ever expected. He had heard of such things happening. That a person lost their spouse and then not too long after died themselves. Not by illness and not on purpose, just somehow, they got into a situation they couldn't get out of. Were individuals like him drawn to more risky situations after experiencing the young death of their life partner? This was not a line of thought Joe wanted to explore right now – if ever. Kitt, Halloran and Grace were counting on him to offer some kind of support. It was time to step up, whether he was ready or not.

Thankfully, he did have a furry mascot to gee him on as he'd decided to bring Rolo along to the meeting. Joe had hesitated initially, concerned that the dog might be put in jeopardy. But then, he reasoned, they needed all the allies they could muster in that field and a dog's self-preservation instinct was usually pretty strong. He trusted Rolo would have the sense to run for it if things went south.

'This is the spot,' said Kitt. 'We're a minute or two early so no need to worry about the fact she's not here yet. I'm sure she can't be far away.'

They'd all agreed not to say anything that might give away their agenda for the meeting once they left the car, which was why Kitt's comments were so superficial and casual. Smith said they couldn't rule out Carly listening to their pre-meeting conversation via a parabolic mic so they had to keep things seemingly light and breezy.

'Those files were likely the reason her uncle was killed. I'm sure she'll be with us before we know it,' said Halloran.

'You're absolutely right,' Carly's voice said from behind them. Joe blinked in surprise at the sight of her. He couldn't quite work out how she had snuck up on them like that.

They were in an open field. Yes, there were crops, but they were only knee-high. Had she been lying low somewhere, watching their approach? Joe tried not to think about that idea. It was too creepy to dwell on.

'I wouldn't miss a meeting as important as this,' Carly added. Joe couldn't quite say what but something had changed in Carly's voice. There was a harsh, almost snide tone to it. Was her mask slipping now that she was close to what she wanted? Rolo definitely didn't appreciate the strange note in her voice at any rate and began growling at her.

'Rolo, stop it right now,' Joe said, deeply regretting having to admonish the dog in order to maintain his cover. After the terrible deception Carly had carried off, as far as Joe was concerned, Rolo could snap at her all he wanted. 'I'm sorry,' Joe said, 'I don't know what's got into him tonight. He's been uncharacteristically growly.'

'I'll try not to take it personally,' Carly said with a smile designed to be warm and friendly.

'Well, I'm so glad you made it,' said Kitt, doing her best not to look surprised at Carly's appearance. 'You weren't followed or anything, were you? I've been so worried that we might have been. My eyes were almost constantly on the rear-view all the way here.'

Joe had to hand it to Kitt. This clearly wasn't her first time putting on a show for someone she was about to apprehend but she was very convincing at any rate. Had Joe not known what was really going on under the surface, he'd have completely believed the note of concern in her voice.

'No, I don't think I was followed,' said Carly. Now that Joe knew the truth about her, every single movement seemed painfully contrived. The look of mild panic that someone might have thought to follow her didn't even remotely convince him now. How had he not seen through her sooner? 'I didn't think to check something like that,' she went on. 'I'm not like you, a seasoned sleuth and all.'

'I should have mentioned it, I'm sorry,' said Kitt. 'In the excitement of finding the USB it fell out of my head to advise you on that.'

'Well, we're all here now,' said Carly. 'That's what matters. I hadn't realized the whole team would be coming along, though. Quite the gathering.'

Was that an uneasy note in her voice? Was she already suspicious that this meeting might not be above board? They couldn't afford to have her suspect a thing before Smith's agents closed in on her.

'We didn't want to come,' Joe said. 'It's bloody freezing tonight. But Kitt was worried that if she came alone and someone tried to take the USB for themselves, she wouldn't be able to fight them off and the USB would be lost for ever.'

'So, here we all are,' Grace said in a convincingly grudging tone.

'This lot are always griping at me,' said Kitt. 'Can you blame me for being cautious? After what happened to your uncle's body, the way it just disappeared like that, I wasn't going to take any chances. I still haven't forgiven myself for not seeing through those officers in the churchyard. I wanted to be sure that this time I made amends for that mistake.'

'You've no need to feel guilty, Kitt,' said Carly. 'It sounds to me like you've blown this whole case wide open. Do you have the USB with you?'

'I certainly do,' said Kitt, opening her satchel.

Joe watched Carly keenly for any sign that she might be on edge. Kitt could pull anything out of her satchel, after all. Including a weapon of some kind. Spies must get training in being ready to expect anything.

But, so far as Joe could tell, Carly was unfazed by Kitt rooting around in her bag.

'Here you go,' Kitt said, making the gesture of handing over the USB as pronounced as she could. There was nothing much on the USB, of course. Some dummy encrypted files Smith and his team had uploaded in case Carly had brought some means of checking what was on the thumb drive.

Joe waited for the shouting to begin. For several armed officers to fall hard upon Carly, subdue her, restrain her and take her in. Then this whole nightmare would be over. Smith and his team would question Carly and get to the truth about what was on the real USB stick. Britain would be saved.

Except, there was no shouting. No gunfire. No sound or sight of anyone or anything.

All four of them stood still, stunned, waiting.

It was then that the most hideous smile Joe had ever seen on a human face, even worse than the one he'd seen on Julius Yeats, spread across Carly's lips.

'I suppose you're waiting for a team of agents to swoop in on me,' she said. There was a hard note to her accent now. All softness had evaporated. She no longer stooped either. She stood tall and straight. She looked solid, assured. Certainly, there was no denying her physical strength. She wasn't broad, but she looked sturdy enough to Joe and he was sure she'd be trained in hand-fighting.

'Wh– what do you mean, agents?' Kitt said, playing innocent.

Something had clearly gone wrong. Very wrong. It didn't look as though anyone was coming to help them. All they could do was exactly what Kitt was doing: play for time. And hope Carly – or whatever her real name was – wasn't in the mood to tie up loose ends.

'I took out the three agents who were lying in wait here before you even arrived. One by one,' said Carly.

'Carly, there must be some mistake,' said Kitt. 'We don't know anything about any agents. We just brought the USB to you, like we promised. If there was someone else here, it must be because they've been surveilling us and knew we were coming to meet you with the files. But . . . wait, when you say you "took them out", you mean . . .'

'I snapped their necks. It's easy when you know how,'

Carly said, pulling a handgun out of the back pocket of her trousers and training it squarely on Kitt. 'And since you've all seen my face, I suppose I'm going to have to get rid of you too.'

'I've got a terrible memory for faces, me,' said Grace, her voice wavering in her attempts to get Carly on side. 'Ask anyone, I can barely remember what Kitt looks like most of the time.'

'Unfortunately, your face is burned onto my memory,' Kitt said to Grace. 'Along with your daft antics.'

Carly held the gun steady but her smile broadened. 'It's a bit of a shame to have to shoot you, I really did quite like you. And if your story about knowing nothing about those other agents is true, well, that is too bad. But a woman in my line of work can't be too careful.'

Joe couldn't think what else to do but yell out a booming, 'Noooooo,' as Carly's fingers started squeezing the trigger.

CHAPTER THIRTY-ONE

'Everybody down,' Halloran shouted as he lunged towards Carly with the taser. He fired it at her before she knew what was happening and she screamed out and threw herself to the side as the pins shot out of the device. Quite unbelievably, they missed Carly, and Halloran had to course correct in a matter of seconds, making a grab for the gun she had.

At first, it seemed like he had control of the situation as he leapt on top of Carly and pinned her wrists to the ground, but his advantage was only passing. Somehow, Joe must have loosened his grip on Rolo's lead because the hound broke free and got mixed up in the fray, biting at Carly's trouser leg and causing one hell of a distraction.

'Rolo!' Joe called out. Not because he was averse to the dog tearing Carly's clothes to shreds but because he was concerned that Rolo would end up injured. Unfortunately, it seemed Rolo was more of a distraction to Halloran than he was to Carly as within a few moments she had gained the advantage. Using her free hand, Carly chopped her hand at Halloran's neck, leaving him gasping for breath. Though he still held tight to the gun, she was able to use his moment of weakness to point it towards his shoulder and before anyone in the group could stop her, a shot rang out.

Halloran bellowed in pain.

'Mal!' Kitt screamed at the top of her voice. It was impossible to see quite how much damage was done but it was clear Carly wasn't going to hang around for a fight.

'Blackbird, I'm going to need extraction in thirty seconds,' she said into a device on her wrist. Giving Halloran one last kick to his ribs as she got up, Carly at once began to run away from the group. Rolo tore after her, barking as he ran. Carly was somehow just staying ahead of him enough to escape his snapping jaws. Joe watched after her while Kitt and Grace ran straight to Halloran's side.

'Mal, my God, there's blood everywhere,' said Kitt, pulling a roll of bandages out of her satchel and immediately putting pressure on Halloran's wound.

'It's just my shoulder,' Halloran said through gritted teeth. 'So long as I don't lose too much blood, I won't die from that.'

On hearing these words, which were a small shred of comfort in a disastrous situation, Joe found himself torn. Should he stay with the group or run after Carly and Rolo?

Then, that question became utterly irrelevant.

'Oh my God,' Joe said, as he looked towards the far end

of the field and struggled to digest what he was seeing. A small aircraft hovered fifty metres or so above the ground and from it a rope dangled. Carly was running towards the rope. She clearly intended to catch hold of it and be pulled into the aircraft before flying away.

'What is it now?' Halloran winced, as he forced himself to sit up.

'She's going to get away,' Joe said, hardly believing that he was saying those words. How had all the agency's careful plans been so easily spoiled? 'She's . . . there's a plane and a rope and . . . she's going to fly her way out of here.'

'No, she's bloody not,' Halloran said. 'Anyone who shoots me doesn't get away that easily.'

'Mal, will you give over,' Kitt said as Halloran made a move to stand. 'You need to stay still until medical help arrives.

'Mal, I've told you, you need to stay still,' Kitt said once again as Halloran made another move to get up.

'I will stay still,' said Halloran. 'Once I've got a clear shot at that plane.'

'You won't be able to take down a plane with a handgun,' Kitt said. 'The logistics just won't work.'

'I'm not going to aim at the plane,' said Halloran. 'I'm going to aim at Carly.'

'But you don't have firearms training,' said Kitt. 'What on earth makes you think you're going to do anything other than aggravate the situation?'

'A little faith wouldn't go amiss, under the circumstances,' said Halloran.

Kitt took a deep breath. 'All right, I'm with you.' Kitt and Joe gently helped Halloran up. Kitt positioned herself under Halloran's right arm to steady him just below where he'd been shot.

Joe watched with some astonishment as Carly grabbed hold of the rope that trailed from the plane. Within a few moments, the plane began to elevate but it was slow and the plane was actually starting to circle a little closer, apparently heading off in the direction of the ocean.

'I think she's just in range, but not for long,' Halloran said, not wasting the opportunity of the plane drawing momentarily nearer. Joe watched as Carly hung from the rope, dragging behind the low-flying plane. She was maybe forty feet above them.

Without another word, Halloran aimed the gun up towards the plane and shot three times. The bullets must have missed Carly because she remained in position, clinging to the rope as the plane flew on.

Joe had no idea how many bullets were left in the gun. Were there twelve in total? Leaving him with nine shots left? No, even if there had been twelve originally that wasn't right. Because Carly had fired at Halloran before. And maybe she'd even fired some shots they didn't know about.

Regardless, Halloran shot again. One bullet after another. Given the tense nature of the situation perhaps it wasn't surprising that Joe lost count of how many bullets Halloran had fired but he didn't stop until, at last, Carly fell from the rope. She dropped down into the branches of a tree that stood about twenty feet away.

Whoever was flying the plane, it seemed they had no intention of coming back for Carly. The aircraft charged through the gathering cloud and a few moments after it vanished, silence descended on the field.

Kitt, Grace and Joe looked at each other and began to walk over to where Carly had fallen. Kitt helped Halloran to stay on his feet despite the bullet wound in his shoulder. When they reached the tree, they saw Carly's body hanging from a branch. She was bleeding but there was no telling from where.

'Is she . . . dead?' said Grace.

'I don't know,' Halloran said, gravely. 'We won't know until someone can check her pulse and I don't know about you but I'm not really in a condition to go tree-climbing right now.' He winced as he reached into the inside pocket of his jacket for his mobile. He dialled the number Smith had given them in case of emergency and identified himself. 'We're going to need an ambulance to our location as soon as possible,' said Halloran. 'The Snow Queen has been shot, and so have I. She is currently stuck in a tree so we are going to need hydraulic ladders too . . . How did she get stuck in a tree? It's . . . a long story.'

Joe swallowed hard as he looked at the woman hanging

from a tree branch, a gunshot wound weeping on the right side of her stomach. They may not have found all the answers but at least they could be sure that Carly Lewis, or the Snow Queen, whatever her real name was, could do no more harm to anyone else.

With that thought, Joe called out for his dog.

CHAPTER THIRTY-TWO

Smith was the first person on the scene. As soon as he'd realized contact had been lost with the agents, he'd instructed another team to move in but it had taken them too long to reach the group to stop the dreadful situation playing out between them and Carly.

By some miracle, Carly had survived the gunshot wound and the fall from the plane, but wasn't conscious when she was wheeled away into the back of an ambulance.

'We'll be keeping her under very tight surveillance,' said Smith once he could be sure Carly was out of earshot. Clearly, he wondered if even while unconscious she might overhear something she shouldn't. 'Hopefully she'll pull through and once she's deemed fit and healthy, she'll be fully interrogated over her part in what's played out here. She has killed three agents; four if you include her orders to follow and execute Holmes. And that's just what we know about. With someone like that, there's likely to be more we've yet to learn of.'

'I'm sorry,' said Kitt, 'that we didn't know who she really was, that we didn't work out that she was the enemy sooner. We could have saved lives if we had.'

Smith shook his head. 'You could not reasonably be expected to have known that she was a spy. Most people deem these kinds of things too outlandish. The stuff of James Bond films, you know.'

'Or John le Carré novels,' said Kitt. Joe saw Halloran roll his eyes at Kitt's reference to books.

'Quite,' said Smith. 'You will need to be fully debriefed, all four of you, which might not be the most pleasant experience. There'll be a lot of personal questions, I'm afraid. The powers that be need to be sure you weren't willingly helping a foreign agency. But you'll have my report to back you up and so long as all your stories support and corroborate each other, all should be well.'

'They're not going to put the thumb screws to me, are they, Governor?' said Grace, in a tone that, even for her, was surprisingly mock-dramatic. 'I'm too young and tender for such torture.'

'Grace, why are you talking like a street criminal in a nineteenth-century novel?' said Kitt, shaking her head.

Grace shrugged. 'Just felt like it.'

'Yes, well, I can see the shock of all this business has worn off and you're back to your usual self,' said Kitt. 'I'm sorry, Agent Smith. Though I did train Grace in investigative work, I'd like you to know that the silliness comes all from her.'

'For the record, there'll be no thumb screws,' said Smith. Again, he almost looked like he might crack a smile but, as seemed to be his custom, decided against.

'Will stopping Carly help you stop the spy network she's a part of?' said Kitt.

'Any blow we can dish out to these agencies is a win in my book. How hard the capture of Carly will hit them will depend on how much information she's willing to give up. Believe it or not, that plane flew out of the naval base. I was there and saw the damn thing take off. Which means at least part of their operation must have succeeded. That they've already got agents on the inside there. As you might imagine an investigation of epic proportions is about to be launched to root out anyone else in their midst. But one less foreign agent on British soil is no bad thing and without you, we wouldn't even have that.'

'I'm glad to have helped, though from what you say there is much work left to do,' said Kitt. 'I just wish I could have uncovered the USB stick with those files on them.'

'If a spy trained to locate such things couldn't dig it up for themselves, I don't think you should be too hard on yourself about that. Sooner or later, in this business, such things have a habit of turning up. Holmes must have hidden the package somewhere after all. I'm sure it's just a matter of time until we uncover where that is.'

At this point, Halloran returned from the ambulance he was being treated in. 'They've patched me up. It's a clear wound, the bullet went straight through, but they're insisting I go to the hospital.'

'Of course they are,' said Kitt. 'You've been shot. If I get the all-clear to go, I'll go with you.'

'I'd say you'd earned some recuperation time before your debrief,' said Smith. 'Just don't leave the country.'

'Doubt he could get travel insurance with that wound,' said Kitt with a wry smile.

'Halloran,' Grace said, sidling up to him.

'Yes . . .' Halloran said, an obvious note of suspicion in his voice, and who could blame him, knowing how silly and strange Grace could be at times?

'On balance, I've decided to upgrade my assessment of you from pretty competent in high-jeopardy situations to impressively competent in high-jeopardy situations.'

Halloran looked at Kitt for some clue as to how to respond to this. When she offered him none, he simply replied, flatly, 'Glad to have gone up in your estimation.'

'Come on,' said Kitt. 'Let's get you to the hospital and then hopefully we can make tracks home once we've been debriefed.'

Joe turned and looked down at Rolo then, who had been happily sitting by Joe's side, wagging his tail and panting since Joe had retrieved him from the car. 'You're certain Holmes had no next of kin who might want the dog back?' he said, still in slight disbelief that he might get to keep the dog.

'Holmes, like many field agents, didn't have any family,' Smith said. 'It's not a condition of recruitment, you understand. But the agency tends to attract people with few familial links, if any. Holmes was an orphan, no wife or family. Just Rolo here. But I'm sure you'll do a good job of looking after him.'

'I certainly will,' Joe promised. 'I suppose since I haven't got a bullet in my shoulder, I should expect my debriefing sooner rather than later.'

Smith nodded. 'We've got the use of some offices nearby. We'll need to get the interview on record, you understand. I can drive you and Grace now, if you're ready?'

For once, Grace didn't have a mocking comment to make. She merely nodded her agreement and followed Smith, Joe and Rolo over to the car.

Before getting into the vehicle, Joe took one last look around the field. In the distance, he could see a series of posts lit up with red lights. That must be the naval base at Anthorn. The one Carly and her network had been trying to infiltrate. Other than that blip of civilization, the scene was a quiet one. Nothing but the flit of bat wings and the low rumble of conversation from the clean-up crew could be heard. How strange, Joe thought, that such catastrophe could fall upon such a small, quiet place. It left him wondering, if even the people here weren't safe from international threats, was it possible to be safe from them anywhere?

CHAPTER THIRTY-THREE

'How's Halloran's wound healing?' Joe asked as he, Kitt and Evie walked Rolo along the banks of the River Ouse, towards the Millennium Bridge in York. It had been ten days since they had returned from the borderlands and they had all rather welcomed getting back to quiet normalcy after the events surrounding Ralph Holmes's murder. It was a crisp autumn day and, as such, it had seemed a shame to spend their lunch break indoors. Grace, however, had decided she would prefer to stay at the agency and hold the fort while Evie joined Kitt and Joe for a walk with the dog.

'He's not a quick healer,' said Kitt. 'But he's not doing badly all things considered and the doctors do expect him to make a full recovery.'

'Why is it that Halloran always seems to get wounded?' said Evie. 'Isn't he supposed to be the most responsible one out of all of us? He can't seem to turn around without getting injured.'

'He is one for self-sacrifice, perhaps a little too much so,' said Kitt, though there was no missing the admiration gleaming in her eyes. 'But you're right, I really do feel it's my turn for some life-altering injury and I will tell him as such so he knows what the score is next time we're in mortal danger.'

Despite the darkness of Kitt's joke Evie giggled and Joe found himself chuckling along with the pair.

A moment later, however, his smile faded.

'Everything all right, Joe?' Kitt said. She had done her best to be subtle about it, but it hadn't escaped Joe's notice that Kitt had kept an extra close eye on him since they had returned from their trip. Few people understood what the life of a young widower was like. But Kitt made a special effort to try and understand and support Joe, knowing that once upon a time he would have had somebody to tell about his adventures near Carlisle. And, moreover, that now the only audience he had for such tales was Rolo. He wagered that she also felt some responsibility in inadvertently leading him into a difficult set of circumstances after he had spent six months trying to come to terms with an already problematic lot. He didn't blame her one bit for that, of course, but from things Kitt had said here and there, he had gleaned she wished his time at the agency had been less eventful.

'I'm OK, as close to OK as I come these days,' Joe said. 'But I'm not going to lie, there is something that haunts me about the events of the last few weeks.'

'Only one thing?' Evie said. 'I wasn't even part of the investigation and I'm traumatized on several levels by what I've heard since you got back. Enough to make anyone paranoid, it is.'

Kitt chuckled at Evie's comment but then asked, 'And what might that haunting element be, Joe?'

'Two words: Julius Yeats. Whatever he was up to when we got there, whatever made him think that we were the police rather than some touring visitors asking for the owner, he's still doing it. I've no idea what it is but I know enough about that man to know it can't be good.'

'We can't be responsible for bringing everyone to justice, Joe,' said Kitt. 'Frankly, we shouldn't have to be responsible for bringing anyone to justice. But that's the world we live in. I don't think people realize how different society could be if we all held ourselves to higher standards, aligned ourselves with greater goods. I meant what I said to Yeats when we were back at his establishment. People like him, sooner or later, pay terribly for the things they have done. I don't think he will be an exception.'

Joe was just about to respond to Kitt's sage words when Rolo began barking and scarpered at breakneck speed away from the trio.

'Where's he going?' said Evie.

'Oh God, he's seen a squirrel,' said Joe. 'I'll have to go after him. He won't stop running until he either catches the thing or is satisfied that he never will.'

'I'm sure he won't get too far,' said Kitt.

'You'll have to forgive me, Kitt, but, on this point, I'm afraid you are mistaken.' With that, Joe set off in a light jog after the dog. The canine was still just about in view, but he was tearing away at a wild pace, and for a moment Joe wondered if he would be able to catch the beast.

As mercy would have it, the squirrel in question dived through the slats of a wooden fence seemingly to safety. At this juncture, Rolo came to a screeching stop and began to gnaw at said fence in an attempt to reach his target. Joe had no idea who the fence belonged to, but he sensed they wouldn't be thrilled about the damage his dog was currently doing to their property. Now he'd have to knock at their door to apologize and offer to pay for any destruction.

Quickening his pace, Joe started to close in on the dog, who had not lost any enthusiasm for chewing at the wood and breaking down the only perceivable barrier between him and his bushy-tailed foe. Joe was almost upon Rolo when he saw the mutt at last stop gnawing. Unfortunately, he replaced this action with headbutting the fence, and to Joe's horror, the wood was starting to crack and split. Joe just managed to grab Rolo's collar before he gained entry to the most beautifully landscaped garden he had ever seen and Rolo was not best pleased at being kept from victory. He began to thrash around, trying to loosen Joe's grip on his collar. Rolo was a large dog with a strength he did not understand, testing Joe's biceps in the struggle. Joe couldn't do much else but cling desperately to the collar, pulling with all of his might in an attempt to get the dog under control.

Something odd happened during all this, however.

Joe's hand rubbed vigorously against the medallion that hung around Rolo's neck and noticed something he had not realized before. The medallion was not completely smooth: there was a seam of sorts along the edge of it. Joe didn't know much about dog accessories but this seemed a strange detail.

'Are you all right?' Evie said as she and Kitt caught up with a now very muddy Joe.

'Put his lead on for me, will you?' Joe said, letting go of Rolo with one hand momentarily to pull the lead out of his jeans pocket.

Evie obliged and within a minute or so of being put back on his lead, Rolo's frenzy subsided, giving Joe an opportunity to examine the medallion a little more closely.

'Is something the matter with his collar?' asked Kitt.

'I don't know,' Joe said, running his finger again along the strange seam along the side of the medallion. 'It looks like . . .' He gently tugged at each side of the medallion and to his surprise the two sides came apart and something small, and square and thin, dropped down into the mud.

Reaching down, Joe picked the tiny little square out of the mud and dusted it off. He frowned, placed it in the palm of his hand and held it out for Kitt and Evie to look at.

'What is that?' asked Evie.

'It's a microchip,' said Kitt, before a look of realization flashed over her face. 'We can't know for sure but if I had to guess, I'd say that little piece of silicon is what Carly was looking for all along.'

CHAPTER THIRTY-FOUR

The very next day, Agent Smith walked through the doors of Hartley and Edwards Investigations and Joe was there to greet him. Unfortunately for Smith, Joe wasn't the only other person in the office. Kitt and Grace were there, of course, but so was Ruby Barnett, who was trying to convince Kitt to come to a festive party she was hoping to hold on the winter solstice, a night, she had explained at great length, which had huge significance for pagans such as herself.

'Let's get Halloween out of the way first before we start planning the festive season, eh, Ruby?' said Kitt. Clearly not willing to give Ruby a straight answer.

'Eeeh, well, I know you're busy, lass, and I just wanted to get the date in yer diary as soon as possible.'

'Mmm. Yes, all right, I'll see if I can make it,' said Kitt, at last admitting defeat on the subject. 'I'm afraid this gentleman's here on a private matter, Ruby, so we'll have to say goodbye for today.'

'Oh, say no more, say no more, lass,' said Ruby. 'Ruby understands the top-secret nature of your business. Not that anything's top secret from me, of course, given my incredible powers of clairvoyance.'

At this, Smith flashed a bemused look at Joe. Joe, for his part, had been working long enough at the agency to know the correct response was simply to shake his head in such a way that let Smith know he shouldn't take what he was hearing too seriously.

Ruby stood from her seat and reached for her walking stick before steadily striding towards Smith. She was just a pace away from him when her eyes widened, and she grabbed his arm.

'I've just had a vision about you.'

'Oh, good grief,' Kitt said, raising her eyes to the ceiling.

'A vision,' Smith repeated.

'Yes,' Ruby said. 'Don't eat the cheese scone.'

Joe bit his lip in an attempt not to laugh. He had become very fond of Ruby in the short time he'd been working with Kitt and Grace but comical as she was at times, he'd done his utmost not to laugh openly at her. It was tough when she came out with 'visions' like this but he didn't want her thinking she was a laughing stock when a person only needed to spend a minute with her to know she had a big heart.

'I'll keep that in mind,' was all that Smith could find to say.

'You do that, good lad,' Ruby said, patting him on the arm and calling out her goodbyes as she left.

'Pity,' Smith said after Ruby had left. 'I was always rather fond of cheese scones.'

'I wouldn't worry,' said Kitt. 'I don't think Ruby's prediction requires any serious changes to your diet.'

'I don't know so much,' said Grace. 'She has been right once or twice.'

'A stopped clock is right twice a day,' said Kitt.

'Trouble is, in my line of work, you never know if food has been poisoned. I think I'll give cheese scones a miss, for a while at least,' said Smith. 'But anyway, on to your discovery.'

'Here,' Joe said, handing over a small brown envelope.

Smith accepted the package, opened it and shook a microchip out into the palm of his hand. 'And you really found it in Rolo's collar?'

'Yes, it wasn't Rolo's finest hour as he'd run off and I was struggling with his collar.'

'A stroke of luck. We've had so few of them on this case, it was about time we had one,' said Smith. 'And it's very typical of Holmes to have hidden the chip somewhere that was so in plain sight nobody would think to look for it there.'

'I hope it helps with taking down Carly's network,' said Joe.

'I've no doubt it will,' said Smith. 'As you might imagine, Carly, which is still the only name we have for her other than her codename, was less than cooperative for some time. She has in recent days, however, come to realize that she's going to have a very miserable time of it if she doesn't give us something. She admitted having Holmes followed. And it seems that the killing of Holmes was actually accidental. As Grace suggested, it would have been much better to keep him alive in order to locate the package. According to Carly, her agent called her and explained that he and Holmes had got into a physical altercation. He'd been holding his gun and it had fired by accident, killing Holmes straight away. The agent buried Holmes and then called Carly to tell her the news. She had told the agent he was better off killing himself than suffering through what she would do when she got hold of him.'

'I can't believe we spent so much time in that woman's presence,' said Grace. 'We were lucky to get out of it alive.'

'That much is certainly true,' said Smith. 'She's definitely cold-hearted, to put it politely. No amount of interrogation has made her give up what she knows about the network's plans either. There must be someone higher up than her in the network that she fears more than she fears us. But now that we have these files, well, we might learn a little more about her and what plans they had for Anthorn naval base.'

'Holmes died trying to get those plans to you,' said Joe. 'I can't tell you how good it feels to know they're in your hands now, just as he wanted.'

Smith nodded. 'From what I knew of Holmes, there was

no greater honour you could pay him than completing the mission he couldn't.'

'Will you stay for a cup of tea, Agent Smith?' said Kitt. 'We're always on the brink of putting the kettle on round here. We'll take any excuse, really.'

'I'd love to but I'm afraid duty calls.'

'Maybe another time,' said Kitt with a nod.

'Maybe indeed. We certainly count this agency among our allies in the North. And you never know when you're going to need a little extra help,' said Smith.

'Well, I can't say that this country is perfect,' said Kitt. 'It is a capitalist, patriarchal society after all, but I think you know that when it comes down to it we're willing to fight for it as hard as we can against threats, domestic or international, should you ever need us.'

At last, Smith cracked a wry smile at Kitt's comments. 'I'm assuming you didn't mention your disapproval of the capitalist, patriarchal nature of our society in your debriefing with HQ.'

'Funnily enough, that didn't come up,' Kitt said, returning his smile.

Nodding at Grace and Joe in turn, Smith said his goodbyes and left almost as suddenly as he'd appeared.

'You did a good job in finding that microchip,' Kitt said to Joe. 'I know you're in two minds about whether going into business as an investigator is for you, but I'd think carefully about hanging your hat up for good at the end of the week.

It's been a rocky work experience project, I understand. But you've learned more in four weeks than many learn in years of practice.'

'I know,' said Joe. 'I have been thinking about it and finding that chip really did restore my faith in my ability to at least have a good go at the profession. I suppose it's just coming to terms with how high the stakes are.'

'Oh well, if you ever manage that, do let me know the answer,' said Kitt.

Joe smiled. 'You know what I mean. The stakes are high and there's no guarantee you get to win out in the end. I'm going to have to figure out how to take the losses as well as I do the wins.'

'That is everyone's struggle in this world,' Kitt said. 'Whether they happen to run a private investigation agency or not. We don't get a say in the wins or the losses. Only in how we handle them.'

Kitt looked at Joe for a long moment as she said this.

And, of course, she was right.

Investigating the death of Ralph Holmes hadn't been an easy ride by any stretch of the imagination. It had made Joe recalibrate all of his ideas about trust for a start. But it had done something else too. It had shown him that, difficult though it was, he could carry on contributing to the world even now Sarah wasn't physically a part of it. It still wasn't a thought he liked to dwell on. In fact, he could still barely even acknowledge that he wouldn't go home to find her in the kitchen, baking, as he used to do.

But there was no denying the fact that Joe had done some good during his time at Hartley and Edwards Investigations. And maybe, on the days when you woke up mournful about all you had lost in this strange, cruel world, pouring some goodness back into it took the edge off the sting. Just a little bit. In his heart, he knew Sarah would want him to keep contributing, keep socializing, keep doing all the things she could no longer do. And if he could help a few others along the way who'd suffered similarly to how they both had when they knew her time was coming to an end, Joe was certain that Sarah would be proud of him. Under the circumstances, he couldn't ask for anything more than that.

ACKNOWLEDGEMENTS

These acknowledgements must start with heartfelt thanks to my publisher Quercus, specifically Stef Bierwerth and Kat Burdon, for their continued support of both myself and the series. Especially given the difficult times I have faced personally in recent months.

Ongoing appreciation is also due to my agent, Joanna Swainson, for all the positivity about each and every new Kitt Hartley adventure. The power of such enthusiasm cannot be overstated.

As ever, I'm left to ponder how I would write books without the support of my writing partners, Dean Cummings and Ann Leander. The answer is, it would be a lot less fun and possibly may not happen at all.

Much gratitude goes to Hazel Nicholson for her diligent feedback about police procedure. What a support it is to have such an eagle eye on your work.

And lastly, to my beloved husband, Jo. You are not here to

see these words in print, but you were there to brainstorm conspiracy theories with me while walking the Solway coast and I will be grateful for those days, and all the others we spent together, always. I know you are reading this, somehow. In life, reading was always your favourite pastime and, wherever you may be now, I know your very first job will have been to locate the library. So thank you, darling. Thank you.